SKIN GAME

KARNE AND LUNDIN

SUBTLE DECEPTIONS
BOOK 3

ELLE KEATON

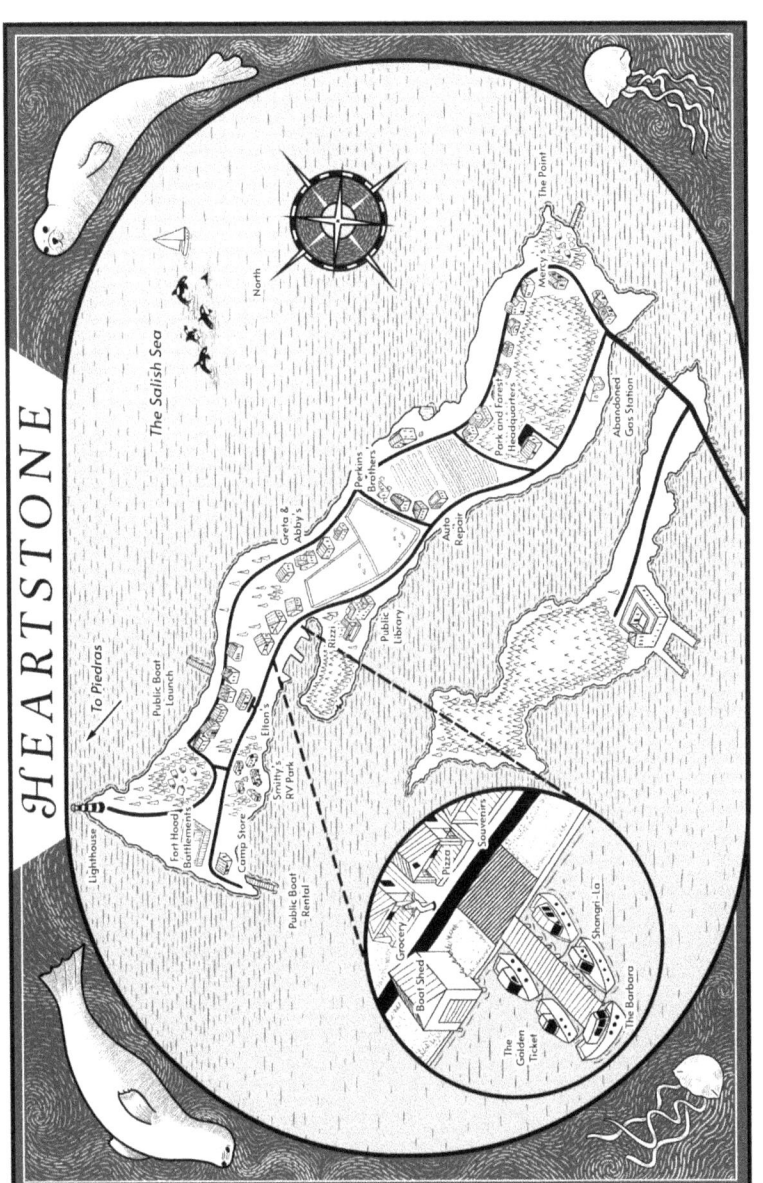

ONE

GABE – MONDAY PART ONE

Gabe's eyes popped open, the popcorn ceiling he loathed glimmering overhead, taunting him. He strained his ears for the sound that had disturbed him. There had been something. Maybe a branch had fallen on the roof.

"I'm never playing cribbage with Elton again," Gabe muttered to the otherwise empty bedroom.

He didn't know how the old man managed it, but he cheated. Gabe was almost positive. If Gabe drank these days, he would have blamed the string of losses on too many gin and tonics. But he didn't drink anymore, and Elton had still managed to Win. Every. Single. Game.

"Cheating bastard."

The soft light coming in through the blinds informed him it was early morning, around seven or so. The pitter-patter against the roof said it was raining. Again. Still? Big shock there. The park was coming awake too. He heard the bark of a dog and the slam of a car door, probably Bill or one of the other park residents heading off to their gainful employment. Gabe was currently gainfully unemployed, and semi-retirement had its perks—like sleeping in on a Monday. Fingers crossed Mondays would continue to improve.

Rolling over, he grabbed his phone from the bedside table and checked the time. Seven fifteen, so much for sleeping in. Then he heard it again, a soft tap-tap coming from the direction of the living room. An early morning door-to-door salesperson? Not likely around this neighborhood. The person would go away eventually. Gabe flopped back onto the bed.

His head had barely hit the pillow when yet another round of knocks started up. Who needed him so desperately? It wasn't Casey or Elton, both of whom would have texted. Or they would have just let themselves in without waiting for Gabe to come to the door.

"The fuck. Keith, get the fricking door."

Keith, Gabe's rescue cat, did not deign to reply. The fluffy orange beast stayed tucked in behind his knees, an anchor. She was purring too. It was probably a crime to move her.

"How do you do it, cat? You normally weigh ten pounds, but when I need to move you, it's more like fifty."

Keith just rumbled louder, a hemi engine warming up.

There was another knock, a bit louder but also hesitant, as if whoever was out there was having second thoughts about showing up this early.

"They should be fucking nervous and having third and fourth thoughts too."

Groaning, Gabe started to pull the other pillow over his head to block out the noise, but it was too late. Even worse, his curiosity was wide fucking awake now too. Additionally, since his car was parked in his assigned spot, whoever was out there had to think he was home.

Maybe the knocker *was* Casey? He could be oddly formal sometimes. "You have your own key, why are you knocking?" Gabe called out. "I'm not doing anything unseemly. I save that for when you're here."

There was no answer. Gabe relaxed a tad; had the phantom knocker gone away? Then he heard another knock.

As if his luck would ever swing that way.

"Really?" Gabe grumbled. Whoever was out there, waiting for him to open the door, it absolutely wasn't anyone who knew him. "Give me a damn second."

For fuck's sake, how often did he lie in bed in the morning doing nothing? Hardly ever. And yet, the one time he decided to revel in his false retirement, somebody showed up on his doorstep.

"Yeah, alright. I'm coming. Give me a fucking sec-minute."

Grabbing a relatively clean pair of jeans from the top of his dresser, Gabe tugged them on. The anonymous annoyance would just have to deal with the rumpled t-shirt he'd slept in. He looked down at himself.

On second thought.

"This better be fucking worth it. This better fucking be Ed McMahon back from the dead." Gabe peeled the sleep shirt off and dropped it to the floor, then grabbed the first shirt in his closet off its hanger, a plain black button-up shirt. Whoever wanted him *this fucking early* couldn't claim he hadn't made some kind of effort. He had tried.

Maybe that was what he should have carved on his gravestone: *Here lies Gabriel Karne. He tried*.

Staring down at his bare feet, Gabe decided against socks. His house, his rules. Departing the bedroom, he padded the short distance to his living room area. He debated for a half second whether to peek outside and see who was so impatient to see him at the ass crack of a Monday morning but decided against it. The blinds were closed. Fuck it, the effort was too much before coffee.

Live on the wild side and all that.

Unlocking the door, he pushed it open. Cool morning air rushed inside, giving him immediate goose bumps. A girl—no, Gabe corrected himself, a young woman—hovered on the cement patio that passed as a porch. She had a hood pulled up over her head and she was trying to appear confident, but unease lurked in the back of her gaze.

"Gabriel Karne?" she said before he could ask what she wanted.

"Yes, that's me. Gabriel Karne. What can I do for you?" He ran a hand through his rumpled hair in an attempt to make it look like he cared about bedhead. Wait, did he care? No, he didn't. Gabe dropped his hand.

The woman was likely in her twenties, Gabe estimated as he took in her appearance. The first half of them. Her dark brown hair was cut short, into what Heidi would've called a pixie, and she had light brown eyes. And she'd known his name, so she wasn't lost.

This stranger had discovered Gabe's new-to-him home address. He'd only put the change into the post office a couple of weeks ago, but it wasn't a state secret, was it? Nevertheless, if something wasn't rotten, it was approaching its pull-date. His Spidey sense was pinging hard.

"Um." She jabbed a pale hand toward him. "Good morning."

Gabriel considered not shaking it.

It never hurts to be polite, Chance. At least until you find out what they want.

Reluctantly, he took it and found her palm sweaty. She *was* nervous. Another reason to shake a hand was that you could learn a lot about a person from their grip—or their sweaty palms.

"You don't know me. My name is, uh, Juliet. Juliet Carter." She jammed both of her hands back inside the pockets of her light blue Columbia parka. That was some purebred Pacific Northwest outerwear. "It's cold out here. Do you mind if I come in for a moment? I won't take up much of your time. I think you'll want to hear what I have to say."

Gabriel looked over her shoulder out into the damp world of Smitty's RV Park. He was going out on a limb and assuming the crappy dark blue Ford Focus parked next to the Honda was hers. Across the road, Bill Floyd was rolling his trash and recycling containers out. Spring mist lingered in a few of the lowest spots, only inches above the ground, like a floating blanket.

Someone's dog barked.

He returned his attention to the young woman. She was watching him warily, her pupils huge, and one booted foot kept shifting back and forth.

Gabe figured he might as well learn what it was.

Turning around, he led the way inside. "Welcome to my abode, such as it is. Make yourself comfortable, just not too comfortable." Gabe pulled the door shut, making sure the latch caught.

The visitor didn't sit; instead, she stood awkwardly in the center of the living room. A shoulder bag Gabe hadn't seen before was now tugged around to the front of her body.

"Coffee?" Whatever she was here for, Gabe needed a strong cup of coffee regardless.

"Um, no. Thanks for offering though." She was looking around now, taking in the smallish room. There wasn't a lot, and he made a note to take a little road trip to the Thrift Shop in Cooper Springs for something to hang on the walls, maybe stop at the pub, talk to the chatty owner.

Moving over to the counter that split the living room off from the kitchen, Gabe pressed the power switch on his espresso machine, pleased as always when the little red power light lit up.

"Why don't you tell me who you are and why you're here while I make a drink for myself?"

He pretended to be focused on the machine and coffee beans while watching the young woman out of the corner of his eye. If she was trying to play it cool, it wasn't working. She was twitchy, squeezing and releasing the top of her purse thing. If her name was really Juliet, then his was Sylvester.

A grifter by any other name is still a grifter, Chance. You've got yourself a baby scammer.

Juliet dropped her gaze and looked down at her bag. She'd come to a decision. She fiddled with a clasp, unzipping it, keeping her dark head bent while she rummaged for something inside the deep pocket.

"You don't have a gun or anything in there? Because that would not make my day."

"What? No." She looked back up at him, brandishing a sheaf of papers she held in her hand. "I have this to show you. It's paperwork."

"I'm not a big fan of paperwork." Gabe set his special demitasse cup underneath the magic caffeine spout. Soon, he'd have caffeine coursing through his bloodstream. He had the feeling he was going to need it this morning.

Paperwork and letters were closely related in his mind. The word paperwork made Gabe feel slightly dizzy. There was no doubt in his mind that this was a pitch of some kind. When she finished, he'd gently usher the young woman out the door and erase her from his memory. Then he'd get ready for the rest of his day.

"You're my father," Juliet announced, the sheaf of papers rustling as her hand shook.

Staring back at her, Gabe blinked several times, his espresso forgotten as he repeated the girl's words inside his head.

"I'm sorry, what did you say? Maybe you could repeat that?" He was proud of himself for not laughing. This was not the sales pitch he'd imagined.

"You're my father," she said, more firmly this time. She stepped closer, making it easier to wave the papers under his nose. "I've been researching using a genetic family tree site, and you came up as a hundred percent match."

Was a one hundred percent match even possible? Gabe was no DNA expert, but he thought one hundred percent was overstating things. Even he knew that a one hundred percent match would be an actual clone. Gabe sucked oxygen in through his nose and deep into his lungs, a habit he'd picked up from Casey.

"I really doubt that." Sure, he'd had sex with women, but condom was practically his middle name. He decided to play along for a bit and see where she was heading with this. He also had many, many questions, the first of which was, "Who's your mother?"

Shit, would he recognize her mother's name? There was a time when he pretty much slept with anyone who looked sideways at him. But never without a condom. Just call him Gabe "Condom" Karne.

The banana and condom demo when you were fourteen served its purpose, Chance. Along with the lectures about parental responsibility.

"She's dead now, but her name was, ah, Laurel. Laurel Carter."

Gabe didn't even have to think hard. He had zero recollection of a Laurel Carter. Plus, the way she said it, with a slight upward inflection at the end of each name, gave him more reason to be suspicious. "Mind if I take a look at the papers you've got there?"

"I want them back," Juliet said, holding them out.

"Sure," Gabe agreed, taking the sheaf from her. "I just want to see what you have here. It's a pretty big deal to be accused of being a father at this stage in my life."

Juliet remained silent and clutched her bag tight enough that her knuckles went white. Gabe sighed and looked down at the pages.

At a glance, the paperwork looked to have been printed off some internet site—there was even a dot-com address at the bottom of each of the three pages. Which, he supposed, could be how these things were done, but he'd never visited one of those sites himself, so he didn't know. Gabe took few minutes to scan over the pages more carefully while "Juliet" rustled nervously in place.

He was looking at a jumble of meaningless numbers and a bunch of names he didn't recognize, up until he reached the bottom of the page. A graphic of a family tree had Gabe's name with Juliet Carter listed below it. He did note that the name above his own was *H. Pritchard*—that information he set aside for later consideration. Pritchard was not a name he was familiar with.

H could stand for anything. Harriet, Hattie, Hortense. Not necessarily Heidi.

Regardless, his initial impression didn't change. These records had to have been faked or altered to make it look like Gabe was a father, but some of the information seemed legitimate. And wasn't that interesting.

But no way was he a father. A snort escaped Gabe, causing the girl to glance sharply at him.

Not only had he never forgotten to glove up, but he had never spit in a tube and sent his DNA in for testing. And he knew for an absolute fact that there was no way in hell Heidi would have. She'd had strong feelings about sharing personal information, and DNA was about as personal as it could get.

What game was this girl playing at? And did he want to find out? Dammit, he did. The curse of curiosity.

"I'm sorry, I don't recall a Laurel Carter," he finally said, sliding the papers across the counter in Juliet's direction. "What's the motivation for coming here to my home and telling me this? You're what, eighteen? It's not as if there's gonna be a happy family reunion."

"I'm twenty-two," Juliet shot back. "We could still build a relationship, maybe be a family."

Gabe looked carefully at Juliet. Try as he might, he didn't see any sort of family resemblance. Maybe she took after this Laurel person. Gabe certainly didn't look much like Heidi. But no, he just couldn't believe it.

"I would've been around twenty-four." He shook his head,

ignoring the mention of a relationship. "Yeah, still don't believe it. Why don't you tell me why you're really here and how you found me? And I don't suppose you remembered to bring along a picture of your dear mother?"

Various emotions flitted across her face. Panic was the most predominant, but he also saw fear as she tried to come up with something he might fall for. Juliet had hoped he would swallow her story hook, line, and sinker.

I raised you smarter than that, Chance.

Indeed, Heidi had.

"Look, if you insist, we'll go to a clinic or someplace and have a real test done. But I think we both know what the outcome will be."

A lone tear escaped from the corner of Juliet's right eye, and her bottom lip trembled. It was very convincing, but Gabriel Karne wasn't born yesterday.

"I don't have any pictures. She died in a house fire. Everything was destroyed."

Gabe sighed. "House fire, that's original. But also, no. How about if you take yourself back to wherever you came from and concoct another story, then come back. Or better yet, tell me the truth about why you're here. If I don't know the truth, I can't help you." He couldn't put his finger on why he thought Juliet was in a jam of some kind, other than the fear he'd seen. Why else would she have come knocking before nine a.m.? Why his door? Why the fake papers? It wasn't as if he had anything. All she needed to do was take a look around.

Swiping the fake tears away, Juliet glared at him and jammed the sheaf of papers back into her purse. "Men. They're all fucking assholes."

She's got something right, Chance.

"Can't deny that. I'm serious about helping you out of whatever jam you're in, but I need the truth."

On the other hand.

"The Colavitos didn't send you this way, did they?" he asked.

He still had the duffle bag hidden away with a substantial amount of cash remaining, and he knew that Larry and family had been put away for a very long time. But would prison stop a man like Larry Colavito?

She frowned at him, her hand on the doorknob. "The who?"

"Never mind. Come back if you come up with a better story," he called after her.

The door slammed shut behind Juliet. Gabe moved back over to the front window and watched her get behind the wheel of her tin can of an automobile and drive off way too fast. Bill was going to be pissed if he was still outside.

Keith chose that moment to saunter into the living room, stopping and staring at him in a very catlike way.

"What the fuck was that all about?" he asked the cat. With a hoarse meow, she padded over and wrapped around his ankles in a blatant effort at assassination.

He rubbed his hands together gleefully. "Now that we've sent 'Juliet' on her merry way, I have that job to do. But first, breakfast for you, coffee for me."

As for the new-to-Gabe fake daughter, this was going to be a great story to share at the next death-match cribbage night over at Elton's. Because dammit, Gabe wanted a rematch.

TWO
GABE: MONDAY MORNING: PART TWO

Shivering slightly in the too-thin jacket he'd decided to wear that morning, Gabe peered out the Honda's mist-coated windshield. He'd already cracked the driver's side window an inch or so to try and keep the glass from fogging while he waited, but the heavy mist surrounding the town of Westfort and this particular hill was cold, cloying, and persistent.

Gabe was fucking freezing. But a favor was a favor, and Gabe was particularly suited to this one.

The address he was focused on sat across the street and to his right, at about one o'clock, maybe one fifteen, and Gabe was just a guy, sitting in his car, watching a house. As one does. Doing his best to appear unremarkable and commonplace. Not casing the joint. Not waiting for the creep inside to leave.

"Come on already. You're going to be late for work, dude."

Maybe Gabe's idea of being on time and this guy's were wildly different. Possibly it was fine for Randy to show up whenever he dragged his ass in. Gabe's own job history was not the nine-to-five version, and he suspected that he also might not have excelled on a set schedule, but one thing Heidi had impressed upon him was being on time. A few more cold minutes passed before the front door opened with a loud scrape and rattle, as if it didn't fit the frame properly.

"Finally," he whispered.

A youngish man Gabe recognized from a selfie that Althea Mortine had shared with him emerged. Gabe lifted his cell phone to his ear, pretending he'd pulled over to answer a call. Randy Witherspoon didn't appear to notice that he was being watched from the Honda.

In his late twenties, Witherspoon was of average height and carried a not-quite-to-term paunch that bulged under his blue Mariners hoodie. This was the springtime uniform for many of the less fashion-forward in the Pacific Northwest. The only things missing were sandals and black socks. Instead, he wore a pair of battered leather sneakers and socks that were possibly gray.

Gabe hoped he wore socks because wearing sneakers with no socks was truly disgusting and having that color of ankles was even more so.

Gabe shuddered.

Blissfully unaware there were eyes on him, Randy pulled the door shut with a slam that echoed across the street and proceeded to lock it with a key he then shoved into the front pocket of his jeans. Althea had given Gabe a key, one that was supposed to fit the back door. He hadn't asked where it came from, but the likelihood that her granddaughter had provided it was high. She was the reason Gabe was there, after all. Which had him wondering if she suffered from self-esteem issues because, based on what Althea had told him via Elton, Randy W. was no prize. He pushed those thoughts away for another time.

Tucking one hand into the pocket of his hoodie, Mr. Oblivious traipsed across the ragged green-brown lawn to the sidewalk, his attention held by something on the cell phone in his other hand. He then turned to his right, heading toward Westfort's down-town area. While he walked, he shoved his phone away and pulled his hood up, presumably with the belief that the material would protect him from the misty rain. It would not.

Gabe knew where Randy was going but wanted proof he'd made it there before letting himself into the house. Technically, he wasn't breaking in since he had a key, but he certainly hadn't been invited.

Potato potahto.

"IT IS, in fact, breaking and entering," Casey had sternly informed Gabe the night before.

The thing was, Gabe never cared much about *possibly* breaking the law when Casey crossed his arms over his chest in that way he did. Ranger Man's biceps were always distractingly sexy.

"But is it? Is it really, if the key fits and all that?" He'd held up the key, waggling it so the light hit it. The *possible* breaking and entering was a favor for Elton's woman-friend, Althea Mortine, and Gabe would never say no to Elton.

Ranger Man, on the other hand, was pissed at both of them.

He'd been rewarded with a long stare and then a shake of the head. Casey should've known that Gabe would do just about anything that Elton—and, by extension, Althea—asked of him, even enter an empty house that he wasn't maybe invited into in order to retrieve personal belongings.

"Gabe, be careful. Please?"

"I'm always careful."

So here he was, being careful and making extra certain that Randy Witherspoon really was out of his house. And now he finally was.

Starting the Honda's engine, Gabe continued to surreptitiously watch Randy over the top of his cell phone until he was almost out of sight. At the last second, Gabe pulled away from the curb, the phone still pressed to his ear, and drove slowly enough that he wouldn't pass Randy right away.

After heading east and downhill for a couple of blocks, the guy turned right again and disappeared down a steep cement staircase that led to Water Street and downtown Westfort. Gabe knew that at the bottom of the steps, on the far end of a short street that dead-ended where the staircase stopped, was the pot shop where Randy Witherspoon was supposed to be spending the next few hours.

"Excellent."

The time had come for some entering and retrieving. If he hadn't been behind the wheel, Gabe might have rubbed his palms together again and possibly cackled. Instead, his phone vibrated, rattling against the hard plastic of the drink holder in the console, and scaring the crap out of him.

"Maybe I should cut down on my coffee intake," Gabe muttered as he looked down at the screen and pressed Accept.

"What?" he said.

"What?" Gabe could hear the frown in Elton Cox's voice. "What kind of greeting is *What*?"

"It's the greeting I use when some people are interfering with my stakeout."

There was a choking sound, as if Elton had been in the middle of a sip of liquid—undoubtably, coffee.

"Yes, I said stakeout."

While on speaker—because he knew if he ended the call, Elton would just call him back until he answered—Gabe performed a three-point turn and directed the car back toward Oblivious's address. Just in case someone else *was* inside, he pulled over and parked a block or so away.

The intel had been a bit vague seeing as Hero Mortine—not for the first time, Gabe thought Althea's granddaughter had a very cool name—had dumped Randy over a month ago, as soon as she discovered he was a petty thief. Why she had been with him in the first place was a question, especially considering the strong likelihood that he did not wash his socks.

On the other hand, Gabe could relate. Over the years, he'd rarely made good choices when it came to romantic partners, although his bar had been set a tad higher than the likes of Randy Witherspoon. The situation with Ranger Man was a bit of an anomaly. Would it last? Gabe wanted it to. But thinking about Casey Lundin was not what he needed to be doing right now.

"Focus, Gabe," he muttered.

"What?"

Crap, he'd hadn't meant to say that out loud.

"Nothing. I'm heading over to the house now."

Taking one last careful look around, he got out of the car and tucked the phone into the front pocket of the too-light jacket. The cold of the afternoon once again made him regret that he hadn't grabbed the fleece-lined flannel one he'd permanently borrowed from Casey. Stuffing his hands deep in his pockets to try to warm them a bit, he began trudging back toward the Witherspoon house, which was situated on prime real estate at the top of one of Westfort's many hills. Property taxes up this way had to be pretty high, even if Randy's place didn't scream "prime."

A few houses away, Gabe paused, only sort of pretending he was short of breath, and surveilled the neighborhood, checking for twitching curtains, pale faces staring through windowpanes, and the like. Elton was still on the other end of the line.

"There's no one out and about. The house feels empty, and the neighborhood is quiet," he told the old man. It was a Monday, so any kids should have been at school, and most adults were probably at work. Fingers crossed.

He'd started walking again while giving Elton the rundown, and now he was almost directly in front of the address.

"I've arrived at the target." Elton had told him to stop acting like the job for Althea was some kind of spy operation, so of course he had to use words like target.

"There is no target, Gabriel. You're finding Althea's locket and bringing it back here, that is all."

"Karne's Acme Retrieval Service," Gabe quipped as he saun-tered down the cement walkway to the front door, glad that the mist had stopped for the time being. "Nah, I don't like that one. I need something catchier."

Randy's place could have been nice. Years ago, it must have been a lovely home, but those days were long gone, the structure having been neglected for decades. The exterior paint had long ago peeled like an August sunburn, and although he could only see the moss-covered eaves clearly, the roof was probably the same.

The front lawn was a tangled mass of overly long grasses and other weeds. At some point, a push mower had been abandoned near the front of the house and weeds had grown up through the thing, anchoring it to the ground. A spring morning glory vine had wound its way through the handlebar, a single white bloom bobbing jauntily in the slight breeze.

"Maybe it's art?"

"What?" Elton said.

"Nothing."

Up close, the front door also did not look great, which explained the noise he'd heard earlier. Sometime, fairly recently if the newly exposed wood along the frame was anything to go by, the house had been broken into. Or maybe Randy'd forgotten his key one day and decided to inflict violence on the door. Randy or someone else had done a half-assed repair involving a sheet of plywood and a nail gun. Gabe raised his fist and knocked, wincing as the door vibrated in the frame.

"Hello! Anybody home?" Gabe called out. "My name's Gabriel Karne. I'm here about the vintage glass insulators? The ones you advertised on Marketplace." That was the story he and Elton had come up with in case anyone was listening.

There was no answer, thank fuck. He was feeling uneasy, but he'd come this far, and he wasn't going back to Heartstone empty-handed. Althea was depending on him, and he had to admit he was flattered by the trust she placed in him. Casey, not so much.

What was Gabe supposed to have done? Tell Althea that the heirloom necklace with the only photograph of her daughter was gone forever? When Gabe put it that way, Casey'd done his best glowering and had made him promise to be careful. He'd agreed because Casey's glowers were almost as sexy as Casey's biceps.

Gabe suspected that Casey's definition of being careful and Gabe's were of opposing origins. *Be safe* versus *don't get in trouble.* But he'd gone ahead and promised Casey anyway.

Gabe inflicted another healthy knock on the door, listening closely for the sound of someone inside. "Glass insulators? Marketplace? Does this ring any bells?"

Gabe didn't care much about glass insulators, although they were kind of cool looking. The intel was that Randy claimed to be a picker, one of those folks who went around to garage sales and abandoned barns and "picked" stuff they could sell to collectors for exorbitant amounts of money. Not a very good one though, which was probably why he had a part-time job at the pot shop. But picking was also how Randy found his victims.

"You two are positive about this? The locket is here?" Gabe asked Elton quietly. "He wouldn't have sold it yet?"

Not that he didn't trust what he'd been told, but something felt off, and Gabe almost always trusted his instincts. It was the *almost* part that often got him in trouble. Right now, this was starting to feel like trouble. The tale of how Randy acquired the locket was wobbly, but this was Elton's friend—and she worked at the Twana County Sheriff's Office—so what could go wrong? Gabe could almost hear Casey's derisive snort.

"Althea says that Hero thinks not. When the jerk wasn't mooching off her, taking up space at Hero's place so he could steal personal items like the locket, he lived in Westfort. It's the family home, apparently, and she can't imagine anywhere else he'd take it."

Picker really did mean taking the pick of things that weren't his. Huh.

"Nice," he muttered under his breath, knocking one last time for good measure. There was nothing, no rustles or soft footsteps. Not even the bark of a dog.

"I'm heading around back," he said. "This key from Althea better work on the back door because I am not breaking the door down. If it does, I'll be in and out before you can say boo." He still spoke quietly, just in case. At least the lots at the top of the hill were large, which meant the space between houses was more than just a few feet.

"Remember, Hero—"

"Told Althea the locket was last seen hanging on a mirror in the downstairs bathroom. But Elton, it could be anywhere by now. You know as well as I do that Randy could have pawned it already," Gabe said.

He should never have agreed to keep the phone on. But Elton Cox had assigned himself as Gabe's guardian angel. Angel wasn't quite the right word, but something along those lines, and Gabe felt like he owed it to him. *It* being reassurance that Gabe wouldn't get in too much trouble and there would be someone to call 9-1-1 if needed.

As if Gabe had never been on a job on his own before. As if he hadn't regularly run high-dollar cons and come out pretty okay in the end.

As if there isn't an overworked guardian angel watching over you 24/7.

Could a memory scoff? Because Gabe could hear his mother's special scoff.

"That locket has one of the only pictures Althea has of her daughter and granddaughter together. She doesn't even have another photo of her daughter," Elton told him for possibly the hundredth time.

Gabe really did hope it was still in the house.

"I've got this." Gabe reached into his jacket and thumbed his phone off as he rounded the corner of the house to the backyard. "Oops, lost the connect—Jesus Christ."

The overgrown backyard was a serial killer's wet dream.

At least no dog, so things were not going sideways. Yet. Gabe liked dogs—Casey's dog, Bowie, was a case in point, as were the rescue dogs Mickie Lundin worked with. But the canines Gabe tended to interact with when he was doing something like this were not inclined to play nice. They were a tad bitey and often had anger management issues.

Human-caused, for sure, but anger issues nonetheless.

The backyard was enclosed by four-foot-tall chain-link fencing. A slightly ajar gate beckoned him, and Gabe slipped through it, wincing at the squeak of the hinges. Did everything around here have a complaint?

A sigh of relief escaped him when the provided key fit perfectly.

"Thank St. Fuck."

Twisting the key, Gabe was rewarded with a satisfying pop and release of the lock. The back door opened surprisingly easily considering the state of the one at the front. Gabe stepped inside, blinking as his eyes adjusted to the gloom, then got his first glance—and whiff—of the kitchen and regretted it, slapping a hand over his mouth and nose.

"Jesus Christ," he repeated.

The stench was literally eye-watering. The grubby linoleum floor was close to impassable, and not only because of cardboard boxes stuffed to bursting with empty and partially empty takeout containers and other paraphernalia. Cabinet doors gaped open, and broken glasses and cutlery were strewn across the flooring.

"No fucking wonder he liked Hero's place better."

Gabe couldn't bring himself to shut the door to the outside, not with the rancid smell of unidentifiables lingering in the air. His gut told him to find the locket and get the hell out of there.

With care, Gabe stepped around the scattered remains and

headed for a short hallway across from where he'd entered. He had studied the floor plan sketched out by Hero and was pretty sure the downstairs bathroom was midway down the hall and near the bottom of a staircase that led up to the second floor. He fucking hoped that was as far as he had to go.

The reek did not lessen when he left the kitchen.

As he approached where the bathroom was supposed to be— tiptoeing, for fuck's sake—he passed a gallery of Witherspoon family mug shots, nearly knocking one of them off the wall with his shoulder. The snapshots were protected by cheap-ass frames and plexiglass. They hung at jarring angles because the hallway was narrow and no one of adult height would miss bumping against them.

Out of habit, Gabe paused to straighten them. And judged each one. The Witherspoon family had stopped memorializing themselves when Randy looked to be ten or so. At the time, he did not look pleased to be clutching the hand of a genderless blob of a toddler. The toddler's face was red and scrunched up in mid-scream.

"That haircut was the beginning of the end," Gabe said to Randy's face before moving into the bathroom.

Unsurprisingly, the small room was filthy, equally as bad as the kitchen but in a different way. How could Randy live like this? How could Hero stay here? It seemed like she would have said something about the state of things, but maybe this had happened after she'd left. He accidentally inhaled a waft of stench, and Gabe's stomach churned. Holding his breath again, he glanced quickly around the small room, which was enough to tell him there was no locket hanging on the mirror.

You should've known it wouldn't be so easy, Chance.

Pulling open the top drawer underneath the shallow sink, Gabe regretfully breathed in a sigh of relief, nearly coughing on the inhale. There, tangled in with dental floss samples, a razor, a black hair comb, and Band-Aids in rarely needed sizes and shapes, sparkled the necklace. Scooping it up, Gabe stuffed the piece of jewelry into his pocket and stepped back into the hallway.

That was when the distinct sound of a key turning and the subsequent click of a lock opening reached his ears.

Gabe froze.

Shit.

The front door creaked open, and Gabe recognized the slope of Randy's shoulders and the hoodie they were encased in.

Triple shit.

Spinning back the direction he'd come, Gabe abandoned stealth and raced for the still open back door. He'd never known if there was a patron saint for ex-grifters, but in that moment Gabe decided there had to be, and he prayed to them loud and hard.

"Hey! Stop, you asshole!"

Gabe did not stop. He raced through the kitchen and out the door he'd fortunately had the forethought to leave open. Behind him, he heard Randy's heavy footfalls. It seemed like they were gaining ground. Why was he always being chased?

"I'm gonna kill you," Randy shouted, thundering after him.

"Was it something I said?" Gabe yelled over his shoulder as he took off toward the side of the house. The grass was wet, and the mist had returned. He slipped and had difficulty finding purchase but made it through the gate.

Fucking Mondays.

THREE
CASEY – MONDAY AFTERNOON

"Casey, it's time for some Greta Real Talk."

Casey groaned and almost swore. Real Talk was an irritating hobby of his coworker's. He wished she'd get off her butt and start that podcast she kept talking about instead of practicing her underutilized psychology minor on him.

"Look," Greta began, "you're worried about Mickie, I get it. But maybe stop envisioning what you think he's up to and have a talk with him. Get to know your brother."

It was proving hard not to worry about his brother after nearly twenty years of wondering when the call would come that something terrible had happened to Mickie, something worse than being sent to prison. But Casey didn't say that; he just plastered a bland expression on his face.

"He doesn't want to talk to me. Mickie made that very clear. I think his exact words were, 'I need some space.'"

Settling back in her chair with her hands resting in her lap, Greta cocked her head at him. "You have to admit, there's been a bit of helicoptering on your part. A lot of helicoptering. He's an adult, he's gainfully employed, and he has money in savings."

"He was also behind bars for almost twenty years! What does he know about real life?"

"He was, yes. We know this already and can't change it. This is not the first or even second time you and I have talked about this." She nodded sagely, and Casey could tell she was enjoying herself. "But he's out now, completely exonerated. I know it's been difficult, especially since you were the only family on the outside who believed in him. That said, it's beyond time for you to step back a tad, give him room to breathe. And heal. If Mickie needs help, you have to trust that he will ask you for it. Space doesn't mean he wants you out of his life, it means he knows how to drive and go to the grocery store by himself."

As if realizing he needed an interruption, Casey's phone vibrated against the top of his desk. He glanced at the word *Charming* and a picture of Keith taking up the screen. Why was Gabe calling? His heart rate ratcheted up, and Casey held up a finger to pause the conversation. Lecture.

As if he didn't know his brother couldn't shop for groceries on his own.

"Gabe?" he said, a tad breathlessly.

"It's not as bad as it looks, I swear."

Gabe spoke loud enough that Greta heard him, and she smirked. Greta was the vice president of the Gabriel Karne Fan Club. In spite of himself sometimes, Casey was the de facto president, even if it meant getting phone calls like this one.

Gabriel, Casey had realized early on, had the tendency to downplay the important things and that tendency was coming through strong now. He had been hurt somehow, and he was going to try and play it off.

"What happened? Never mind, where are you?" Casey asked, expecting him to say the emergency room. Maybe jail. Truthfully, Casey wouldn't have been shocked by one or both of those answers coming from Gabe.

"I'm back home already," he said.

Right. Because he'd gone off to Westfort on that "job" for Elton and Althea. Casey shut his eyes for a moment, took a breath, then opened them again. Greta was still watching him, still smirking.

"I'll be right there."

"Casey, there's no emergency," Gabe protested.

But Casey clicked off. He would be the one deciding whether there was an emergency or not.

"I need to get over to Gabe's. There's been some kind of incident," he told Greta.

For her part, Greta rolled her eyes and practically chased him out of the office. "Go away and don't come back until you can go five minutes without glowering or looming. I'll finish up this report and take a look through the new-hire files. You should take the rest of the day. Maybe tomorrow too, jeez."

Casey hesitated. He felt guilty about leaving Greta on her own.

"Go on." Greta waved emphatically toward the office door. "Get out of here. But maybe take Bowie on a hike before you find out what kind of trouble Gabe managed to get into this time. And don't forget to call me back and tell me what it is too," she added while laughing.

Casey grabbed his keys and coat and headed out, waving Bowie into the back of the Wagoneer. A quiet hike in the woods sounded sublime, and maybe that's the choice he should have made, but he didn't take Greta's advice. Instead, he headed toward the RV park, not the woods.

Gabe *had* been hurt. No matter how much the infuriating man tried to make it sound like nothing, Casey could tell he was trying to sugarcoat it, and he didn't appreciate the effort.

"I DON'T KNOW which of you two I am more pissed off at."

Casey shot a laser glare at Elton first, because this was all his fault, then Gabriel. Neither one of them appeared particularly quelled by it, which shouldn't have surprised him. He was losing his edge, getting soft, his glare had wiggle room these days.

For his part, Bowie trotted across the room, giving Gabe a thorough once-over sniff and a lick on the hand before plopping down onto the dog bed in one corner, the special extra cushy one Gabe had spent a ridiculous amount of money on. He'd excused the purchase with some comment about Bowie being the best doggo who deserved the best. Which, of course, Casey couldn't argue with.

He could, however, argue with Gabriel.

"It's not as if I don't have enough to worry about without Gabe gallivanting off to—to—" he sputtered, unable to come up with a descriptor that suited the occasion.

What the fuck had they been thinking? Answer: They had not. Together, Elton, Gabe, and yes, Althea too, he wasn't about to leave her out, had hatched an outrageous plan, and it had gone sideways. Why had he let them go ahead with it? Because he was losing his edge, that's why.

Regardless of what Gabe and present company wished to be true, having a key did not give the holder carte blanche to enter another person's home without their permission. Randy could press charges. If he ever figured out who Gabe was and where he lived. That was unlikely, so they were probably safe on that front. Small mercies. Casey rubbed his forehead and pinched the bridge of his nose.

Gabriel Karne was genetically wired to tread the thin line between legal and illegal but had a huge soft spot for underdogs, the quintessential modern-day Robin Hood, and Elton Cox and Althea Mortine had tapped into that aspect of his personality. Because *of course* they had. Convincing Gabe to use his "skills" for good and not evil, something along those lines.

"I warned you. You can't just go breaking and entering, Gabe,"

Casey repeated. He doubted his admonishment was going to be acknowledged or possibly even heard.

Gabe rolled his eyes. "Not even to retrieve an irreplaceable treasured necklace with great sentimental value?"

That was a first. Casey tried not to show his surprise at Gabe almost admitting to breaking the law and refused to think that maybe Gabe's values were changing slightly.

The bag of frozen peas being held against Gabe's forehead didn't fully conceal the purple bump and scrape underneath it, and a previously frozen droplet rolled down the side of his face. He swiped at it with his free hand while waiting for Casey to respond.

"You look like you were dragged through a hedge backward," Casey added, knowing the retort was pathetic.

"It was this close to being a hedge drag." Gabe raised his hand, index and thumb about an inch apart. "Randy wasn't fucking around. I slipped and had to slow down when I went through the gate. He managed to shove me into an inconveniently placed evergreen shrub, made me trip, and I stumbled. That's when my face hit the holly tree branch. The guy was set to commence with the violence, lots of yelling and profanity floating around. Good thing no small children were nearby. Luckily, he was distracted by a car going by or something and let go. Too bad for Randy though. I kicked him in the kneecap, scrambled off to the Honda, and drove away before he could get me again."

Blowing out another breath, Casey ran that imagery through his head. Then he added it to the fact that Gabe was proud of his breaking and entering. "I give up. Did someone call the police?"

"Maybe," replied Gabe. "But if they did, I didn't see them. I sure didn't call them on myself."

Casey stared at Gabe's off-white, sparkly sprayed ceiling, sucked some air into his lungs, and let it out slowly. In the past, Elton had hosted these post-disaster tête-à-têtes at his place. But with the demise of *The Golden Ticket*, Gabe had his own address now, 183 Bayview Drive, just down from Gordon MacDonald's place at Smitty's RV Park. Casey was surprised Gordon hadn't shown up for this debrief.

The park hosted fewer recreational vehicles these days, but the name stayed the same from when it first opened. Since learning this fact, Gabriel had started a low-key campaign to change it to something more appropriate. But the names he'd come up with—Shady Acres, Riddle Hollow—were no better. Casey thought they sounded like cemeteries.

"Look, I got the locket for Althea, didn't I? You can't deny the success of my mission."

Across the room from Casey, Elton smirked. Ignoring them all, Bowie stood up, turned three times, and lay down again.

Casey jabbed a finger in Elton's direction. "You've created a monster. Breaking and entering? For crying out loud. I just—" His attention drifted to the bag of defrosting produce covering Gabe's forehead. "That looks nasty. Have you cleaned it up yet?" He shifted his butt off the windowsill to start toward the bathroom where Gabe stored the basic first aid kit Casey had given him as a housewarming present.

"It looks worse than it is, I promise," Elton said before Casey could take a step. "I checked."

Fine.

Casey settled his butt back against the sill.

Gabe shook his head. "I didn't break anything. Besides, it looked like someone who was not me really did break in the house fairly recently and Randy hasn't bothered to clean it up. I didn't add to the chaos. Honestly, it was disgusting." Gabe glanced over to where Elton had made himself comfortable on the other end of the couch. "How did Hero meet him anyway? Did she stay overnight there? Maybe she needs a tetanus shot. *I* need a shower, and I was in there less than five minutes."

Casey took in Gabriel's general state of dishevelment. The

holly tree had done a real number on him. He supposed he should be glad; at least he wasn't posting bail.

As he ran his eyes over Gabe again, the scrape, the deepening bruise, and the bag of defrosting peas told Casey he hadn't been wrong. Gabe was in pain. Maybe he should grab the first aid kit anyway.

"You didn't need to rush over here. I told you, it's not as bad as it looks. Elton took a look at it, and I don't need stitches. I even let him pour an ungodly amount of hydrogen peroxide on the cut. If I get an infection, it will be some kind of bacterial miracle. A second coming, a bacterial rapture. You do know I'm not that breakable, right?"

Instead of answering him with words, Casey huffed and turned to look out the window. Gabe was, in fact, entirely too breakable.

A Steller's jay, its feathers so black that the blue was merely a hint, flew past the window. It careened downward to land on a stump and loudly announced its displeasure with the world in general. Casey could relate. The jay cocked its head and seemed to look directly at Casey, its beady eyes glittering as if to say *Get it together, big guy* before it fluttered off with a loud squawk toward a stand of trees.

Sucking in a breath, Casey tried to marshal his thoughts. He didn't need Greta's Real Talk to tell him the emotion he was feeling was fear. Fear because he'd let Gabe past his barriers, and caring for Gabriel Karne was fucking frightening. Fear because he had no control over the chaotic bumper car ride that was Charming Fucker, a man for whom rules were suggestions and not regulations.

The few times in his life before now that Casey'd envisioned being in a relationship, he'd seen himself as part of a safe—on the cusp of boring—couple. Fictional days off together spent hiking or planning hikes. Maybe volunteering to count that year's salmon run or helping to rebuild the boardwalks at the local wetlands.

Gabe was not safe. There was no control switch. Casey just needed to hang the hell on. And, for reasons he hadn't quite figured out yet, he wanted to.

Gabe patted the seat cushion next to his thigh. "You're looming again."

"Greta said the same thing," he said with a halfhearted grumble. Crossing the room, Casey took the spot next to Gabe. Elton rose to his feet with a "Coffee?" and headed toward the kitchen.

"The answer is almost always yes, as you are fully aware. Do you need me to demonstrate how to use the espresso maker again?" Gabriel asked.

"No, I think I've got the damn thing figured out. Why you had to buy a coffee machine that costs more than your rent and has more buttons than the space shuttle, I will never understand."

They watched Elton trundle out of the living room into the open concept kitchen, where he'd be able to make the hot beverages and still participate in the conversation.

"I'm not going to bother answering that." Gabe turned to Casey. "So, what's going on with you?"

Casey inhaled a deep breath, getting enough oxygen to start in on a decent safety lecture.

"Besides my face, I mean," Gabe added hastily.

Casey deflated, letting his shoulders droop.

"I'm worried about Mickie. I've told both of you that. He asked me to give him some space, and I'm giving him space even if it kills me." Casey tried not to cross his arms and pout. "This morning, Greta told me I'm helicoptering."

Gabe wrinkled his nose, clearly thinking. "I mean, maybe? Not to me though, babe. He's your brother and you love him. You're the one who's been there for him over the years, the one who believed. It was a lot for you to handle. But for what it's worth, I also don't think him asking for space means he's cutting you out of his life."

Factually, Gabe was right, but emotionally, Casey was having a hard time coming to terms with his brother's need for emotional elbow room. He promised himself—again—that he would let Mickie be Mickie. If Mickie needed Casey, he had to trust that he'd reach out, even if it killed him to stay away until his brother asked.

Which left Casey with Gabriel to worry about. Who, if Casey was being honest with himself, was much more likely to induce some kind of medical emergency than Mickie, Elton, or Greta, although they all had their moments. Why couldn't the people he cared for behave and stay where he put them?

"What exactly happened in Westfort this morning?" he asked, changing the subject away from him. "And I don't want to hear the Cliffs Notes. Why aren't the police here, ready to escort you to the county jail?"

CASEY – MONDAY
AFTERNOON TO EVENING

"Well." Gabe glanced toward where Elton was standing in the kitchen and fiddling with glossy nobs. "Althea asked Elton to ask me if I could retrieve that necklace for her."

"Keep talking, I know this part."

"Yeah, so Hero's douchebag—"

Elton interrupted with a throat-clearing sound and Casey suppressed a chuckle.

"I can't think of a better word. You come up with one, Elton, and I'll start using it. Anyway." He turned his attention back on Casey. "Hero's *tool* of an ex-boyfriend took something that didn't belong to him, and I took it back. It was almost like falling off a log." He pursed his lips. "Actually, it was a lot like falling off a log. Long story short, he left for work, so I thought it was safe to go inside, but he must've forgotten something or been fired for being late. Anyway, he surprised me at his hovel and tried to take me down." He nodded in Elton's direction. "But I got it, didn't I?"

Elton reached over and lifted a gold-colored necklace from where it had been sitting on the counter. A thumbnail-sized locket dangled from a gold chain and shone in the light. Setting it back down, he pressed a switch on the espresso machine, grunting as he did so. They listened to the hum and chug as hot caffeinated beverage dribbled into the hedgehog cup Gabe had found at a local thrift store.

From the pleased expression occupying Elton's face, he at least thought Gabe's adventure had been a success. Maybe he *was* the glass-half-empty guy, but Casey had the feeling that this morning's undertaking was going to come back and bite Gabe in the butt. Or all of their collective asses, as Gabe would say.

Elton pushed the mug across the counter. "First one's up."

"You have that one, Casey. You look like you need a pick-me-up."

"What I need is not to get phone calls that begin with 'it's not as bad as it looks.'" And not have his boyfriend breaking and entering.

"I assure you, it isn't." Gabe pointed at his forehead. "This here is just a memento that will soon fade into nothing."

"That sounds like wishful thinking, but what do I know?" Rising to his feet, Casey crossed the room to lean his hip against the living room side of the counter.

From the bounce of Gabe's knee and the barely suppressed grin, it seemed to Casey that he was riding high on adrenaline and the success of his undertaking in spite of the encounter with Hero's ex. Shooting Elton a sideways glance, Casey saw that he too looked pleased with himself.

Great. Now Casey needed to keep his eye on both of them.

He watched Gabe push to his feet, then carry the bag of peas into the kitchen and toss them back into the freezer. Note to self: Don't use the peas.

"Hey, not to change the subject or anything, but have there been any sightings of Calvin Perkins?" Gabe asked. He'd moved to stand next to Elton on kitchen side of the counter, leaning forward so his elbows rested against the countertop.

"Not that I've heard." Casey was fine with Gabe changing the subject if that's what he wanted, but he was watching that bruise. "Why do you ask?"

"Huh. I could've sworn I saw his truck or one just like it on my way back here today. Mind, I'm no Calvin Perkins expert, thank god, but a massive tricked-out red truck like the one I remember him driving in the fall passed me heading north. It even had the offensive flags flying from the windows."

"You didn't get a good look at the driver?" Casey said, taking a careful sip of his java. The hunt for Perkins had ended before the turn of the year. The assumption was that the man was dead or well hidden. Casey figured it was fifty-fifty. Perkins was an idiot, but he had the skills to survive off grid for as long as he wanted. The forest was arguably the single place Perkins felt most comfortable. He wouldn't have many issues subsisting as long as he wasn't hurt.

Gabe shook his head as he also sipped at his coffee. "It wasn't until the truck passed me that I had the thought. I suppose there are a lot of red pickups around here."

Casey nodded, because yes, there were hundreds, perhaps thousands, of red pickups in the region. As he set his mug down, his gaze landed on a letter-sized envelope propped up against a bowl about half filled with red apples. The slightly grubby packet was addressed to Gabriel Karne, Care Of Elton Cox. "What's this?"

"I don't know," Gabe said eyeing it warily. "I haven't opened it. Maybe I won't. Can't be good. And also, this is a Monday, which, considering the Karne Monday Fuckery tradition, has been very strange, even for me. I'm considering avoiding them altogether in the future."

"Maybe you should just abstain from breaking and entering." Gabe sputtered a protest, but Casey interrupted him by asking, "Who's the letter from?"

Who from Gabriel's past, beyond Heidi who was dead, knew how to contact him through Elton? As far as Casey understood,

Gabe had left Seattle and never looked back. Furthermore, if Casey was letting the breaking and entering go—*for now*—he deserved to know what this letter was about.

"I don't know the return address, and we all know nothing good comes from an address you don't know." Gabe eyed the missive as if it might contain something evil.

"Maybe you won the lottery," Elton said, his tone remarkably snarky.

"As if. I'd have to buy a ticket to win the lottery."

"Did you do a search on it?" asked Casey.

"Nope. It arrived at Elton's a couple days ago, he tells me. I knew nothing about it until just now when he brought it with him." He shot the letter another dirty look.

"Might as well get it over with," Casey said, raising an eyebrow in Gabe's direction. By now, he knew this song-and-dance fairly well; left to his own devices, Gabe would put off opening that letter until it was conveniently forgotten or "accidentally" tossed in the trash. Casey could understand Gabe's reluctance after the past few months, but ignoring the letter wouldn't make whatever was inside go away.

"You are ruthless. Both of you." Regardless, Gabe reached and slid the envelope toward himself. "Fine. I'll open this Pandora's box, and you will all rue the day."

"I'm sitting back down for this," said Elton, taking his drink and returning to the couch.

Casey moved around to Gabe's side of the counter so he could read over his shoulder. He leaned into him a bit, offering silent support.

"The address is Seattle." Casey mentally rolled his eyes at himself. Way to state the obvious.

"Yeah, I saw that much, Watson." Gabe flipped it over and inspected the back, then slid his thumb under the flap.

"Why am I Watson?" Casey asked.

"Because I get to be Sherlock in this role-play, that's why."

Peeking out from the inside of the envelope was what appeared to be a single sheet of yellow legal paper, the top ragged where it had been ripped off the pad. Gabe shot Casey a glance and pulled it out, setting the envelope to one side.

"I'm not a big fan of letters," Gabe muttered.

Casey knew the letter Gabe had gotten from his mother after her death still bothered him, and with good reason. "At least your mom's words brought you here. Where would you be without me and Elton?" He gave Gabe's bicep a quick squeeze.

"Ugh." Gabe shot him another look and bumped his shoulder against Casey's. "Why are you so cute and sentimental?" Casey did not roll his eyes, even though he recognized that Gabe was trying to distract them all from the task at hand.

"Fine." Gabe flattened the paper against the counter and began to read. "*Dear Mr. Karne*. Hah, proof this person doesn't know me *at all*."

"Keep reading, kid." Elton pointed at the paper. "Casey and I are dying of curiosity."

Gabe sighed and started again. "*Dear Mr. Karne, you don't know me, but I was a friend of your mother's*—I have to say, this is the first person I've known claiming to be Heidi's friend."

"Gabriel." Casey did his best to shoot him a stern look. His response was a mischievous grin and waggle of his eyebrows.

"I'd like to think that I was her friend," said Elton, ignoring the awkward flirting Casey was working on.

"Okay, that's two. Anyway, blah blah, friend. *Heidi left a few belongings with me with instructions to notify you via Mr. Cox if my circumstances changed and I was no longer able to watch over them. I am moving into an assisted living facility at the end of the month, and my house is going on the market. I'm sure you realize this means you need to come and collect your mother's things. If you choose not to or I don't hear from you in a timely manner, I will donate the furniture to charity and put the paperwork through a shredder as she requested.*"

"What is this?" Wide-eyed, Gabe stared at the handwritten

letter and then at Casey and Elton. "Who the hell would Heidi trust enough to keep stuff? Other than you, Elton." He turned the letter over a couple times, like that would make it offer up more clues.

"Sounds to me like you have a field trip to Seattle if you want to find out," Elton said.

"Fuck Seattle."

"We can go together," Casey offered. After all, Gabe had gone with him to pick up Mickie. "I can take the day off tomorrow. Greta's a bit fed up with me right now and has made it clear she wants a break. We'll take the Jeep and load it up with whatever your mom left behind." He gestured at Gabe's blank walls, gray sofa, and ugly coffee table. "Maybe it will be something interesting you can add to your décor." He gently nudged Gabe again. "If you want the company, that is."

Gabe didn't seem to hear him. "But why didn't Heidi just tell me this in the first letter? Why add in a second third party?" He turned the paper over and then back to the front again, seemingly exasperated by its existence.

"I guess you'll never know," replied Elton, "unless you actually go and get the stuff. The shredding comment implies there might be something important."

Gabe's shoulders sagged. "Fuck me."

Casey wrapped one arm around Gabe, tugging him to his side. Surprisingly, considering his childhood, Gabe thrived on physical contact, something Casey was getting used to offering and, until now, hadn't realized how much he enjoyed as well. Gabe's tight shoulders slowly relaxed under Casey's touch, which always felt a little bit like magic. Plus, it didn't hurt that, even if Gabe had been in a scuffle that morning, he always smelled damn good.

Casey breathed him in before saying, "I'm happy to go with you. Maybe we'll learn something more about your mom. Is there a number or anything for you to call and let them know you're coming?"

"Are you sniffing me? That's my sneaky habit." Gabe teased, but didn't move away. "Yeah, there's a phone number there." He pointed to the bottom of the page.

"Call now," Casey urged.

Gabe made a growly sound deep in his throat. "*You* call now."

Without giving him time to protest, Casey pulled his phone out of his pocket, tapped in the nine-digit number, and held the device to his ear. "It's ringing."

"Give that to me." Gabe held his hand out.

Smirking, Casey handed him his cell phone. He'd known Gabe would step up; he had just needed a little nudge.

"Hello," said Gabe. "This is Gabriel Karne. I received a letter with this phone number at the bottom." There was a bit of a pause, then Casey heard a higher-pitched voice but couldn't make out the words. "Okay, yeah—yes, thank you. I can be there tomorrow." He looked at Casey, who nodded. "Yes, this is a good number for me." He made a face at Casey. "Is your address the same as the one on the envelope? Right, great. We'll text you when we're a few minutes out. Sure, not a problem, um, see you tomorrow afternoon."

Clicking off, he handed the phone back to Casey. "I guess it's gonna be road trip Tuesday. We'll need snacks."

FIVE

GABE – MONDAY EVENING

Gabe felt slightly guilty at the sense of relief he felt when Casey left to head back to *The Barbara* for the night with Bowie in tow. They were still working out the who-stays-where-and-when part of their relationship. He hoped they'd eventually get to the point of moving in together, but both of their places were very small, and Casey's absence meant that Gabe was able to do his brooding in private as needed. Undoubtedly not healthy. Wasn't he supposed to share the good and the bad with his boyfriend? No clue. He was making up this serious relationship stuff as he went along.

Because, in all seriousness, what the fuck with another letter, Heidi?

The most recent letter-from-not-quite-beyond-the-grave unsettled him more than he was willing to admit to Casey, Elton, or anyone alive. Casey was a smart man; he'd figure out that Gabe's current weirdness had nothing to do with their relation-ship. As per usual, it was All About Gabe time, which he felt guilty about. Heidi had kept so many secrets, and here was a-fucking-nother one popping up, like she left him his own personal game of whack-a-mole.

They'd never had the kind of mother-son relationship where she made him a nice hot chocolate after he fell off his bike or gave him stickers when he got good grades, but it hadn't been adversarial either. However, it had, as Gabe was discovering over and over again, been wrought with duplicity.

Con artist, Chance.

Whatever. And he meant that in the most passive-aggressive, dismissive way possible.

Gabe was tired of secrets. What would this one turn out to be? He swallowed, realizing he was having trouble breathing past the weird lump in his throat that had been sitting there since he'd read the contents of the letter and talked to whoever the hell she was on the phone.

How was he supposed to look back in time and know what was real and what was deception? He purposefully breathed in and held his breath for a few seconds before letting it back out. Why had Heidi believed she needed to live that way, even with her own son? Gabe suspected he might not want to know the answer but was about to find out.

After Casey and Bowie left for the marina, Gabe ate a quick dinner consisting of boxed tomato soup and a stale dinner roll. When he finished, he dropped the bowl and spoon into the sink to clean the next day—he was not going to turn into Randy Witherspoon—took a couple of Advil, and crawled into bed.

In the comfortable darkness, he forced himself to think back over what he knew for sure about Heidi's life and his own childhood. There had to be something, a clue or hint that would unravel the mystery of Heidi Karne, but if there was, it wasn't immediately apparent. Maybe some direction would present itself when he eventually went through her belongings. After all, whatever this newest haul ended up being, she'd wanted Gabe to get it at some point.

Could have just given it to me when you were alive, Heidi.

There was no answer—thank fuck—but Keith decided to bless

him with her presence at that moment, jumping onto the bed and curling up behind his knees.

"Where have you been hiding?" he asked. Keith, of course, did not answer. "And why couldn't you have intercepted the letter and eaten it or something?"

Again, no response, so Gabe closed his eyes and did his best to fall asleep.

SIX
GABE – TUESDAY MORNING

"Your forehead looks lovely. That's sarcasm, by the way," Casey said as he came through the door.

"Yeah, it looks worse this morning," Gabe agreed before Casey could add another snarky comment. "Maybe I should have put a slab of rib eye steak on it like Elton suggested. And I think I may have sprained a rib. But don't worry, I took some pain killers."

Casey shot him a look, one that telegraphed, *You are possibly an idiot,* his stupidly sexy eyebrows drawing together. Why had Gabe been relieved that Casey hadn't stayed over?

"Does it hurt when you laugh?"

Gabe considered that the correct response for him was probably *It always hurts when I laugh,* but Casey was already wound up tight, so he decided to skip it. "It twinges, I guess? Not that I've been ha-haing much since I rolled out of bed though. That first step was a doozy."

"Personally, I think that's a waste of a perfectly decent steak. Is your head bothering you?" Casey asked. "No nausea or dizziness?"

"No, it's really not. I am fine, I swear."

"Are you ready for Seattle, then?"

Gabe eyed him. Ranger Man never missed a damn thing. He especially never missed things Gabe wanted him to. Because no, Gabe was not ready for this.

"Fine. You busted me. I'm not ready, and if it weren't for you and Elton, I would have ignored the letter. Huh. Maybe that's why Heidi used him as a liaison?"

The other thing Gabe wasn't ready for was telling Casey about the young woman who had dropped by and claimed to be his daughter. It wasn't true, but he didn't want Casey to think poorly of him. Gabe didn't need more sympathetic glances or worse, pure pity. He wanted his life to be normal.

Really, Chance? Normal?

Fine. Normal-ish.

It had been difficult enough for him to get on Ranger Man's good side, but they were together now, and Gabe wanted things to stay that way. Casey didn't need to know there was someone out there peddling complete fabrications about Gabe's past. If Juliet Carter returned with something more than printouts, then he'd tell Casey. Until that time, he was the only one who needed to know about yesterday's visitor, mostly because he could not figure out the *why* of it.

"Let me finish getting dressed, then we can blow this popsicle stand."

GABE FELT Casey's gaze on his forehead again as Casey shifted the Wagoneer into reverse and started backing out of the gravel driveway. "You're sure that doesn't hurt? We can call and tell her we're coming another day."

"I swear, it doesn't hurt. And I just want to get this next Gabriel Karne side quest wrapped up," Gabe replied. He clipped his seat belt and settled back for the ride. "If it makes you feel better, I did slap some more antibiotic ointment on it. It's all good. Let's get this over with. I, for one, am not looking forward to this trip to Seattle." Gabe glanced into the back, expecting to see a familiar fuzzy face there. "Where's my dog?"

"We might need the space for whatever we're picking up, so Bowie's with Elton for the day. I was going to ask Mickie to watch him, but"—Casey breathed out a sound of frustration and pressed on the gas pedal—"I thought Mickie might think I was using it as an excuse to check up on him."

Gabe suppressed a chuckle when Casey flipped on his indicator before turning onto the main road. There was no one else in sight, not even Juliet Carter's beat-up Ford Focus coming back with more lies.

"Try for the ferry first?" Casey asked. "If it's full, we'll drive around."

"Sure, I like the ferry as much as the next person. Plus, there are jigsaw puzzles to entertain ourselves with."

Either way, they would be crossing over several long bridges and various bodies of water between here and their destination, which would also give Gabe plenty of time to dive into the problem that was Mickie Lundin. He'd much rather talk about Casey's brother than his own new crop of problems.

"Are you checking up on Mickie?" Gabe asked after a chunk of scenery had been passed by. "When we talked about this the other day, you said you were going to give him some space. Would you be? Using Bowie as a way to check up on him, that is?"

Casey was quiet for long enough that Gabe thought maybe he wasn't going to answer. Which, fine, he could understand.

They passed by Norskland General Store, currently on limited hours since it was a weekday during the low season. He frowned at the closed sign. Yes, Gabe had a fancy espresso machine of his own, but he still liked stopping by for a coffee and a chat, so Mercy and Barry's absence bugged him. He even liked talking to the teenagers; it was always good to keep up with what they were into.

"No. At least, I don't think I am," Casey finally said. They'd crossed onto the mainland and were headed toward Hood Canal Bridge. "I just worry."

They'd had this conversation a few times since Mickie had been exonerated by Eli Rizzi's confession to the murder of Maya Crane and finally released. After years of worrying about his brother, Casey was having difficulty finding the Off switch. Gabe understood, at least he thought he did, but he knew for sure that Casey needed to let his brother do his own thing. For both their sakes.

"You spent years doing everything for Mickie. It's hard to give that up." Gabe figured a lot of what Casey was currently feeling had to do with his almost primal need to protect those he considered his people. His family.

"Don't I know it."

"But Mickie needs to figure out his life on his own. You know that?"

"Yeah, I guess."

Gabe had gone along with Casey to collect Mickie when the older Lundin had been released from prison. He'd been mildly surprised when Casey had accepted his offer, but his acceptance had backed up Gabe and Elton's theory that Casey didn't know what to do with Mickie now that there were no bars or plexiglass between them. A theory that was being confirmed over and over.

It still boggled Gabe's mind that the Powers That Be had just sort of pushed Mickie Lundin out the gate, no offer of transportation or even decent bus service. Just opened the doors, watched him walk out, and locked the gate up behind him. Again, Casey had been the one there for his brother. Their parents hadn't even bothered to show up. What the fuck was with that? Casey and Gabe had been the only people waiting in that desolate parking lot.

"Oh, hey." Gabe pointed to the side of the road. "The coffee stand is open. Let's stop."

"I've literally never met anyone else who enjoys coffee as much as you do."

"Except Elton, and you say that like it's a character flaw," Gabe pointed out. "This place has great pastries too. They get them from one of the bakeries in Westfort."

"Only you, Gabriel Karne, Charming Fucker himself, would have chatted up a barista for intel on the baked goods," Casey said. "How do you manage it?"

"Pastries are important. Life is meant to be enjoyed."

Casey grunted and veered off the road to where Watershed Espresso was doing brisk business. The Shed's owners had tapped in on the local need for caffeine—and baked goods—between Heartstone and the canal. Or Westfort, depending on which way a person was driving.

"I counted once, and there're at least fifteen roadside espresso stands between here and the ferry."

"Bet you missed one or two."

"Shall we bet on it? Closest to the correct number buys coffee for a week?"

"Nope, I'm not taking that bet."

"Coward," Gabe said with a laugh.

They were lucky, just third in the line, more cars arriving while they waited. Eventually, the barista handed over two twenty-ounce Americanos, a glazed lavender-lemon tea cake for Gabe, and a toasted bagel for Casey.

"Are you ready to get going now?" Casey asked, pulling back onto the road.

Apparently, he'd clued in to Gabe's delaying tactics.

"You have a blob of cream cheese on your nose," Gabe said, popping a bit of the cake into his mouth.

"I do not." But Casey swiped at his nose anyway.

"Made ya look."

"Asshole."

"Yes, but I'm your—"

"Don't say it," Casey ordered.

Smirking, Gabe took a bite of his lavender cake and groaned long and loud—several times. "God, these cakes are delicious. I should have gotten two of them."

Gabe glanced at Casey, who was shaking his head at him. But a half smile curved his lips as he focused on the road. Yeah, he'd do a lot to make Casey happy, even pull out a Meg Ryan impression. A rather good one, if he had to say so himself.

SEVEN

GABE – TUESDAY: SEATTLE

"Well, here we are. And here goes nothing," Gabe grumbled, staring up at the house.

The structure was an older one, probably built during the post-1944 construction boom that many cities, including Seattle, experienced. A For Sale sign was stuck into the grass that grew along the parking strip.

"We've got this," Casey said.

"Right. Okay."

Taking another deep breath, Gabe headed up the cement stairs that shot from the sidewalk straight to a large front yard and then along a curved walkway that led them to yet another set of stairs. Definitely not ideal for an elderly person, so maybe this wasn't a scam or some kind of ambush. That depressing thought had occurred to him last night: What if this was an elaborate setup by friends of the Colavitos? He didn't think he'd ever quit looking over his shoulder for those assholes.

The front door opened before they could knock.

An older woman, probably somewhere between Althea's and Elton's ages, peered out at them. After glancing between Gabe and Casey, she spoke to Gabe. "You must be Heidi's son, Gabriel. You have your mother's skeptical expression, and it's just not possible that the handsome redhead with you is related to Heidi. It's lovely to meet you in person, Gabriel. My condolences on your mother's passing."

She was tiny, diminutive even. The temperature today was pleasant, with off-and-on sprinkles of rain, as was its custom during the first false spring in the Pacific Northwest. But the woman was bundled up as if there was frost on the ground and snow in the air. She even wore a pair of fingerless gloves.

Gabe climbed the stairs and stuck his hand out toward her. Shaking it with one gloved hand, she waved them both inside with the other.

The front door opened to a living room that had moving boxes stacked around its perimeter and a narrow pathway running through them. A shoulder-height wood mantel had Gabe suspecting a fireplace was hidden behind the boxes that extended into a dining area.

The boxes and lack of overhead lighting gave the rooms an uncomfortable, deserted feel, and any natural light was thwarted by heavy curtains that looked to Gabe to be decades old. The whole setup made him appreciate just how—

Crap. He realized he still didn't know what to call Heidi's friend and their host. The letter had been signed with an indistinguishable squiggle.

"I missed your name," he said, trailing after the older woman. "I mean, I could come up with something on my own, but I'd rather use your correct title."

"Oh," she exhaled the word as she turned and looked at him, her eyes moving upward. "That looks painful."

Gabe shook his head. "Nah, just had a run-in with a hedge."

"Looks like the hedge got the better of you. Anyway, just call me Lynn."

Not, Gabe noticed, *my name is Lynn* but *call me Lynn*.

Sure. What was it with people lying to him about their names this week? Was it his face? If her name was Lynn, then he was buying several hundred dollars of Power Ball tickets the next time he stopped at the gas station. In fact, he'd have Casey stop at one on the way home this afternoon. On the other hand, maybe she had good reason to keep secrets. She was a friend of Heidi's, after all.

But perhaps he was being paranoid, and Lynn really was her name. Why did he have the feeling she wasn't being honest? Did it matter? He felt like his mother would have an opinion, but he couldn't imagine what it was.

In spite of himself, Gabe asked, "How did you know Heidi?" Who knew, maybe the two of them had come up with pseudonyms together. That they'd met through *business* seemed obvious.

Lynn shot him a conspiratorial smile. "Oh, you know." She waved a knit-covered hand. "We sort of found each other, you might say, back in the day. Kindred souls, I guess."

Ah. Yep.

Let it be, Chance, you don't need to know everything.

"She must have trusted you quite a bit if she left belongings she valued with you," he persisted.

That odd smile emerged again. "We trusted each other and moved in the same circles for a bit of time. Years ago, when she left these things with me, she asked me to look up someone named Elton Cox if she passed before I did, said he'd know how to find you. Honestly, it's a bit shocking to me that I'm still here and she's not. This Elton person must be at least as old as I am, but I sent the letter anyway. And here we are in the nick of time!" She lifted her arms, dramatically gesturing at the stacks of moving boxes. "I was relieved to hear from you. I thought I might have left it until too late. The movers are coming tomorrow and most of this shit is going to the Goodwill. Now." She brought her hands together with a muffled clap. "Do you boys need something to eat or drink? Or do you just want to grab the boxes and head out?"

Abruptly, Gabe wanted to get out of there and away from "Lynn" and secrets that didn't want to be brought to light. Normally, he was the one who was very good—excellent, even— at pumping people for information. He'd been a reasonably successful grifter and could tell when someone was not going to easily give up whatever they knew. Lynn was definitely in that category. Plus, the house was oppressive and cold, and he wanted to be out of there. He glanced at Casey.

"I think," Casey replied, correctly reading Gabe's expression, "that we'll pack up and get going, if you don't mind." Casey shoved his hand out for her to shake. "Sorry, my name's Casey."

She smiled and accepted his hand, saying, "It's nice to meet you, Casey. Now, if you want to come this way, everything's in the basement."

They followed her into a dimly lit kitchen and out into a hall on the other side, where she opened a door to yet another set of stairs, this one disappearing into a murky and without a doubt cobweb-infested darkness.

Fucking spiders.

His stomach sinking, Gabe stared downward. This was definitely a serial killer cellar. He didn't like it one bit. At least Elton knew where they'd gone. Someone would find their bodies— eventually.

"Oh, sorry!" Leaning past the door, she flicked on a light switch above the top stair. A single bulb illuminated the descent. If Lynn thought that made the basement seem less serial killer-ish, she was wrong.

"There, it's a bit less Bates Motel now. Heidi's things are stacked over by the water heater." She made a vague motion to the left of the staircase.

Here goes nothing, Gabe thought.

Lynn always did have a flair for the dramatic, Chance.

"Come on, Ranger Man." Ignoring the pain radiating from his knees, Gabe started down the stairs. "Let's get this loaded up." He wished he'd thought to bring along the entire bottle of pain relievers. After the holly tree incident yesterday, his body was not going to forgive him anytime soon.

EIGHT
CASEY – TUESDAY AFTERNOON

The return trip to Heartstone was unnerving, and there was one single reason for it.

Gabe was quiet. Too damn quiet.

Casey was not used to his—his *Gabriel,* for lack of a better word—not engaging in an almost endless stream of chatter.

Casey had expected a running commentary on a variety of road trip topics. The significant amount of terrible and distracted drivers. Potholes the size of hippopotamuses, possibly leading to alternate dimensions. Billboards advertising ambulance-chasing lawyers in the most accident-prone section of Interstate 5. Which previously presumed dead seventies bands were playing at the casino or the Tacoma Dome. Even more prodding about Mickie. But no, Gabe kept his mouth firmly shut, appearing to watch the scenery, such as it was, flash past.

A trickle of concern took root and quickly bloomed in Casey's stomach, driving away all thoughts of stopping for five-star pad see ew or pad kee mao. He briefly considered forcing the conversation, but his last interaction with his brother came to mind, and he decided it was fine to let Gabe brood until they got back to the island.

Gabe played the carefree ne'er-do-well almost perfectly, but Casey knew that he worried, and he cared. Deeply. As much as Casey's life had been, and still was, upended by Mickie's wrongful imprisonment and their parents' inability to deal with it in any remotely healthy way, he at least hadn't been brought up to unearth people's weaknesses and take advantage of them. Gabe had been, yet he'd managed to retain his core decency, which, of course, if Gabe knew Casey thought that, he'd make gagging sounds.

But Casey was onto him.

Gabe was Casey's Charming Fucker, but he wasn't a natural cheat. He had to work at it. A few months on Heartstone and his con artist veneer had worn away, revealing—well, a man who didn't mind flaunting the law but only for what he considered the greater good. Gabe's gift was that people took to him without much effort on his part.

About halfway home, Casey's cell phone vibrated, and both he and Gabe glanced over to where it sat in the cup holder. *Elton* lit up the screen. Casey thought that Gabe might answer the call, but he just turned his head again as they crested Narrows Bridge, his attention focused on the swirling dark waters far below. Casey would return Elton's call once they arrived at Gabe's.

Finally, Casey turned into the RV park. They'd made decent time on the return trip, with the sun just now starting to sink behind the Olympics and sending a swathe of red and yellow ribbons into the atmosphere. As always, he felt incredibly lucky to live and work where he did.

"Sorry," said Gabe, reaching for the door handle.

His first word in a solid two hours, and it was sorry? "I was going to ask if the cat got your tongue, but Keith stayed home," Casey teased.

"Ha, ha." Gabe clicked the lock and elbowed the door open. "Thanks."

"Thanks for what?"

"For driving my sorry ass to Seattle, for braving the serial killer basement of doom and carting this shit back here." Gabe dragged his fingers across the top of his head, tugging at his hair like he did when he was perturbed about something. "What the hell am I going to do with it? And what the fuck is with that chair?"

Casey pinched his lips together, trying not to laugh, and shrugged. The chair in question was remarkably ugly. "You don't remember it from when you were a kid?"

"Oh, come on," Gabe scoffed. "Would you forget a chair that ugly?"

Casey had to admit he wouldn't. The chair in question was antique, there was no doubt of that, and sort of looked like a throne, except without the gilt and precious gems he randomly associated with something like that. The piece was heavy and awkward too. It had taken both of them to get it out of the basement and to Casey's car. Jamming it in the back had been an event in itself. Thank god Bowie had stayed at Elton's.

"Nope, you're right," Casey said. "It's definitely unique."

"Which then begs the question: What, and I do mean, *The Fuck*, was Heidi doing with something like that?"

Gabe was out of the car now, his hands clasped together on top of his head, conveying his utter and complete exasperation, as if he'd spent the drive trying to figure out what the stuff they'd picked up meant and yet was still clueless. Casey got out from behind the wheel and came around to join him.

"Maybe you'll never know. But I'm guessing there's a clue in one of those boxes."

"Har, har." Gabe dropped his arms and turned to glare at the moving boxes visible through the passenger windows. They'd been packed long enough ago that Casey suspected the moving company was out of business and, by the look of the logo's style, had been for at least thirty years.

"How do you want to do this?" Casey asked.

Gabe was quiet for a moment, then a more familiar mischievous glint lit up his eyes. "Gasoline would probably work best. A couple of gallons and poof! My problems would be solved."

At last, a glimmer of his Charming Fucker. A man willing and ready to torch his problems with gasoline. And god help him, Casey loved him. Hadn't said the words to Gabe yet, but the truth was there.

Gabe was probably just kidding, but in case he wasn't—

"You would regret not finding out what your mom thought was so important that she stored it safely with a friend and did her best to make sure it got to you at some point."

Casey stepped in close to Gabe, his hands landing on his hips so he could tug him even closer. The bruise on Gabe's forehead had darkened, making Casey wonder once again if he had a headache. Gabe would never admit it if he did. "Although I have to admit that the fact she made it happen after her death is a bit worrisome."

"See! That's what I'm talking about! And I didn't tell you what happened yesterday morning!"

Casey lifted both eyebrows. "You mean something more than going one round with a tree and losing?"

"Yeah—"

The crackle of gravel interrupted them before Casey could ask him what exactly had happened. He dropped his grip on Gabe's hips and twisted around to watch Elton's truck pull in and stop behind Gabe's Honda.

"How did he know we were back already?" demanded Gabe. He sounded a tad outraged, a bit more like his usual self.

"You're the one who bought him a phone with tracking capabilities and spent hours teaching him how to use them," Casey reminded him. "I'm sure he knew exactly where we were the entire day. And he did call, I just didn't answer."

The incident late last fall when Casey had been attacked up near Gordon McDonald's place had finally convinced Elton to get a cell phone, and not just the burner one Gabe had picked up for him. The old man didn't welcome all the "fancy interwebs shit," but he did like to know where his family was. Casey wasn't entirely sure how *he'd* managed to slip from friend and into Elton's family group, but he was fine with it.

They watched Elton let Bowie jump over his lap and out of the truck, then the man himself slowly emerged. Bowie raced over with a waggle and proceeded to give Casey and Gabe a good sniff over.

"Bowie probably smells all the bodies that woman had hidden down in that hellhole of a basement." Gabe then huffed a hearty sigh, still watching Elton. "Fine, you're right. I've created a monster teaching him how to use his phone."

Elton started inching his way to the ground, and Gabe murmured, "The man seriously needs a ladder. Why haven't we made that happen?"

"Or a vehicle that isn't four feet off the ground," Casey said out the side of his mouth.

"How was the trip?" Elton asked when he was closer.

"Fine," Gabe lied, crossing his arms over his chest.

"It was—interesting," Casey filled in. "We were just discussing next steps."

"I'm all for ignitable petroleum products, but Casey says that a big no. Spoilsport."

"That's my middle name, Casey 'Take the Fun Out of Everything' Lundin."

Elton's eyebrows drew together. "There's something that Heidi wanted you to have or at least know about. Aren't you curious about what it is?"

"Of course, I'm curious. Am I breathing?" Exasperation dripped from Gabe's tone. "But I'm also considering the Pandora's box angle. Do I really want to open these? Also, why now? Why didn't she get them to me when she was still alive?"

"What's the worst that could happen?" Elton asked, ignoring

the unanswerable questions. He jammed his hands into the pockets of the puffy jacket Gabe had bought for him and walked toward the house.

"You ask this question like there aren't multitudes of answers," grumped Gabe toward Elton's back. "And with my luck, I won't like any of them."

"Start unloading and I'll get the coffee going."

Keith must have been watching them through the window because Casey saw the cat jump away, presumably to hide under the couch or Gabe's bed, as Elton used the key Gabe had given him to unlock the front door.

"You only like me for my fine espresso machine," Gabe yelled after him.

Elton, wisely, did not respond. Bowie bounded inside ahead of him.

"THIS IS ALL OF IT," Casey told Elton a few minutes later. He accepted the hot espresso held out to him and wrapped his hands around the mug.

"That's quite a chair," Elton commented, eyeing the oak monstrosity.

Black with age and grime, the piece of furniture took up a significant amount of floor space in Gabe's front room. They'd done their best to place it out of the way, but Casey suspected that soon enough one of them would stub their toe on the damn thing when the lights were out. Bowie was certainly eyeing it with distrust.

The leather upholstery on the back and seat was faded and cracked, and the wood arms, sides, and legs were carved with a repeating flower and vine pattern. Maybe a tulip, Casey wasn't certain. The arm supports were boxy enough that Casey figured they were hollow and meant for storage. As far as he could discern, this was the original E-Z chair. A man—because honestly, who else would design or want something so uncomfortable looking—could have everything he needed within arm's reach.

Elton had taken off his coat and draped it over the back of one of Gabe's mismatched chairs. Gabe had picked them up from the hardware-slash-secondhand store in Irondale. Supposedly, there was a plan for a table, but it hadn't materialized yet. Elton moved to sit on one end of the couch, his coffee in one hand, clearly planning to stick around for the unboxing.

"Not to be brutally honest or anything, but that thing is fucking ugly," Gabe repeated before sipping at his double espresso—black, no sugar. Casey could tell he was amused by ordering coffee drinks from Elton as if the old man had trained as a barista. Even better, Elton had risen to the challenge.

Gabe glared at the offending containers for a solid minute. "The one time I want a laser glare to really do its thing, and I get nothing. Fine." He set his mug on the counter. "I might as well get this over with." With that bold statement, he stepped across the floor, chose one of the boxes, and plopped it onto the battered coffee table.

None of the boxes were labeled except for having *Heidi* scrawled in thick permanent marker followed by a sloppy *K*, like the writer's hand had slipped or been bumped. If they hadn't known better, the *K* could've been an *R*, possibly a *P*. Maybe an *H*? When they'd been loading them into his car, Casey had noted that the boxes were of varying weights, leading him to speculate that perhaps some had paperwork and others held books or similar heavier objects. There'd been no clinking sounds either, so any breakables were well wrapped or there were none.

They were about to find out what Heidi had thought important enough to store for her entire life and make sure her son got it.

"There should be music for this," Gabe commented. "I bet

there is. Maybe some depressing synth-pop from the late nineties, like Belle and Sebastian."

"Gabe," Casey said.

"Fine."

The contents of the first box seemed innocuous. It contained a few spiral notebooks and an unorganized slew of paperbacks. Casey spotted copies of *Interview with a Vampire* and *All Creatures Great and Small,* but he'd never seen those particular covers before, so they were older, maybe even originals. Gabe flipped through the notebooks, finding the pages filled with flowy but faded cursive writing. Were they journals or schoolwork? At the bottom was a wooden cigar box that held what appeared to be gaudy costume jewelry: several bejeweled pins in the shape of birds—a peacock, a swan, and a swallow—a few rings, a wide beaded bracelet.

"God, this shit is ugly. I think the cigar box is worth more than the jewelry inside it." Gabe tossed the pieces back into the cigar box and carefully placed it back inside the larger container.

The next two boxes were equally mundane except they did learn that Heidi had been a reader, judging from all the paperbacks she'd saved. Otherwise, the containers were packed with the detritus of a young woman barely out of her teens. Gabe had snorted when he found a dried-up tube of Lip Smackers sparkly strawberry lip gloss.

"I cannot even imagine Heidi using this," he said, flinging the tube back into the box before he reached for the next one.

Casey realized he was holding his breath, as if this last box of the six they'd found in Lynn's basement might contain the Answer to Everything. He slowly released it and forced himself to relax.

"I feel like what's-his-name from the eighties," Gabe said as he scraped at the adhesive tape with a fingernail. "Cue ominous music. What's in the box? Have we discovered Capone's secret lair?"

"I wasn't born in the eighties," Casey pointed out.

"Don't remind me, you'll make me feel old."

Casey coughed into his fist. As if. Most of the time, Casey felt a million years older than Gabriel.

"Fuck you," Gabe said with a grin. "Not that I remember much before I was eight or so, to be honest."

"Geraldo Rivera?" Elton interjected. "Is that who you mean?"

"That guy!" Gabe pointed at Elton. "You win the grand prize, a superbly dreadful chair. It will be delivered Monday."

"The vault was empty. What a disappointment." Elton shook his head, probably re-experiencing his disgust from 1986 or whenever that had occurred. "National TV and everything. Complete waste of time."

Chuckling, Gabe ripped the tape off the box and pressed back the flaps. Casey edged closer so he could peer inside it too. A manila-style envelope sat at the top, and Gabe slowly extended his hand and picked it up.

He looked at them. "I also now hate envelopes. What if Pandora's box was an envelope?"

"I read that it was actually a jar," mused Elton, "but why couldn't it be an envelope?"

"Since when are you reading about Pandora?" Gabe asked, obviously willing to be distracted from his task.

"Since I'm retired and can do what I want with my time. Open the damn envelope."

Gabe blew out a gust of air but turned the envelope over and unbent the metal brackets so he could lift the flap. He bowed his head and peered inside it, then tilted it and let the contents slide out onto the coffee table. Several black-and-white snapshot-sized photos slipped onto the table's pitted surface. Casey and Elton let Gabe look through them first, but it didn't take him long. He shook his head after a minute or so.

"I don't recognize anyone in these. Do you, Elton?" He handed the pictures over.

Elton took his glasses off so he could peer at the photographs Gabe thrust into his hand, his nose almost touching the photo paper. Casey felt like they were all holding their breath and the various ambient background sounds became loud, almost too much. The tick of the fridge. The click of an old antenna wire against the roof. He swore he could hear Keith and Bowie breathing.

"Nope," Elton finally said, handing them back to Gabriel. "I don't recognize any of them right off the bat. Not sure why I would. That last one seems familiar, but I can't place it. These look like maybe they were taken in the late forties or fifties if that car is anything to go by."

Impatient to see, Casey tugged the photos from Gabe's grip and stared down at the black-and-white shots, like he, the youngest of them all, would be able to discern something Elton and Gabe could not.

The top one showed a young man and woman standing close together in front of what was now a collector's automobile. An Edsel or Oldsmobile, some kind of massive American car with fins, maybe a Chrysler. The background was out of focus, but there were a few trees and an indistinct building off to one side. Were they married? Were they setting off on a honeymoon or just celebrating a special day?

The next was of a baby, old enough to crawl through grass toward the photographer. Boy or girl, they had a bonnet on their head, the strings tied under their chin to keep it from falling off. The child grinned toothlessly at the camera. Again, the background was indeterminate—grass and tree shapes, nothing identifiable.

Last was a forested landscape with a body of water in the foreground. Casey narrowed his eyes; something about the shot made him think he *did* know where this had been taken. Unfortunately, the Olympic Peninsula had changed so much over the decades—and not in all good ways—that he wasn't positive.

Stooping, Casey dropped the pictures on top of the table and tapped the landscape. "This last one feels familiar, like Elton said, but I can't place it. Maybe the baby is your mom?"

"Might as well see what else is here," said Gabe, ignoring Casey's baby comment.

A few minutes later, he'd reached the bottom of the box and had haphazardly laid the contents out on the coffee table.

"Mixtapes!" Gabe picked one of the cassette tapes, turning it over in his hand to read the handwritten playlist and nodding while he perused it. "Nothing earth-shattering here. The Beatles, Elvis, Joni Mitchell—Heidi always did like her—Donna Summer, Patti Smith. Oh, Velvet Underground. Wow."

"What's that?" Elton pointed to a slim volume.

It looked to Casey like a product manual or a catalog, but the title was obscured. Gabe set down the cassette he'd been holding. Casey knew he'd seen the booklet when he'd first reached in but had decided to ignore it. The cassettes were probably more interesting to him, more of an insight into Heidi as a young person.

With reluctance, he pushed the other papers aside so they could all read the title.

"Oh, lookie here, a yearbook. Mom was sentimental after all."

NINE

GABRIEL – TUESDAY EVENING

Across the top of the oversized booklet in faded lettering was *Westfort High School 1978, Home of the Puffins*.

"The Puffins?" Gabe said. He looked at Casey and then Elton, his eyebrows reaching for his hairline.

"Yep. One of Washington's best-kept secrets, the tufted puffins. Unfortunately, the population is dwindling for reasons we don't understand," Casey replied, coming around to perch his hip on the arm of the couch. The couch creaked under his weight.

"Do not break my furniture. This thing is vintage."

"Vintage Ikea maybe," Casey muttered, shifting again.

"Maybe so, maybe so. It keeps my ass off the carpet, so don't break it."

He glanced down at the yearbook, where a tufted puffin floated serenely across the cover, bobbing in the waters of the Salish Sea. "How did I not know about this?" Gabe waved the booklet. "Puffins! Real puffins."

Gabe was not any kind of birder, but he could filibuster with the best of them. Learning that puffins were a local high school's mascot was officially the best part of this weird-ass week so far, and it was only Tuesday. Much better than possessed furniture and strange young women claiming he was their father.

"Quit your stalling and see if Heidi's in that book," Elton ordered. "Or else hand it over and let one of us take a look at it."

Gabe narrowed his eyes in response to Elton's bossy but correct assumption that he was avoiding opening it. Heidi had saved the damn thing for a reason. Still, Gabe felt apprehensive, his natural curiosity at bay for the time being. If Casey and Elton hadn't been there, he would've stuck the boxes in a closet and ignored them forever. Which both of them probably knew.

"Fine." He sat down on the opposite end of the couch from Elton and flipped the book open to the first page.

"Like ripping off a Band-Aid. Oh look, they had a band." He pointed to the photo of kids with French horns, tubas, and trumpets that took up the first page. "I bet they still do. Do high schools have marching bands anymore?"

"Gabriel," Elton growled, reaching for the book.

Rolling his eyes and catching Casey's amused glance, Gabe gave in and skipped forward a few pages to where the student pictures began. Six to a page, the shots were, of course, printed in black and white. He appreciated that Casey shifted so he could look over Gabe's shoulder while he searched for his mother.

"She could have left a damn clue, maybe thrown another letter in one of these boxes."

What fun would that be, Chance?

All the underclassmen years were lumped together in alphabetical order, while the senior class was listed separate from the rest. A quick glance informed him that there was no one with the last name Karne. Not a big shock. Gabe had long suspected that his surname had been created out of thin air.

"No Karne. Why am I not surprised?"

"Keep looking," said Elton. "Do you want me to drive home and get my magnifying glass?"

"No, I do not need a magnifying glass." Maybe he did, but he wasn't admitting that right now. The pictures weren't so small he couldn't focus on them. He just didn't want to.

"Suit yourself," Elton said with another huff.

Gabe ran his index finger under each shot of the impossibly young-looking students, searching for the one who might be Heidi. Why else would she have kept this yearbook? Gabe had never been one hundred percent certain of her age, but his mom would have been what, sixteen or seventeen in 1978?

A quick calculation told him there'd been no more than two hundred students that year, less than fifty in the senior class. Gabe's final high school had had a population of over two thousand, allowing him a comfortable level of anonymity at the time. Less than two hundred? Everyone knew everyone else's business, which Heidi would've hated.

"She wasn't a senior, or she didn't have her picture taken," Gabe said to his audience. "Hang on while I go back through the rest of the riffraff."

He flipped the pages back to the start of the undergraduates and forced his finger to move slowly down the page and not skip past anyone. There was nothing on the first few pages.

At the next one, Casey bumped Gabe's shoulder. "Oh, check it out, third row, middle."

Staring out from the yearbook page was Eli Rizzi. He'd been a junior, which meant he was somewhere around seventeen years old. Gabe would never have recognized him, proving that he also might not recognize his own mother.

"Who knew he'd grow up to be a POS. Does he look like a criminal to you? Although look at those weaselly eyes." Gabe said, peering closer at the grainy picture of the former Twana County sheriff. "Why did I think he moved here from somewhere else?"

"Westfort is somewhere else. Back in those days, it seemed far away," Elton told them. "The bridge over the isthmus wasn't built until the early 1980s, so if the weather was bad or the tide high and dangerous, people didn't come or go from here to there."

"What a pig. I hate that he probably knew Heidi."

His attention strayed up the page, and he sucked in a sharp breath. There, nestled in between O and Q, was his mother. At least, he thought so.

"Shit, there she is." He jabbed a finger toward a black-and-white image with *Holly Pritchard* underneath. Holly. Holly wasn't a name he'd noted when Juliet Carter had stopped by with her faked paperwork, but Pritchard was.

He stared at the photo, narrowing his eyes. Unless Heidi had a doppelgänger, this was his mother. This very young version of his mom reminded him of Marcia Brady—she'd had long, straight hair of an indeterminate dark blond or brown, held back with what looked like plastic clips. She wasn't smiling. Which, to be fair, Heidi hadn't done often over her life. A true-life case of resting bitch face.

You smiled enough for the both of us, Chance.

Elton and Casey leaned in to get a closer look, their heads momentarily blocking his view.

It was Elton who nodded first, saying, "You're right. She couldn't have been much older when she showed up looking for work."

"Holly Pritchard. Huh. There you are, Mom. Why did you decide to use the name Heidi Karne?" She'd claimed she'd never married, but Pritchard had been a name she decided to shed. Gabe looked away from the picture to Elton, as if the old man he considered to be family might have the answer.

"Can't say. Heidi Karne is the only name I knew her by. But I'm not surprised to learn she was from around these parts. How else would she have known about Heartstone Island? We aren't exactly the center of the universe."

"And she never said anything to you about Westfort or her family?"

"No, not that I recall. And I don't think she ever used that name with me, but that was a long time ago. I could have forgotten. I've heard the name Pritchard, there's plenty of them around, but never had any reason to connect Heidi to them." Elton pursed his lips and shot Gabriel a complicated glance. "Heidi was not someone I would describe as open or warm. As you know, she didn't invite many people to get to know her. Frankly, I'm still scratching my head over David Delacombe. I suspect he was a one-time-only incident of letting her guard down."

Ah yes, Gabe's sperm donor, David Delacombe. In a way, it was nice to know Heidi had had what he was going to imagine was a steamy affair at least once in her life. It made her a bit more human to him. David must have been something to get past Heidi's barriers. Or a fast talker.

"And she ended up saddled with me."

Elton waggled his head. "I understand that Heidi wasn't perfect, but she kept you. She didn't have to. And now it's starting to look like she was trying to get away from something. What, we don't know—"

"Family makes the most sense," Casey interjected.

Elton nodded again. "Family, most likely. But she kept you, Gabe. There were other options for single mothers back then. She kept you, kept a roof over your head, brought you up the best she knew how. Whatever you take away from this"—he gestured at the unsmiling picture of his mother—"don't forget that. Heidi did the best she could with what she had to work with."

"I think I want a reason to be angry with her." He really did. Gabe wanted to be furious, to rail at his mother for her shortcomings and the decisions she'd made. But Elton was right, she had done the best she could. Maybe his childhood could've been better, maybe not.

"Not all my memories are bad. Actually, most of them aren't, and the bad ones I most likely brought on myself. Let's face it, I can be impulsive sometimes."

Casey was unable to repress a smirk. "Sometimes?"

"Yeah, yeah, so sue me." A smile played at the corner of Gabe's lips. "Unless there's a set script, I improvise. And okay, yeah, it *occasionally* doesn't go quite right. But in all seriousness, I'm a bit unsettled by all this and the possibility that there's more I don't know. That she hid so much from me. I thought I had a pretty good idea of what made Heidi tick, and it turns out I didn't know anything, not even her given name."

He felt like he should be angry, but what he felt instead was exhaustion coupled with a sense of loss. A history had been hidden, one that he had no real tools to connect back to. Gabe glanced down at the yearbook. Maybe that was the point of this? What if the solution was to meet Heidi-slash-Holly while trying to discover the truth?

It's not pretty.

Yeah, well, that wasn't a surprise.

"There are those who would argue that a taken name has more meaning than a given one," Casey pointed out.

"Ergh, fine. You have a point. Although *Heidi Karne*? I always thought our surname was a riff on carny, like our forbearers worked the circus circuit. Who knows." He sucked in a breath, blowing it back out almost immediately. "I might as well finish going through this stuff. AC/DC though? Who would've figured Mom to have a wild side? Aside from being a professional grifter."

Casey stood from his spot on the arm of the couch. "What I'm wondering is, did Heidi make those tapes or did someone make them for her? And could that person still be in the area? If she grew up in Westfort, or at least went to school there, it's highly likely someone may still be around who knew her. I suppose it depends on just how much you want to know about your mom and any blood relatives you may have in the area."

"Ugh, this is literally the worst." Gabe set the yearbook down and plucked one of the cassettes off the table again, examining the handwriting. Heidi had distinctive, odd, loopy handwriting. "This doesn't look much like her handwriting to me. But it evolves, doesn't it? Maybe she purposely changed it." Dammit, he wished that first letter hadn't been destroyed when the *Ticket* mostly sank.

"How about we see if anything is up with that chair?" Casey suggested. "From the thickness of the arms, I'd say there's a possibility of hidden compartments."

Oh, hidden compartments could be fun. "Fine, but if we're poisoned by a secret poison-powder blower, it's not my fault."

Dropping the cassette back onto the coffee table, Gabe rose to his feet again and moved across the room to where the chair waited for him. *Them.* Not for the first time that day, Gabe was very glad that Casey Lundin hadn't been scared off. Not yet anyway. And from the expression on his face, Elton was getting a kick out of this. At least one of them was enjoying himself.

Stepping in front of the massive piece of furniture, Gabe set his hands on his hips and stared at it. "That thing is begging for a name. Alfred, something like that."

"You need to get a move on," Elton groused again. "Pull it out more so I can see better."

"Give me a hand?" Gabe said to Casey.

Together, they dragged the weighty piece closer to the center of the room. Casey was probably right about the arms being hollow, but it still was a huge monstrosity and heavy as fuck. Gabe spotted small but ornate hinges along the outside edges of the rests.

"Yep, this monster's absolutely an Alfred." Gabe circled the chair now, taking in every angle. Then, with a sigh, he crouched down and started to poke and prod Alfred as if it were a recalcitrant patient and he was a doctor checking its internals.

"Hey, check this out."

He pried one of the armrests upward. Years of sitting in a damp Seattle basement had not done the piece of furniture much good, and the hinges were a bit rusty, but they still moved. At least the chair had been stored on a raised concrete pad.

"Anything inside?" asked Elton, who then heaved himself up and stepped closer to supervise.

Gabe peered into the cavity. "Nothing that I can see. Who has a flashlight? I'm not sticking my hand in there."

It was Elton who handed him a small pocket light he had stashed in his coat pocket.

"Always prepared." Switching it on, Gabe shone it into the hidden recess. "There doesn't seem to be anything in this one."

Casey had opened up the other arm while Gabe and Elton checked out the first one, so Gabe moved to shine the light into it.

"Nothing here either. Check this out though. There's a chess-board on the side. It flips up and out like an airplane tray. I wonder if there were pieces that went with it?" Dammit, now he was curious in spite of himself.

"Do you even play chess?" Casey asked, his tone laced with skepticism.

"Hell no, I do not have that kind of patience. But it would be cool to have them."

He fiddled with the seat cushion and discovered it also lifted. They all leaned forward, and Gabe ended up breathing in some of Casey's hair. Gross. But he still smelled good.

"One at a time, one at a time."

Nothing in that hidden space either.

"Well, this was a fun mystery while it lasted," Gabe said, brushing his hands together to get the invisible grime off them. "I guess the thing to do now is take some pictures of it and see if the thing is worth anything as is or if refinishing it would be a better decision. One of those folks at Pick Me might have an idea."

"Anything is possible, I suppose," said Casey.

Gabe smirked and sent him a wink. Casey, he suspected, was

wrongfully jealous of the owner of Pick Me, although he refused to admit it. Yes, Colton Bernard was good-looking, personable, and had a rainbow tattoo on his shoulder. But Casey was the only plaid-wearing, redheaded lumberjack type in the area that Gabe was interested in.

What was it with plaid anyway? Grunge was dead. Gabe seemed to be one of the few in the region who did not have a closet stuffed with plaid flannel shirts of all colors—mostly shades of red—and all patterns. Even Elton wore plaid.

Setting the plaid issue aside, Gabe's gaze landed on Alfred again. "Why did she save this hideous thing though? Why store it for *literal years* with someone I've never heard of, then make sure I got it and the rest of the crap after she died?"

Stepping toward the kitchen area—or maybe it was a kitchenette, he hadn't decided yet—Gabe snatched his no-longer-warm coffee from the counter and swallowed the cold brew down in one nasty gulp. He wished he could head to Norskland General Store later for a quart of some ridiculously named angsty ice cream from Jewel Creamery. Damn them for their odd winter hours. After today and yesterday, he deserved it. Maybe he and Casey could have another ice cream date night.

Elton reclaimed his spot on the couch. "What was she like? The gal who had Heidi's things?"

Gabe shot a look at Casey, urging him to please field the question. He didn't feel like the best judge of character today.

"She was—odd," Casey said slowly, thoughtfully. "Hard to read, not really forthcoming."

Gabe snorted. Maybe he wasn't the worst judge of character.

"Odd, how?" Elton asked.

Casey mulled over his answer for a moment, then said, "Like Gabe's mom, I suspect Lynn wasn't her given name. There wasn't anything specific, she didn't come out and say, 'I go by a pseudonym.' It was more how she shared things—what she did and didn't say, and the vague reference to how she and Heidi met.

The whole thing was weird. Although we didn't actually talk with her a whole lot. Gabe was ready to leave when we arrived."

"I was glad to get out of there," Gabe added, plopping his ass back down on the couch next to Elton.

"Well, what are you going to do now? Have you thought about next steps? Do you want to know more about Heidi?" Elton asked. "You don't have to follow up on any of this, you know."

The question was framed with kindness; Gabe knew that Elton would support almost any decision he made regarding Heidi. And Casey would support him too. The issue was that Gabe didn't know what he wanted. He'd brooded about it the entire drive from Seattle to Heartstone and still didn't have an answer for himself.

Did he want to uncover his mother's backstory? She'd kept it hidden from him while she'd been alive, after all. Was her history so terrible that she'd made sure he didn't know anything until after she'd passed away for his safety? Could the truth be so terrible?

"I don't know," he said with heartfelt honesty. "I just don't know."

"Well, you don't have to decide anything now. Or ever, for that matter. You can just let sleeping dogs lie and all that."

"Yeah, no." Gabe drew the second word out. Even if he wanted to ignore the boxes and their contents, he couldn't. *The Golden Ticket* led to my sperm donor. Great, yeehaw. Now she's made sure I took possession of this haunted Alfred chair, mixtapes, and other stuff she saved. What does she want me to learn this time?" He slumped back against the couch cushions. "She wanted me to know her past but not until she was dead, which cannot be good. This would have been so much easier if she'd just sat me down and told me. I guess that means I'll be poking around a bit in Westfort. They have a public library, right?"

And then there was the—as yet undisclosed—appearance

yesterday of Juliet Carter. While she was on his mind, Gabe picked up the yearbook again and checked to see if there were any Carters at Westfort High in 1977.

Casey snorted. "Yes, there's a public library. There's one here too."

Gabe did not point out that it was probably in some old lady's garage and smelled like mothballs. Not finding any student with the surname of Carter, he tossed the yearbook down again.

Straightening quickly enough that his spine snapped and crackled like a xylophone, Gabe looked first at Casey and then Elton. "It's settled, then. I'll start at the library in Westfort."

He slapped his hands together. "Tomorrow. Now, raise a hand if you want to hear what happened yesterday morning *before* the locket incident?"

TEN

CASEY – TUESDAY EVENING

"I cannot believe we drove to Seattle and back and you didn't tell me about this." Casey hoped he was managing to sound mild and not flabbergasted. Gabe was an adult. There was no requirement for him to share every moment of his life with Casey. So what if some young woman appeared on his doorstep claiming Gabriel was her father?

But, as Charming Fucker would say, What The Actual Fuck.

"Honestly, Casey, I needed some time to process." Gabe did look apologetic. "Driving home today, I was trying to think back if it was at all possible that I'm a father." He shook his head. "I don't see it. Not the way I was raised. I suppose there's always a chance. But you have to admit, the timing is fucking weird."

Casey had to agree with him on that last point.

"Maybe I'm overthinking this and her popping up has nothing to do with anything and is just a random scam, nothing to do with my retrieval services Monday or the trip to Seattle to pick up Heidi's belongings. Is it coincidence that we just learned my mother is from around here? I think not. And"—he shook a finger Casey's direction—"she just seemed fishy."

"How could this person have anything to do with Seattle?" Casey asked him.

"I don't know! But what if there's some kind of connection between the Lynn person and my fake daughter? And you know what else? You know what really pisses me off? If I was this girl's father, I'd do the right thing. I really hate deadbeat dads, fucking David Delacombe comes to mind as a prime example. I'd make an effort, try and get to know her. But I'm telling you, I'm not her father."

"We know you would," said Elton calmly. "Can you describe her?"

Casey had to appreciate that Elton was taking Gabe's news in stride.

"Your basic young woman in her early twenties. Dark blonde hair, slender. Brown eyes, I think. Five six or seven. Nothing remarkable. Which I suppose is remarkable in itself. No visible tattoos or a pierced nose. Perfect blending-in ability."

"Mm, she doesn't sound familiar to me."

"Not to me either," said Casey. "I suppose the question to ask now is, what would she gain from you being her father? What's her endgame? Did you agree to see her again?"

"No idea, no idea, and not really. I told her to come back with more convincing evidence."

"Do you think she will come back?" asked Elton.

"Six of one, half dozen of the other. Anyone up for another cuppa?" Gabe had picked up his empty cup and was waggling it in their direction. It was Casey's opinion that Gabriel had had quite enough caffeine.

"No more coffee, thanks for the offer. A man's gotta sleep at some point," Elton said, pushing to his feet. He retrieved his jacket from the back of the chair and started to pull it on. "Almost forgot to pass along Althea's thank-you, Gabe. It meant a great deal that you stuck your neck out for her. That locket is important to her. She says to plan on dinner at her place soon." He smiled. "Althea's fried chicken is incredible."

Casey's attention drifted back to the prominent and colorful bruise on Gabe's forehead, but he stayed silent. He'd already made his opinion about the adventure clear to them both. Gabe, for his part, beamed like he hadn't been chased off by the angry and possibly unhinged resident of the house. He'd retrieved Althea's jewelry, and nothing was going to take away from his success.

"It was nothing. Any time," Gabe said to Elton.

The thing was, he meant what he said. Gabe would do it again, even returning to that same house if Althea or her daughter remembered something else special that needed to be reclaimed. Yesterday a locket, tomorrow missing silver. He'd probably offer his services to anyone else who thought they needed them too. And still quibble about the definition of breaking and entering.

Casey almost shook his head but bit the inside of his lip to restrain himself. Who would've suspected that this man, whom he first laid eyes on while attempting to illegally camp at Fort Hood, would turn out to have such a big Robin Hood complex?

And end up being so important to him.

"If you want me to ask around about Heidi or this Carter girl, I'm happy to," Elton said, his hand on the doorknob. "It's been a while since I've hung out with the codgers during game day. I think there's a spring training game tomorrow, and if there is, they'll have it on the TV at the boat shed. Maybe one of them remembers Holly Pritchard."

The boat shed was basically the Heartstone community center. It was a large, covered shelter rather than a structure with four walls. A flat-screen TV and thick plastic sheeting that rolled down when the weather was bad had been installed. All the local sports games played on the big screen there, and gossip was exchanged. It was, Casey thought, a great place to ferret out information if you were in your eighties.

"Sure, why not? The more eyes the better. I'm going to head into Westfort and see what records the library has that I can go through, maybe check the public records too. If the game is still on, I'll stop by on my way home and let you know what, if anything, I find out."

They watched through the window as Elton climbed into his ladderless truck, backed out of the driveway, and headed toward home.

"Maybe he'd use a step stool? I should get going too," Casey said. At the words *get going*, Bowie hopped up and trotted over to wait by the door.

"Sure, sure. It's all good. Leave me alone with the haunted chair. I'll be fine. Are you sure you don't want to stay over tonight? Although admittedly, I don't know how good of company I'd be. I know I've been difficult the past few days."

"The chair is not haunted," Casey said with a sigh and a smile. "I should get a few things done on *The Barbara* tonight, and they might take me a while. How about I check in with you later? I can always come back here, or you can come to mine."

"Sounds good. And how do you know Alfred is not possessed? An expert on haunted chairs all of a sudden, are you? How did I not know that about you?"

This time, Casey did shake his head, and he added an eye roll for good measure. His eyes had been getting a workout since Gabriel crashed into his life. "If it turns out to be haunted, I'm sure you'll find a way to exorcise it. Threaten to chop it into firewood or something. Do you want me to go into Westfort with you tomorrow?"

"Don't you have a job? Like, you know, actual work? Greta's been pretty patient with you the past few days."

"I suppose she has. I just worry you'll get into some kind of trouble if I'm not there."

Gabe grinned. "I bet I could get into trouble with you along as well." He waggled his eyebrows. "Have you ever made out in the stacks?"

"Made out in the stacks? How old are you, really? Who says made out anymore?"

"So, you haven't. Maybe you should convince Greta to let you tag along so we can remedy that."

"I think not."

"Killjoy." Gabe began to pick up the things that Heidi had stored away and return them to the boxes. "I don't know what to do with all this shit. Like any emotionally aware male person, I plan on finding a place to store it that's out of sight, so I don't have to think about any of it. I mean, who even has a tape player these days?" he grumbled, then brightened. "I know, I'll stop by Seaside Records. I bet Ed has one he'd let me borrow for a little while."

Gabriel never failed to boggle Casey's mind. He had lived most of his life on Heartstone and worked in the region since returning after graduating from college. Yet it was Gabe who was on a first-name basis with just about everyone he came in contact with. Ed—record store guy, Colton—secondhand store, Mercy and Barry—the general store, Otto—Otto's Erotica, Greg—the kite-shop guy. The area's teens seemed to have taken to him too. It was weird. Even his brother liked Gabe.

A half grin curved Gabe's lips. He stepped into Casey's space and lifted his hands to cup his face, then stared into his eyes for a long moment, making him feel a bit vulnerable, exposed. Still, Casey returned the gaze, distracted, trying for the hundredth time to figure out exactly what color Gabe's eyes really were. They seemed to alternate between hazel, green, blue, and sometimes grayish. Changeable, just like the man himself.

"What?" Casey finally asked. What he really wanted now was for Gabe to kiss him already. Maybe then he'd forget to worry about all the people in his life who seemed determined to rush headlong into the unknown.

"What, what?" Gabe responded, his eyes glinting with humor.

"What. What, what?" Casey growled back.

Now Gabe was grinning. "You know what."

Another three seconds of eternity passed before Gabe *finally* leaned in to capture Casey's lips with his own.

When Gabe broke off the kiss, Casey wasn't prepared for it to end, and he felt slightly off-kilter, like he'd forgotten to breathe. Maybe he had.

Who needed oxygen when they had Gabriel Karne?

"Go on, get out of here," Gabe said. "I can tell you want to be alone for a while. If you change your mind, come back or give me a call, and I'll come right over." He waggled his eyebrows suggestively. "If not, I'll text you in the morning, but after I've checked out the library. Stop worrying about Mickie and Pedro."

How had Gabe known that he'd started thinking about Mickie again? After managing not to think about him all day, Mickie had popped up in his brain.

"Checked out the library?" Casey repeated, not responding to the comment about his brother. "Very funny."

Casey pulled his cell phone out of his pocket and checked the screen, just in case. But there was nothing from Mickie. No calls, no texts. He shoved it away again.

"I'm a funny guy," Gabe quipped. "Now, get going and leave your brother to his own devices. Trust that Mickie will reach out when he's ready. Look at me, giving out advice. The world must be coming to an end."

In spite of his unreasonably grumpy feelings, Casey planted another kiss on Gabe's lips and then, as instructed, left to attend to his own overthinking. Mostly around wondering what his brother and Pedro, the nice veterinarian, were up to.

He was going to probably regret not staying at Gabe's place.

Life was too short for regrets, especially not those within his control.

"I'll be back later."

"Promise?" Gabe teased.

"Promise."

ELEVEN

CASEY – TUESDAY EVENING

Casey spent the short drive to the marina rehashing his and Mickie's last conversation. It always helped to think something into the ground. The conversation had occurred after Casey had, apparently, checked in on his brother one too many times. Oops.

Gabriel was perceptive. It hadn't taken him long to figure out that Casey was wound up about the possibility of Pedro and Mickie together. *Together* together, as Gabe put it, smiling while he gently teased him. He should have never told him about last Saturday.

Casey's concerns weren't about the gay part, obviously, it was the life experience part. The behind-bars-for-years part. What did Mickie know about real life?

Worse, somehow, it was Casey who'd introduced his brother to the island's one and only small animal veterinarian, Pedro Morales. Mickie had been at loose ends, he'd needed something to do, and he'd worked extensively with the prison's dog training program while he'd been incarcerated.

It seemed like a perfect fit for him, and Mickie had jumped at the chance to work with and train "untrainable" dogs, which were just one of Pedro's many passion projects. Dogs who were lucky to be alive but maybe had been returned one too many times to a rescue or had exhibited negative behavior. Whatever the reason, the prison's program had been a last chance for the canines. And now Mickie was doing the same thing at the clinic.

With likable, nice Pedro. Very rich, very cute Pedro. *Ugh.*

Casey had been thrilled at first. But recently, Mickie had begun to act differently. Secretive. He didn't always reply to Casey's texts or phone calls. And when he finally got in touch, it was quick, almost a brush-off. They'd planned to meet for coffee and Mickie was often late, one time by an hour.

Finally, a couple of weeks ago, he'd met Mickie for lunch and asked him outright what was going on. Was there a problem that Casey needed to solve? That was when the hammer dropped. Mickie told him it was time to back off. The conversation had been painful, and Casey was still feeling a bit hurt.

"Case." Mickie had used his childhood nickname, so Casey knew he was in for it. "You mean well. I know you do. While I was inside losing my mind, you were the only person who was there for me. You fought, gave me hope when I didn't have any. I can never thank you enough for that."

"Of course I did!" Casey had responded. "You're my brother, my family."

Their parents had acted like prison was all about them and not about Mickie being falsely accused of murder. As if Mickie had failed them, not the other way around. Casey's blood still boiled when he let himself think about them. Maybe he should have forgiven them by now, but he still couldn't bring himself to, not yet. Maybe not ever.

"Please try not to take what I'm about to say to you the wrong way." Which almost guaranteed that Casey would, in fact, take what his brother had to say the wrong way. Mickie had stared at him for a long time before speaking again.

Finally, Mickie said, "I need some space. I need you to back off a little and let me breathe."

Casey had opened his mouth to protest, but Mickie held a hand up, stopping him, and continued.

"Prison was terrible, the worst, but now I'm a free man and doing what I can to put the experience behind me, in the past where I want it to belong. I can't and never will deny that it made me who I am today. My twenties and thirties were stolen from me, but I need to make my space in this life *now*. If I make a bad choice or a terrible decision, I can pick myself up, don't worry. It won't be the end of the world, I promise. You're my brother, I love you, but I need you to back off. Please."

Then he had stopped speaking, an expectant expression on his face.

The words were rehearsed; Casey could tell they were. Mickie had been thinking about saying them for a while. Well, shit, didn't he feel terrible.

"Um. Okay. I'm sorry you feel that way, that I've made you feel some way I didn't intend. It's just, Mickie, I worry."

"I know, and that's part of the problem. You worried about me for nearly twenty years. Me being behind bars shaped you too. Think about it. What would you have done, who would you have become if"—he waved a hand—"all that fucked-up shit hadn't happened? Stop worrying about me now. Step back from the job you gave yourself. Maybe try being my brother instead of my parent. Which is way weird anyway since I'm eight years older than you."

What could he have said? What Casey did say was, "Okay, of course."

"Thanks, man. I promise that I'll reach out if I need anything." Then Mickie had given him a quick hug and next thing he knew, Casey was hearing his footsteps as he hopped off *The Barbara* and jogged down the pier to the parking lot where he'd left his van.

Since that conversation, he and Mickie had communicated mainly via cat memes. But just Saturday morning, he'd sort of accidentally-on-purpose driven past the cabin Mickie was renting while he sorted out his future. Casey's plan had been along the lines of saying, "Hey, I was in the neighborhood, do you have coffee going yet?"

The van Mickie drove had not been parked in its usual spot. Casey had headed to Heartstone Veterinary Clinic, thinking he'd gone in to work early. Very early. But Mickie's van hadn't been there either. Unable to stop himself, he'd sped over to Pedro's spread, worried that Mickie had been injured or something worse and hadn't told him.

Honestly, he still didn't know what he'd been thinking because Mickie was a grown man and could call 9-1-1 if he needed to. When Mickie's silver carpenter-style van had come into view, a huge sigh of relief had escaped him. There it was. Parked next to Pedro's white van, the one with Heartstone Vet Clinic painted on the side. Then Casey'd noticed that both windshields were covered with early spring frost.

He could still feel the intense heat of embarrassment that had scorched his cheeks. "For fuck's sake. You are such an idiot."

He'd let himself spiral with worry and had driven all the way over to Pedro's to check in on Mickie when he'd specifically been asked not to. Mickie didn't need to be checked on, he needed privacy. Which was what he'd asked for, and Casey hadn't been able to abide by a simple request. Maybe Mickie was having a morning coffee with Pedro, but it sure looked to Casey as if coffee had started the night before.

Hoping he hadn't been spotted, Casey had slammed the truck into reverse, backed down the driveway, and taken himself away to park headquarters. Hours later, when Greta had asked why he was in "a worse mood than usual," he'd made something up, he couldn't remember what, and she obviously hadn't believed him. Greta was no fool.

And neither was Gabe, who'd been kind when Casey told him about his temporary idiocy. He'd also been right just now;

Casey did need some space to think this evening. Brood. Whatever.

So here he was, heading to *The Barbara*, alone, when Gabe was at his house, alone. He almost turned back right then, but he truly did have a few maintenance chores that he'd gotten behind on. A sailboat always needed something.

Opening the gate, Casey let Bowie in first and then locked up and followed his goofy dog. Casey felt a few drops of rain against his cheeks after a typical early spring day of misting on and off. The mostly hidden sun was slipping behind the tops of the mountains, and soon it would be fully dark.

That was the only reason Casey noticed the red and blue flashing lights. He stopped walking and peered south. From where he was standing, Casey couldn't tell for certain, but it looked like the police were responding to an incident on or near the bridge.

He watched for a few minutes until Bowie returned to nuzzle his hand and let him know he was taking too long.

"I'm coming, silly dog. Are you hungry?"

Bowie woofed and raced back to the sailboat with Casey once again following him.

The lights continued to flash as he climbed aboard *The Barbara* and were still flashing when Casey took the trash out to the dumpster an hour later. An uneasy feeling took root in the pit of his stomach.

Whatever was going on out there, it wasn't good.

THE SINGLE-BULB PORCH light was a welcome sight. Before he and Bowie managed to get out of the car, Gabe had the door open and was smiling at them, beckoning them to hurry up and get inside.

"I wasn't sure you were really coming back," he said, an uncharacteristically shy expression lurking in his eyes.

"To be honest, I wasn't sure either, but then I thought, 'That's plain stupid, Casey.' So, here I am."

"You had something to eat?"

Casey nodded. "Bowie too."

"He's a good boy though, so surely a biscuit is in order."

Shutting the door, Gabe moved to the kitchen, opening a cabinet and pulling down a box of dog treats. Bowie, who knew he was a darn good boy, followed him quickly and sat down on his haunches in the middle of the kitchen floor, his tongue lolling out of his mouth.

"Who's a good boy? Are you?"

Bowie woofed, just the one time. Gabe tossed the biscuit into the air, and Bowie caught it with practiced ease and chomped it down. Returning the box to its shelf, Gabe turned back to Casey.

"And you? What can I get you?" He sauntered to where Casey stood watching his two favorite beings. "I'm sure I can find a cookie to throw in the air for you somewhere around here."

"You're ridiculous, you know that right?"

"I prefer fabulous, thank you very much."

"Well." Casey eyed Gabe's handsome face. "You are sort of fabulous."

"Sort of?" Gabe fake frowned and pulled a skeptical face.

"There could be a better descriptor. You know I'm not good with words."

"I've heard that actions speak louder than words."

"You are demoted back to ridiculous."

"Nah, I'm not. You know what I am? Tired. I was just thinking about changing into PJs, but I could be convinced to sleep in my birthday suit. As long as you do too."

Hooking a finger through the belt loop of the jeans Casey wore, Gabe tugged him down the short hallway to his bedroom. Since sleeping with Gabe in his bed was what Casey wanted the most and had brought him back here, he did not protest.

"Your head?" he asked.

"My brains are perfectly fine, and I will feel even better after this. Sleep better too. Endorphins," he said with an eyebrow waggle and a wave of his hand. "First, let's get rid of these pesky clothes."

Sex with Gabriel was much like Gabe himself. Unpredictable. Changeable. Variable. Sometimes it was a breathless, wild ride that left them both panting and in need of a shower afterward. Other times, like this one, they came together slowly, gently, savoring the connection between them. But Casey had the feeling they would still both need a shower afterward.

Occasionally, Casey was in the driver's seat. But many times, like this night, it was Gabriel who led the charge. Gabriel who pushed Casey back against the mattress and peeled his clothing off. Slowly and with intent. Savoring. Tasting. And, yes, snuffling. For whatever reason, Gabe had a habit of running the tip of his nose against Casey's skin, from shoulder to hip, as if he could literally breathe Casey in like a backward genie.

By the time Casey was fully naked and exposed, he was rock hard, needy and desperate.

"Need you. Now," he groaned. Lifting one hand, he ran his fingers across Gabe's sexy back and down underneath his hips to gently caress Gabe's balls. It hadn't taken Casey long to figure out that Gabe loved that kind of touch too.

Gabe's body jerked, and the wet tip of his cock stuttered against Casey's arm, leaving yet another damp spot on his skin. "Fuck, Casey. Me too."

Casey didn't need to be a rocket scientist to figure out that the intense foreplay was Gabe's way of getting Casey out of his head. The tantalizing light touches, the swipes of his tongue across Casey's nipples and other sensitive spots.

Gabe teased Casey mercilessly with his cock, positioning himself so that it would occasionally dip downward to glance briefly against Casey's abdomen, thigh, or forearm, all of which was intended to make Casey lose his mind. And it worked. He was panting now, his chest rising and falling as he tried to maintain control of himself. But he had some remaining dignity, and he wouldn't be coming before Gabe did.

Gabe grinned, also breathing heavily. "Yeah, me too," he repeated.

With a lazy grin, Gabe slowly scooted up Casey's body.

"Faster," Casey demanded.

Finally, they were lip to lip, chest to chest, thigh to thigh. Gabe's weight held him down, and any remaining coherent thoughts fled Casey's mind. Then Gabe's hot mouth closed over his, invading him with licks and gentle nips while Gabe's hand snaked down their bodies so he could wrap his fingers as much as he could around both of their erections.

Casey arched into his grip, reveling in the slide of his cock against Gabe's. The silk and iron. Gabe's fingers kept them together as their movements became more frantic. Casey's hips pistoned as he drove himself, over and over, into the palm of Gabe's hand and the top of his thigh. He'd been so close to coming before this, and now he felt the final incendiary spark at the base of his spine.

"Gabriel," he managed to groan as an orgasm ripped through him. His balls released, come exploding from his cock, the slick covering Gabe's hand and Casey's abs.

"Fuck. Yes, yes."

Gabe was right there with him. His body shuddered before he stilled and threw his head back, and Casey's stomach was covered with warm come seconds later. The visceral feel of it had Casey's cock twitching again, an aftershock that left him gasping for breath.

For several long moments, he lay there, floating in what Casey could only describe as an orgasmic dream state. He imagined that their hearts were beating in tandem, sending blood and oxygen through their veins, their own contained universes, a synchronized rhythm.

"God, you're incredible," Gabe finally said, rolling off Casey after a few seconds of being flopped on top of him, presumably enjoying his own post-orgasmic haze of pleasure.

"I think I had oxygen deprivation for a few minutes," Casey muttered.

"Did you forget to breathe?"

"I generally forgot."

"That's good. That's exactly as it should be."

Casey had the niggling feeling there had been something he'd intended to tell Gabe, but whatever it was, it had literally been fucked out of his mind.

"Shower? Separate or together."

Casey turned his head in Gabe's direction. "Is that a trick question?"

Gabe laughed, which had been Casey's intention.

Shower orgasms were almost as good as bedroom orgasms, the only downfall being that Casey had to prop himself up against the shower wall in order not to fall.

"The right answer is always together."

TWELVE

GABE – WEDNESDAY MORNING, WESTFORT

In hindsight, waiting for the scrape on his forehead to fully heal before heading back into Westfort to seek information about Heidi Karne, née Holly Pritchard, might have been a smarter plan. But Gabe hadn't been thinking about his recent foray into town when he parked at the end of Water Street and walked over to the public library.

And to be fair, Casey had been a distraction that morning. All hot and sexy and right there in Gabe's bed before he headed off to do ranger stuff for the day.

He stopped for a moment to take in the magnificent architecture from a bygone time before climbing the steps that led to the grand two-story structure. He certainly wasn't thinking about the identifiable scrape and greenish-black bruise, he was thinking about Heidi and her Big Fucking Secret. About Juliet Carter. And about the inscrutable Lynn who'd cared for Heidi's belongings for decades.

Last night in bed with Casey asleep beside him, Gabe had thought about his childhood. The longer he lay there thinking, the more irritated he'd become. Because a pattern emerged.

Admittedly, he'd never noticed it because he never taken a lot of time to think deeply about how he'd been raised. But it seemed to Gabe that, if he was going sort out this current fuckery, he was going to have to dive into their shared past in order to get to know his mother a little better.

He'd learned early that there were only two good things about the past: learning from one's mistakes and getting to where one needed to be in the present. Thus, Gabe rarely looked over his shoulder; it had always been about moving forward to the future and the next mark. And that was one hundred percent a habit set for him by Heidi.

Do you like where you are now, Chance? Then it's all good.

As a kid, he'd known they'd moved more often than other families because of Heidi's "jobs." Maybe the mark had become suspicious, either legitimately or not, something along those lines. Maybe Heidi had gotten what she wanted. Or maybe the target had flat-out disappeared.

Which *had* happened sometimes.

When he was twelve, they had lived in Laguna Beach for a year or so. Heidi had landed a gig working in an art gallery and "had an understanding" with the owner, an art collector with deep pockets and a cocaine habit.

So very late eighties of him, Chance.

This interlude had stuck with Gabe because he'd been quasi fascinated with the guy, who wore Don Johnson-style suits and a lot of gold necklaces, even a pinky ring. Then one day he'd been gone. Poof. Nowhere to be found. By that point, the guy had trusted Heidi enough to let her have her own set of keys.

His name had been something boring, like Phil Jones. What had really happened back then? Why had the guy disappeared? Had Heidi been involved or merely an accidental bystander? Gabe doubted his mother was ever a bystander, not once she was on her own and savvy enough to practice the art of the con. Gabe himself was probably the last "accidental" event Heidi allowed to happen.

Heidi *had* helped herself to a couple of Jones's paintings. She'd taken them right off the wall while Gabe stood back and watched. She'd told him they were in lieu of payment for services rendered.

I'm sending you a hairy eyeball, Mom.

After wrapping them up and packing them into the trunk of their late model Chevy sedan, they left town without stopping at their apartment and headed due north on the Pacific Coast Highway. Gabe remembered being disappointed at leaving the golden sand and sunshine of California for Seattle clouds and rain.

What had happened to those paintings from Southern California? They hadn't been stored at Lynn's. Gabe wasn't sure he'd ever seen them after they went into the trunk, like a kidnapping gone bad. Heidi had never shown much interest in fine art after that.

And how had she known to keep Gabe home from school that day?

"Seriously, Heidi, some answers would be great," Gabe said aloud as he finished the climb. "I'd even read a third fucking letter."

He'd reached the landing of the Westfort Public Library's stairs and a set of double doors beckoned. Rolling his neck and ignoring the ever-so-slight pulse of pain in his forehead, Gabe looked up and took in the grand building one more time.

You're stalling, Chance.

Maybe he was. But although Gabe was not one who generally appreciated architecture, he could tell the structure had been built with the help of a Carnegie grant. It had that very specific look to it. Like other towns and cities across America, a band of intrepid Westfort townspeople had banded together sometime around the early 1900s and convinced the Carnegie Foundation to help them build a library.

"Hello, gorgeous," he whispered, pulling one of the doors open and stepping into the quiet beauty.

. . .

A CONVERSATION with the librarian at the information desk eventually led Gabe to the local reference section.

"We have a local fiction section too, but that doesn't sound like what you're looking for," she informed him. "And if you want to use one of the computers, you only need to show us your library card, and we can get you set up."

For the first time in his life, Gabriel Karne filled out an application for a library card.

"We're out of cards at the moment. Your permanent card will come in the mail in a week or so," she told him. "Don't worry, this temporary one is good here and in the Timberland library system but expires when the new one is sent out. Since your home address is on Heartstone, I imagine that's the branch you'll end up frequenting most. You can have requests sent there if the library doesn't have it on its shelves." Then she proceeded to slide the slip of paper across the counter as if it was gold.

Smiling at her, Gabe accepted the temporary card. "Thank you."

She turned away to help another visitor, but Gabe stayed put for a moment, staring down at the printout. This piece of paper was one more thing that linked him to Heartstone. To a permanent address. To Casey, to Elton, even Althea. He never thought he'd cared before that he didn't belong, but the funky twinge in his chest said otherwise. Carefully, he tucked the card inside his wallet and returned to the task at hand.

A few older citizens were lingering around the kiosks, waiting for another silver-haired person to finish up on the public computer, so Gabe headed over to the Westfort and Pacific Northwest section at the back of the facility. He had his cell phone with him, but the signal inside the library was crap and he didn't feel like asking for the Wi-Fi password. If he found anything useful, he'd have to take some pictures and follow up later.

What was he looking for anyway? Now there was a good question.

More Westfort High School yearbooks, to begin with. He'd learned those were shelved at the library. But he also wanted to search records regarding birth, death, land ownership, etcetera, and those were stored at the Twana Country Public Records Building, which was just a block west of where he was now. The kind librarian had informed him that, while most records were also available digitally, "for vital records before 1981, you need to go in person."

Maybe he hadn't needed to drive all the way into Westfort to do this research, but Gabe was glad he had. Heidi had been from this town, or at least had lived here for a while, and it made him feel somehow closer to her.

What happened? Why did you leave?

Heidi's trademark derisive sniff was almost audible.

He located the yearbooks and spent several minutes flipping through ones from before and after 1978 but didn't learn anything new. The one Heidi had kept had been the last one where Holly Pritchard had been pictured. She'd been a junior, one year to graduation. What the hell had happened?

They knew she'd stayed in the region because she'd been drawn into Elton's orbit soon after that time. And wasn't that an incredibly lucky thing? Gabe felt oddly blessed.

With not much to show for his research, Gabe walked down the street to County Records. Surely, he could at least discover Holly Pritchard's date of birth and her mother's and father's names. But Gabe struck out there too. Either Heidi hadn't been born in Twana County, or she'd been born at home, and no records had been filed. Nowadays, parents were required to file for a Social Security number within days of the birth of a child, but back then it was still possible to be born off the grid.

Frustrated and not sure where to turn next, Gabe stepped out County Records and into the now glitteringly bright spring afternoon sunshine. And then immediately regretted not waiting for his face to heal.

How else had Dirty Socks Randy recognized him?

"I've got you now."

It was a man's voice, one Gabe hadn't recognized at first. Squinting, he looked around to see who the fuck was talking to whom.

Shit, was his second thought. There, a mere four feet away, at the top of the steps, was Randy Witherspoon. The bozo whose house he'd entered in a not-so-legal way, as Casey insisted on reminding him, just two days ago. Randy even wore the same clothes. Either that, or he had a closet full of matching hoodies and stained jeans.

Which was also likely.

"Is it my face?' Gabe asked him, pointing to his forehead. "This mug brings all the boys to the yard."

"You're the fucker who was at my house!"

"How could you tell?" Gabe edged away from him and toward the opposite side of the staircase. "I mean, maybe I'm talking out of school, but consider hiring a cleaning service to give you a hand. Also, I had a key, so I didn't *break* in, I unlocked the door. But believe me, I have no plans on returning, so you can have it back." He stuck his hand in his jeans pocket. "I don't have it on me, but I'll drop it in the mail. Don't worry, I know the address."

His new friend Randy made an inarticulate sound that Gabe quickly translated as *very angry man wants to rip Gabe's head off*. It was a sound he was familiar with. The guy lunged and Gabe scooted, managing to dodge Randy's outstretched grabby hand. For his part, Gabe darted to the right and careened down the records building's stairs to street level without tripping and falling on his face. He'd have given himself a small cheer, but that would've interrupted his momentum.

There was a scuffle and then a thump, and Gabe risked a glance over his shoulder. Randy had tripped and fallen but, unfortunately, did not appear hurt. Oh, to be that young again. Instead, Randy picked himself up and started after Gabe at a dead run.

Fuck.

It was another mild spring day, and Westfort was a destination town. Sure, it was March and Wednesday, but people in the Pacific Northwest knew better than to waste a single ray of precious sunshine. The sidewalks were not exactly crowded on Wednesdays in early March, but there was a significant number of pedestrians out and about.

"Just what I needed, a damn Weeble," Gabe muttered as he swerved past a couple who emerged from the Pie Shop without checking for traffic.

"Hey!" one of them yelled. "Watch where you're going!"

Gabe did not reply. They were lucky he had been doing exactly that.

Not wanting to lead Randy directly to where he'd parked his car, Gabe kept moving. When there was a break in the line of cars waiting to turn, park, or whatever, he cut across the street and between two red brick buildings.

One of the things Gabe appreciated about Westfort was how hard the city leaders had worked over the years to save the historic storefronts. Original painted signage—GENUINE BULL DURHAM SMOKING TOBACCO and BUHLER MOTOR COMPANY—were among many ghost signs still visible on the sides of buildings. Also, like the "old days," there were doors leading in, up, and out, even into the alleyways. Many of the shops had more than one entrance, and one of those was Windward Kite Shop. And Gabe was friendly with the owner.

He dove into a handy alcove and pressed back into the shadows, hoping that his man Randy couldn't see him and would keep on going, giving Gabe time to catch his breath. He also hoped that Randy had the sense to let bygones be bygones.

Considering Dirty Socks Randy's behavior, chances were seventy-thirty.

If Randy did venture down the narrow alleyway, Gabe could step into the kite shop directly behind him. As soon as he had that thought, a shadowy figure wearing a hoodie paused on the sidewalk and peered down the breezeway.

"Hey, fucker!" Randy yelled. "I know you're around here somewhere. I'm gonna find you."

Well, dammit.

Randy stood still for a few seconds more, then started in Gabe's direction.

Triple fuck.

Reaching back with one hand, Gabe pressed the door handle down, pushing in at the same time. *Thank fuck* the door opened inward. He heard the quiet jingle of a bell somewhere and slipped inside, softly closing the door behind him.

THIRTEEN

GABE – WEDNESDAY, WESTFORT

He was surrounded by a sea of dizzying colors. Kites of all sizes, shapes, and types hung from the ceiling and walls and filled floor displays. This shop was one of his favorite places in Westfort, and regardless of being in semi-mortal danger, Gabe grinned at the visual delight.

"Can I help you? Oh, hey there, Gabe."

Spooked, Gabe spun toward the deep voice. Duh, of course, someone would come and see why the bell had jingled.

"Greg! I was just, um, popping in to check out the new spring kite selection. What are the fashionistas of the kite world looking forward to most?"

Keep talking, Chance, it's what you do best.

Greg Trainor, owner-operator of Windward Kite Shop, was a sexy former college athlete. Not only was he fit, but Greg was also *built* and a genuinely nice person too. Gabe wondered how he managed all that when Gabe could barely get up without moaning some days. Okay, most days, but no one except Casey needed to know that.

"Are you in the market for another kite? I told you, once you start, it's hard to stop," Greg said with a grin. "I knew Casey would love it."

Not long ago, Gabe had been searching for a birthday present for Casey and had ducked in to pick out a kite, although Randy hadn't been on his heels that day.

"We haven't had a chance to fly it yet," Gabe admitted. But if the wide grin Gabe had received was anything to go by, Casey had liked the gift.

"Take him out to one of the hills and he'll be sold on it. But he's from around here, isn't he?" Greg said. "He probably already has a good idea where to go. What's going on today? Need ideas for another gift? I'm sure Otto could help you out." He looked around as if either Otto or Casey might just pop up out of thin air. But Greg's partner, Otto, had his own business to run, and as far as Gabe knew, Casey was doing outdoorsy forest-type things.

Gabe imagined taking Casey to Otto's Erotica and quickly dismissed the idea.

"I don't think we're quite there yet." Or ever would be. Gabe couldn't imagine Casey casually wandering into the local adult sex toy shop, but this truth didn't bother Gabe in the slightest. The fact that Casey Lundin deemed him worthy was enough.

More than enough.

Gabe still kept one ear out for the sound of Randy coming closer. Maybe he should leave and face the music; he didn't want to cause Greg any trouble.

"Ah, well." Greg gave an easy shrug. "Otto's isn't for everyone. Hey, when are you and Casey setting a date for dinner at our place? Wait too long and we'll have to push it to the fall."

While they were talking, Gabe eased around one of the floor displays, placing it between himself and the door. A shadowy silhouette passed by on the other side of the frosted glass door, and Gabe thought he recognized Randy's caveman-style walk and that damn hoodie. Didn't the jerk have anything better to do?

"Are you *hiding* from someone?" Greg whispered, his gaze drawn to the side door and then back to Gabe.

"Sort of? Maybe? Yes. Yes, I may be hiding from someone who thinks I broke into their house the other day."

"*Did* you break in?" Greg asked quietly.

"I had a key. But my appearance possibly could have been misunderstood as breaking in, yes. Of course, if Randy had returned what he'd taken from a friend of mine, well, my services wouldn't have been required."

Greg wrinkled his nose as if he could smell Randy from where he stood, stepped toward the door, and locked it with a decisive click. "Problem solved."

Gabe breathed a sigh of relief although he still had to get to his car.

"At least he'll have to come through the front entrance now. Hold it, are we talking about Randy Witherspoon? That looked like his walk. Is he also how you got that bang on your forehead?"

"Guilty on all counts." Self-conscious, Gabe gently rubbed his brow in a futile effort to erase the bruise. "It's kind of a long story, and I don't know that I have the time to tell it to you right now." On the other hand—"What do you know about good ol' Randy?"

"Eh." Greg wrinkled his nose again. "Most of us along the Strip know him and avoid him these days. I've heard that the Witherspoons were once the big dogs in town. I think Randy is one of the last ones left, but he might have some relatives still kicking around. I don't think anyone will be terribly broken up when he fades into the woodwork."

"Huh." Gabe still listened for Randy. "A friend of a friend's granddaughter was dating him."

"She can do better. Oscar the Grouch would be better, apologies to Oscar. There's something I've never been able to wrap my head around. The jerk doesn't brush his teeth, so what do women see in him? That's a rhetorical question, by the way."

Another thought struck Gabe. "Greg, you know a lot of people in town. Who could I talk to about someone who lived here in the seventies? I've been to the library and County Records so far but haven't had that much luck finding the information I want. I don't really want everyone to know my business, so I'd need someone discreet."

Greg's eyebrows drew together as he thought, then his face brightened. "Jack. Jack Thorne might be able to lend a hand. He's not originally from around here, but he's an ex-police detective and has his own company now. Thorne Investigations. He might know where to start. Is this like a missing-persons thing?"

"Something like that," Gabe conceded. "More of a missing-link thing, present to past."

"Tell him I sent you. Fair warning, he's not exactly sunshine and roses, but he is a good person."

"Grumpy." Gabe grinned. "My favorite."

He peeked out the street-facing door. There was no sight of Randy. "I should go," Gabe said. "Later." He opened the door and eased out to the sidewalk.

With luck, he'd lose himself in the lunch crowd.

FOURTEEN

CASEY – WEDNESDAY, AFTERNOON

To distract himself from the capital-T trouble Gabe was potentially getting into in Westfort that morning, Casey took a deep, calming breath and texted Mickie to ask if he wanted to meet for lunch. That was unintrusive, right? He was pleasantly surprised when the reply came quickly and was a yes.

CHENDA'S PLACE? Casey texted back. NOON?

M: SOUNDS GREAT.

"Wow, okay."

"What?" Greta asked from where she was sitting behind her desk.

"Mickie agreed to meet for lunch."

"That's great! You'll keep it casual, right? You're not going to give him the third degree? Just brothers getting together." She'd been on the phone all morning interviewing potential educators for the park's summer nature program. Interfering in Casey's life was much more interesting.

"Yes, thank you, oh Wise One. I'll take it easy on him."

"Because if you grill him today, he won't say yes the next time you ask. If there is something going on with our gorgeous and independently wealthy veterinarian, he'll eventually tell you. You just need to nod and smile. Or smile and nod."

Casey turned and glowered at Greta. He knew he shouldn't have told her about that. She just smiled back at him.

"Have I ever been known as a smile-and-nod kind of person?" Casey asked.

"It's never too late to start." She grabbed her shoulder bag from underneath her desk and rummaged in it. "Where the heck is that? Aha." She brandished a twenty-dollar bill before holding it out for him. "Bring me back a large phô soup, extra veggies and hot sauce. Please."

Standing up, Casey accepted the cash and tucked it into his back pocket. "I'm just a tool for Chenda's phô."

"Maybe? But I am happy that Mickie wants to see you. And I'd like an update on The Adventures of Gabriel Karne too if you happen to run into him." She looked at her watch. "You should move it if you're getting there in time. Bowie will stay here with me, won't you, good boy?"

Bowie, the traitor, thumped his tail and didn't even bother getting up. Casey suspected that Greta kept a stash of fancy dog treats in the top drawer of her desk, just like Gabe did in his cupboard.

"I should be back before three," Casey said, heading out the door.

THE LONGEST NOODLE LOOKED BUSY. Luckily, Casey had called ahead and asked for a table, and the restaurant just happened to be in Westfort. He wasn't checking up on Gabe. Not at all.

He parked the Wagoneer around the corner from the restaurant and briefly considered texting Gabe anyway but decided against it. He also needed to learn how to talk to his brother without Gabe's help.

Glancing up and down the street, he didn't see Mickie's van, and Gabe's Honda wasn't in sight either. Maybe he was already heading back to Heartstone. Casey hoped he'd learned something about his mother. And had stayed out of trouble.

"Casey!" Chenda exclaimed after giving him a tight hug. "It's so good to see you. It's always too long between visits."

"Yeah, well, at least it's not me delivering purloined fungi this time."

Chenda smiled back at him. "We'll have plenty of time for that later in the year. Follow me, we saved a table by the window."

Casey followed Chenda to a table that looked out onto the sidewalk and took a seat. He still didn't see his brother, but his watch told him it wasn't quite noon yet.

"Thanks, Chenda."

"Sure thing, I'll try to come back and visit, but Mama insisted on coming in today, and someone needs to supervise her in the kitchen."

His phone vibrated. Casey pulled it out of his pocket and checked the screen.

M: SOMETHING CAME UP AT THE CLINIC AND I HAVE TO MISS LUNCH. RAIN CHECK?

Looking away from the text and trying not to let disappointment bring him down, Casey responded to Chenda, "Give your mom my regards."

"I will. Bring that man of yours with you next time," she said over her shoulder as she hurried off.

C: SURE. JUST LET ME KNOW.

Then he tucked his phone away again so he wouldn't brood over Mickie's text.

He told himself it was probably a good thing that Mickie had canceled on him. Casey always seemed to fuck up when he met with Mickie alone. Gabe had the art of casual conversation down pat. He had charmed everyone in Casey's circle, even Mickie.

Casey glanced out the window, and a familiar figure caught his attention. There was Gabriel with his head down, looking a bit furtive. He was quickly passing by the other pedestrians lingering on the sidewalk.

"Speak of the devil."

Casey surged to his feet, nearly knocking the chair over in his haste. By the time Casey got out to the sidewalk, Gabe had almost reached the corner.

"Hey! Gabe! Gabriel!" Casey yelled.

He watched Gabe hesitate before stopping and turning around. When he saw Casey waving at him, his face lit up, and he made his way back to where Casey waited. Having Gabe smile like that for him gave Casey a pleasant little shiver.

"Casey! Even though it's only been a couple hours, you're a sight for sore eyes. What are you doing here? I thought you were working today."

"I was meeting Mickie for lunch, but he had to cancel at the last second. Care to join me?" Casey gestured to the entrance of the noodle house.

Nodding, Gabe brushed past him into the restaurant almost as if he was in a hurry. Or avoiding someone.

"Are you in trouble again?" Casey murmured, stepping around Gabe and leading him to the table with a small Reserved sign on it.

"Excuse me," Gabe said to the nearest table of two as he squeezed behind them and took a seat. He did not confirm Casey's suspicion that he was in trouble, but he didn't have to. Casey *knew* Gabriel Karne.

"How did your trip to the library go? I'm surprised you're still in town, figured you'd be on your way back home by now."

Before Gabe could answer Casey's question or come up with an outrageous lie that no one within fifty miles would believe, the server arrived and offered them menus.

"No need for that. I'll have the yellow curry soup, thanks so much," Gabe told her.

Casey ordered his favorite noodles, "plus a phô to go," and then settled back. He had a feeling this story was going to be good. Or bad. Again, he knew Gabriel Karne.

"The library went fine. I have my own card now. And I made it to the records building too. It was after I left there that I ran into trouble."

"What kind of trouble?" Casey demanded.

"The Randy Witherspoon kind. Ran into him when I was leaving Public Records, almost literally. It was almost as if he was waiting for me, but I don't see how he could have been. And, yes, he chased me."

"I take it he didn't catch up with you." Casey imagined Gabe escaping the Twana County Public Records Building like he was Matt Damon fleeing the super spies in a Bourne movie. It actually cheered him up a bit. Mickie didn't know what he was missing by skipping out on lunch.

Evading Randy Witherspoon explained why Gabe had been walking fast and furtively.

"As if," Gabe scoffed. "No, he did not. I snuck into the kite shop and talked to Greg for a few minutes, gave good ol' Randy the slip. I did worry that he was lurking around every corner on the way to my car. But honestly?" Gabe eyed Casey again. "Why isn't having Dirty Socks Randy chase me down Main Street not the strangest part of this week? It just doesn't seem fair. No way do I have *more* unknown-to-me relatives waiting to be discovered. It just makes no sense."

He sat back and crossed his arms as if he'd finished the concluding argument in a major court case. Gabriel Karne vs. The World. The server returned to set their meals in front of them, and Gabe relaxed, picked up his spoon, and began to stir the fragrant liquid.

"So, both the library and Public Records were a bust?" Casey asked around a mouthful of noodle.

"Not entirely, but I might need to spend more time at Public Records, maybe head to Olympia. *If*, that is, I want to track down supposed long-lost relatives or, you know, my mother's history. Maybe Elton will come up with something because I haven't been able to find any record of Holly Pritchard existing beyond that yearbook so far, and definitely not an explanation as to why my friend Juliet would know enough to have Pritchard on that paper-work of hers."

Gabe was fooling himself, Casey figured. He did have more relatives he didn't know about, and, like it or not, they could be living in Westfort. The young woman, Juliet, might not be his daughter, but having that information meant she could be a cousin some number of times removed. Gabe wasn't ready to hear that yet, but Casey suspected the conclusion would come to him on his own.

Gabe's arrival on Heartstone, and apparently by extension to the Westfort area, had stirred a hornet's nest.

Some as yet unknown event had occurred back in the 1970s, causing Holly Pritchard to disappear and eventually reemerge as Heidi Karne. Additionally, this event was big enough that Gabriel's mother had waited until after her own death to send her son to the area to—to what? Fix it? Solve it? Reveal something? Heidi had known her son well. Gabriel wasn't going to rest until he got to the bottom of this current mystery.

With a start, Casey realized that Gabe was still speaking.

"—but we don't actually live in *The Twilight Zone*. I mean, I suppose I could have a doppelgänger wandering around. That said, I'm pretty sure I'm it for this particular sequence of DNA." Gabe spooned soup into his mouth and moaned appreciatively, then continued. "I did tell her to come back when she had real proof, remember. And I meant it. If she decides to come back and what she shows me makes some sort of sense, I'll send my damn spit in, and we'll go from there."

They were quiet as they continued eating, Chenda's curry being one of the few things Casey knew of that had this effect on Gabe. Casey finished off his noodles, and his bowl was swiftly removed. Casey watched Gabe slurp his curry and make a "yum" sound of satisfaction.

"Any idea what happened with Mickie? And a reason why he bailed?" Gabe asked after he swallowed.

"No. But he said rain check, so I'm choosing to believe something really did come up."

"This is true. So." Gabe tried to look nonchalant and failed. "You haven't been able to confirm if he and Pedro are an item or not?"

Casey, who'd raised his glass to his lips and was mid-swallow, breathed a mouthful of water into his lungs. He gasped and coughed hard enough that Gabe hopped up and came around to pound on his back.

"You okay?" Gabe asked him when he could breathe again.

Casey nodded and rasped out, "Yes. And also no."

"Pedro's a good guy. And cute as hell." Gabe grinned, doing his best Charming Fucker. "If there is a thing going on, I wish them every happiness."

Opening his mouth to say that, of course, he wanted Mickie to be happy, Casey was instead interrupted by the buzz of his cell phone. Frowning, he pulled it out and glanced at the screen.

TCSO.

He looked up at Gabe. "It's the Sheriff's Office."

FIFTEEN

GABRIEL – WEDNESDAY
LATER AFTERNOON

Gabe unapologetically listened in on Casey's conversation. Heidi had always maintained you could learn more than you'd think by listening in on one side of a phone call.

Except for mine, of course.

"I do. He's here with me, actually. We're in Westfort. Uh-huh. Do you want his number so you can call him directly?"

Gabe pointed at himself and shook his head, mouthing, *No battery*.

Casey nodded at him and kept talking. "Ah. Okay. He'll be in as soon as possible."

As he spoke, Casey's demeanor changed from casual to stern. Gabe knew that look and it wasn't the sexy kind of Casey-stern. Something not-good had happened. Casey had many tells, which meant he was a terrible poker player. Gabriel had managed to get him naked both times that Casey had agreed to play.

Clicking off, Casey set his phone down on the table and looked at Gabe.

"A body was discovered this morning."

Goose bumps rose on his arms and a shiver raced down Gabe's spine.

"Whose?" he asked.

"They haven't ID'd it yet. But—" Casey paused, but in his heart of hearts, Gabe already knew.

"It's my visitor from Monday, isn't it? Juliet?"

Casey nodded. "From your description of her, I'd say so."

"Why'd they call you?"

"Deputy Eagan said that she tried your phone with no luck."

"Battery's dead," Gabe confirmed. "Found that out in the library."

"She and Deputy Wycoff then went by your place, but obviously you're not there."

"Shit." Gabe stood up, pulled out his wallet, and tossed enough cash on the table to cover the entire bill.

Aside from Elton, for whom using cash was a lifetime habit, he was one of the few people he'd met who carried cash instead of cards to pay for things. Cash was a habit that he'd found no reason to break. For one thing, it didn't leave an electronic trail. Additionally, servers didn't have to "necessarily" claim their cash tips when tax season came around.

He looked over at Casey. "Let me guess, Eagan wants to question me? I might as well get it over with."

Casey rose to his feet, picking up the plastic bag with Greta's phô packed inside. "Where's your car parked?"

"Closer to the library." Gabe gestured in the general direction of his car. "I was taking a detour."

"Let me give you a ride there just in case Randy is still around. I'd rather you weren't arrested by Westfort law enforcement before you talk to the Heartstone Sheriff's Office."

"Ha, ha. Yeah, one meeting with cops is pretty much all I can handle most days anymore. Let's get out of here." Gabe headed for the door and outside. The Longest Noodle was not the place for this conversation.

He waited for Casey to join him. "But seriously, Juliet's dead? Was she murdered? At the very least, I'm guessing her death is suspicious since they want to talk to me. As if I didn't have enough on my plate this week. Did they say how they connected her to me?"

Casey stayed quiet, and Gabe crossed toward the Wagoneer, trying not to look too furtive about it.

"She must've had that paperwork on her with my name on it," Gabe said, answering his own question. "Did Eagan say anything about what happened?"

At Casey's car, Gabe lingered on the sidewalk, keeping a watch out for Dirty Socks Randy, while Casey climbed behind the wheel and unlocked the passenger door for him. Randy showing up right now would be the last thing he needed. He reconsidered that thought; the last thing he needed was Juliet Carter showing up dead.

And yet, here he was.

"Okay," Gabe said once he was buckled in. "What else did Eagan say?"

"Not much. You heard how short a conversation it was."

"But you think it's bad."

"I think it's bad," Casey confirmed.

Gabe blew out a gust of air. "What the fuck is going on around here?"

And when did Wednesday decide to compete with fucking Monday?

SIXTEEN

GABE – WEDNESDAY

Gabe appreciated that Casey followed him all the way to the Sheriff's Office. Casey pulled in beside the parked Honda and rolled the Wagoneer's passenger window down, gesturing for Gabe to do the same.

"Do you want me to stay?" Casey asked. "I can."

"No, I'm good. I didn't do anything except refuse to fall for her scam. I'll call you as soon as I'm done. But," he added, "my place later?"

The way the week was going, Gabe could use some more up close and personal private Ranger Man time. Casey was very good at taking care of his people, and Gabe was starting to feel a bit delicate, even if he'd never admit so out loud.

A soft smile curved his lips. "Yeah. Your place sounds great. I'll be there with bells on and all that. How about I stop and grab us pizza for dinner?"

"Oh god, yes." Pizza was the world's best comfort food. After talking to Eagan and the new guy, Gabe was fairly sure he would need all the comfort he could get.

. . .

"HOWDY, Althea. I'm here to see Chief Deputy Eagan."

If Gabe understood things correctly, Althea Mortine was the glue that held the TCSO together, especially since the county was still searching for an interim sheriff. She'd been behind that front desk for decades and knew everything there was to know. Whoever the county brought in as sheriff would have to run for the position when election time came around, but in the meantime, Althea was there to guide them.

Both Gabe and Casey thought Bree Eagan would do an excellent job. Elton had told them that she was facing resistance from the Old Codgers Club, but he was working on them to change their minds.

Gabe held the opinion that the Old Codgers Club had fucked up enough keeping Eli Rizzi in place and had lost their chance at influencing who would take the position now.

"Mr. Karne, I'll let Deputy Eagan know you're here," Althea said formally.

"It's Gabriel," he reminded her.

Althea smiled primly at him and pressed buttons on her phone, presumably to alert the deputy. Gabe started to sit in one of the chairs across from the desk, but Deputy Eagan arrived before he could.

"Good afternoon, Mr. Karne," she said. "We appreciate you coming to speak with us. If you don't mind coming this way." She gestured down the hall to the interview room.

Gabe liked Bree Eagan, which was unusual; he wasn't usually a fan of law enforcement. But Bree seemed to fall toward the side of protect and serve, instead of arrest and harass, and he appreciated anyone who understood the true purpose of their fucking job.

And what is Casey Lundin if not law enforcement, Chance?

Fine. Point made.

She led him to the interview room he'd already spent too much fucking time in since first arriving on Heartstone.

"At least it doesn't smell like old sweat socks in here anymore," he commented, taking the seat closest to the door. Old habits die hard.

Gabe thought he spotted a glimmer of amusement in Bree's eyes as she took her seat, but she quickly hid it away.

"Mr. Karne, this isn't a formal questioning"—*not yet anyway*, Gabe inferred—"but if you don't mind, I'd like to record your answers." She indicated the voice recorder set into the table.

"That's fine, but please call me Gabriel. Or Gabe."

"For the purposed of this interview," she said with a brief smile, "I will refer to you as Mr. Karne, but I promise not to in public."

Eagan's response gave Gabe hope that her questions weren't too serious, and even better, she didn't appear to be sizing him up for handcuffs. Not yet anyway. She reached across the table and pressed Record.

"First, Mr. Karne, how did you acquire that bruise on your forehead?"

Gabe lifted a hand and touched the tender area above his left eye, yep it was still there. "I had a run-in with a hedge Monday morning. I think the hedge won. You can ask Elton about it if you need to. He'll back me up." He was not admitting to breaking and entering lite while being recorded.

He was rewarded with a raised eyebrow and an ever so-slight shake of the head.

"The body of a young woman was discovered near the point last night," Eagan began. "The victim was approximately five foot seven with dark blonde or brown hair and slender. Estimated time of death is sometime Monday evening or Tuesday very early. She hadn't been in the water long. We have reason to believe she either knew you or knew of you. She carried no identification, and we have yet to find a cell phone or an abandoned vehicle that could help us determine her identity."

Eagan stared hard at Gabriel, watching for his reaction to her next words. "However, there was a paper tucked into the inside pocket of the jacket she was wearing. Once we got it dried out, we discovered your name and home address written on it. Can you explain this?"

What had happened to the fake genealogy paperwork? And her purse thing?

"Sort of," he said, hating that the dead woman had been so young. She hadn't even finished up Grifting 101. Maybe if she'd had a chance, she could've turned her career around. And why did he have to be associated with yet another body? "She came to my house Monday morning, said her name was Juliet Carter."

Gabe went on to describe their interaction, starting from the time he'd been woken by Juliet's knocking until she had left, pissed as hell because Gabriel didn't believe her story. He even included her statement about men.

Eagan's dimple made another brief appearance, then she opened the file folder she'd carried into the room with her. Inside was a photograph. Gabe's stomach clenched; he did not want to look at it.

Eagan pushed it toward him. "Is this the same person? She was found on one of the beaches on the north end of the island. We don't think that's where she was killed though. The currents around the island probably carried her there, and we think that coat she was wearing maybe gave her some buoyancy."

That made sense. The north end of Heartstone was too busy, what with RV campers set up there all year long. Too many possible witnesses.

"Yes, that's her," Gabe confirmed, wishing it wasn't. People young enough to fake being his kid were too young to be dead.

"Are you certain you don't recognize her from somewhere else? She doesn't look familiar to you at all?"

Gabe shook his head. "I only recognize her as the person on my doorstep Monday morning. I had never seen her before then, and I don't know who she is. As I stated, she gave me the name Juliet Carter. I think it's likely to be false though."

He stared at the photo, refusing to let himself look away. Her eyes were open, staring at nothing, her face was deathly white, and her lips a grayish hue. The collar of the blue Columbia jacket she'd been wearing Monday was visible at the bottom of the photo. Her long hair was obviously wet and obscured the lower part of her face. Seawater had washed away any blood, but the wound that had ended her life was clear to see. Someone had hit her on the left side of her head, hard enough to leave a dent.

Gabe pointed at the damaged area of her skull. "That wasn't an accident, was it." He doubted that Juliet had abruptly decided that March was the perfect weather for a swim, fully clothed.

He wasn't really asking a question, but Eagan answered him anyway.

"No. The coroner thinks she either hit or was hit by a blunt object. Is there anything else you can tell me about her visit? Anything that might help us find out who she is?"

"Her showing up was out of left field. You could've knocked me over with a feather." Damn, Gabe was spending too much time with Elton. He was starting to sound like an old man.

Gabe shook his head and forced himself to refocus. "I told her to come back when, and if, she had evidence that wasn't obviously manipulated. I said I'd take a real DNA test, but she didn't want that. I did get the impression she was nervous. At the time, I thought it was because she'd shown up uninvited and I wasn't giving her the response she thought she'd get, but maybe it was something else. That's all I know. She was only at my place ten or fifteen minutes."

They were both quiet for a moment. An analog clock hanging on the wall ticked, filling the silence. Gabe looked down at the photo again, realizing he was angry. Not angry with Eagan or the sheriff's department, but with the person who had prematurely ended this young woman's life.

Why kill her? What had she done that was so terrible that another person thought she deserved to die?

Maybe she hadn't *done* anything. Maybe it was something she'd known. Or maybe none of the above.

Eagan's voice interrupted his thoughts. "Do you have anything else you'd like to share with me? Anything that might point investigators in the right direction?"

Gabe could think of a few things that could be pertinent, but none of which he wanted to share with the deputy on the record. He nodded at the recorder. After a moment's thought, Eagan reached across the table and pressed the Stop button. Then she leaned back in her chair with her arms crossed over her chest.

"This better be good. I'm waiting."

Gabe stared back at her, debating how much he could reveal about himself, his life, and his mother. Fuck, he had no idea, so he just began talking.

"As you may suspect, I haven't lived a conventional life. And neither did my mother. 'Family tradition' was the most she ever said about it. The con was in our blood. Until this week—and it's only fucking Wednesday—I had no idea that my mother actually grew up around here. She was incredibly secretive." He indicated the photo of the dead person. "Is it odd that she showed up around the same time I learned this? Yes, it is. But the timing is such that I don't know how she could have been aware of Heidi's Westfort connection, unless I'm the last one to learn." He wrinkled his nose and added, "Which is a distinct possibility."

There is no such thing as coincidence, Chance.

"Keep talking."

"Honestly, I just don't get it. Why show up with bogus evidence claiming I'm her father? What would anyone have to gain from that?" He shook his head. It didn't track. "All my mother left me was a now burned-out sailboat and a weird-ass chair. Have I told you this has been a wacky week? Started with a fight with hedge and has only gotten stranger."

Gabe shifted in his chair, meeting Eagan's gaze straight on. "Moving right along, there are many people I've made angry." Gabe leaned toward the deputy now. "The people who feel I *may* have wronged them aren't the type to go after someone else to get to me. If they knew where I was, they would come straight here, no stopping at Go."

"*Do* these mysterious people know where you are?"

"Possibly. But the ones most invested in getting even are behind bars now." Something Gabe was infinitely grateful for.

"Are you currently involved in something that might have led to this person's murder?"

Gabe sighed and ran his fingers through his hair. Dirty Socks Randy came to mind, but he dismissed him. The retrieval gig had been on his radar for a while, and he just didn't see a connection between Dirty Socks and the baby grifter.

"I don't think I am. I just can't see how it's possible that her death is connected to me, but I could be wrong. I'm dealing with my late mother's estate. Did my mother operate on the grayer side of the law?" He waggled his head side to side, acknowledging the whiff of probability. "But she's dead now, and I doubt even Heidi Karne could reach from beyond the grave to kill a girl she never met in her life. I can't speak for the people that Heidi may have wronged, but I seriously doubt they waited this long and then killed someone she had nothing to do with."

"Someone killed this young woman." Eagan pointed at the photo. "And, unfortunately for you, the only name we have is yours."

"There was nothing else on her? She had a pretty big leather shoulder bag with her when she appeared on my doorstep."

"Not that we found. Can you describe it?"

Gabe glanced up at the ceiling, doing his best to recall what the bag looked like. "It was roomy, big enough for a small dog if you're into that sort of thing. Leather, I think, and possibly navy blue or black? It was a shoulder bag, not a backpack, if that helps."

Eagan jotted the information down in the small notebook she always seemed to carry with her.

"She drove an older dark blue Ford Focus. Pretty dinged up, Washington plates."

Eagan's pen scratched across the notepad again.

"What *have* you found? Anything you can tell me about?" Gabe leaned toward the deputy again. "I just assumed you got my name from the paperwork she tried to pass off as legitimate." Not from some random piece of paper inside her coat.

"Nothing else. We were lucky that her jacket was waterproof. Otherwise the piece of paper would have been destroyed."

"Who found her?" he asked.

Eagan considered his question before replying. "A dog walker discovered the body. We haven't confirmed yet if the head injury happened before she went into the water. I'm hoping the pathologist can answer that soon."

"But you suspect she was bashed before."

"I do."

Egan's eyes bored into his like she was trying to read his mind. *Good luck there*. Gabe stared back, but he wasn't thinking about Juliet Carter, he was thinking about Heidi Karne. The tendrils of a shadow of a hunch were starting to form in his mind, and he needed space to tease them out.

"Do you know anything about Jack Thorne?" Gabe asked. "Someone gave me his name. He's a private investigator in Westfort."

Eagan scowled. "Yeah, I've heard of him. Why?"

"Clearly, I have some private investigating I need done." He emphasized the word private. He'd rather not air the specifics of Heidi's probable dirty laundry if he didn't have to.

"As far as I've heard, Thorne is good at what he does." Eagan closed her notebook and pushed back her chair. "Karne, at this point we're not officially bringing you in. I, for one, would like to think I know you a bit now, and this does not feel like your type of crime. Please don't ruin my faith in you."

"As backhanded as it is, I'm going to take that as a compliment. I'm free to go, correct?"

Did he have a type of crime? He supposed he did.

The deputy rose to her feet. "Yes, you are. If we have more questions for you, we'll call. In light of that, please leave your cell phone number with the front desk."

"Absolutely."

"One last question." Eagan reached down and started the recording again. "Mr. Karne, where were you on Monday night?"

Gabe shrugged. "Home alone, with my cat."

"Casey Lundin can't corroborate?"

"Nope. Definitely wish he could. I guess this just means we have to get our shit together and find a place big enough for the both of us." *Before the next body shows up.* "Am I still free to go?"

The deputy nodded, and together they left the interview room and returned to the lobby.

"Thank you for your cooperation," Eagan said, and turned back the way they'd come.

Stopping at her desk, Gabe made sure Althea had his cell phone number. She dutifully jotted it down in an official-looking TCSO notebook and turned back to her monitor and keyboard. He wondered what duties she had aside from basically keeping the station in order.

"How's Hero doing? Is she happy to have the locket back?"

Gabe lingered, his hands stuffed into his jeans pockets. Althea was still a bit of a mystery to him. According to Elton, she and he had been "stepping out occasionally" since the beginning of the year, but Elton hadn't shared much else with Gabe and Casey, which seemed odd. She'd been with the TCSO for a couple of decades and had a good fried chicken recipe. Gabe had a sneaking suspicion that last one was the main reason the stepping-out was still happening. He knew Elton'd do just about anything for decent fried chicken.

Pausing mid-type, Althea looked up at Gabe. "We're both glad to have the necklace back."

"We should do dinner one of these nights, you and Elton, Casey and me. I'd love to hear some stories about Elton and the island back in the day."

She nodded, the corners of her eyes creased in what could have been the start of a smile, but she also made a noise that conveyed *I have work to do and don't have time to talk*.

"Okay, then. See ya around."

Althea gave him a nod in return and went back to her typing.

"Huh," Gabe grunted as he got behind the wheel. He refused to have his feelings hurt because his eighty-year-old friend's girlfriend didn't seem to care for him as much as she had. Maybe she was busy? God, he hoped her attitude wasn't because she was okay with gay as a concept but gay in real life was not a thing.

Not everyone is going to like you, Chance. That's a fact of life.

Gabe reversed out of the parking spot and pointed the Honda toward home. Not everyone liking him was indeed a fact of life, and those who didn't appreciate his style didn't know what fabulousness they were missing out on. Or, like the Colavitos, had personal reasons.

SEVENTEEN

CASEY – WEDNESDAY EVENING

Not only did Casey stop and pick up a large pizza with all two of Gabe's favorite toppings, but while the cooks at The Pizza Joint were busy putting together the order, he jogged over to Norskland General Store, hoping they were open. They were, so Casey picked out a couple pints of Jewel Creamery ice cream. No one could say he didn't know how to cheer up his boyfriend.

"Casey Lundin, you are my hero," Gabe said when he opened the front door.

Impatient to greet Keith or, more likely, to check the state of the cat's food dish, Bowie squeezed past Casey and ran into the house.

"Hi, doggo. Glad to see you too," Gabe said as Bowie completely ignored him and shot into the kitchen. "Learning from Keith, are you?"

Keith was nowhere in sight. She was probably sitting on one of the windowsills in the bedroom. Soon enough, she'd make her appearance and join Bowie, both of them lobbying for a morsel of Italian-style goodness.

While Casey set the pizza down on the counter, Gabe went into the kitchen area to grab some plates. Due to the continued lack of a dining table, the choice was to either stand up and eat at the counter or retreat to the couch. Gabe kept making noises about finding one he liked, but when he returned from his various excursions, his haul was just more kitschy mugs and beat-up paperback thrillers.

The boxes they'd picked up from Seattle were stacked exactly where they'd been left after they combed through them Tuesday evening. Alfred the Ugly Chair glowered in its spot alongside the boxes.

"I got us some ice cream too," Casey announced, opening the paper bag and popping the two precious pints into Gabe's freezer.

The boxes needed to be gone through again, more slowly this time, but that was a topic Casey was going to bring up after pizza and ice cream.

"Is there something even more amazing than a hero?" Gabe asked with a tired sigh. "Because that's what you are."

Casey took another second to really look at Gabriel Karne. Aside from the obvious gouge and dark purple bruise on his forehead that hopefully had peaked, there were dark circles under his eyes, and he seemed dispirited. Tired. "How did it go with Eagan?"

While he waited for Gabe to share his take on the day, Casey transferred a few slices of pizza from the box to the plates and handed Gabe one of them.

"Fine, I suppose," he said, accepting his dinner and staring at the plate without moving to pick up a piece of pizza. A sure sign that Gabe was dragging. "Turned out she had questions for me because my name was on a piece of paper in the dead body's pocket. And yeah, it was Juliet Carter or whatever her real name is. Eagan showed me a picture I won't be forgetting anytime soon."

Morgue photos were never flattering. Casey hadn't seen many, but those he had stuck with him.

"I'm sorry you had to do that. Come on, let's get some food in you."

Casey led Gabe to the couch and plopped down, then patted the empty spot next to him as if it was his couch and this was his house. He was beginning to understand that there were times when Gabe needed Casey to take over for a little while and take care of him, and he was happy to oblige. Gabe was always quick to do the same for him too. "Sit down and put your feet in my lap. I'll balance my plate on your ankles."

The couch was barely bigger than a love seat, which meant only one of them at a time could stretch out, and Gabe got the honors tonight. Once they were situated—without pizza slipping off plates and into Bowie's or Keith's mouths—Casey said, "Tell me what happened."

"Not much to tell," Gabe mumbled around a mouthful of pepperoni and black olives. "They say she was killed Monday night or Tuesday morning, a lot of hours after she left here. No ID on her. I think Eagan will tell me if the name Juliet Carter checks out, although I have my reservations there. You know, it wasn't official, but the usual 'stick around in case there are more questions for me' was mentioned."

"Did you talk to Elton? Did he find anything out from the Old Codgers Club?"

Gabe's eyes widened. "Shit! I totally forgot to call him. I can't believe he hasn't called me already. Unless Althea told him or he heard it on the scanner, he doesn't know about the body. We should talk to him now."

He started to move, but Casey grabbed his ankles, stopping him. "Calling Elton can wait until the morning. If Elton learned anything, he won't forget it by tomorrow. And if he had found out something important from Althea, he would have been here already."

"Truth." Gabe blew out a big sigh and tilted into the back of the couch, semidefeated. "Juliet was absolutely trying to con me, and she wasn't very good at it. Who let the baby grifter out on her own? Where was she between the time she left and"—he waved a hand—"you know. Was she killed because I didn't fall for her con? I'm feeling obligated, like I was the last one to see her alive so it's up to me to get to the bottom of what's happened. No one deserves to have what I saw in that photo happen to them."

"Gabriel, and I cannot emphasize this enough," Casey began, "the ultimate responsibility for her death lies with the person who killed her, not with you."

Casey was starting to see a pattern with Gabe when it came to situations like this one. A dead body showed up, and Gabe would feel like solving the why of it was his burden to bear. For reasons Casey still didn't quite understand, the murder of "the baby grifter" seemed to be hitting Gabriel extra hard.

"It only makes sense that I'm the one who needs to get to the bottom of this current round of fuckery."

"Why?" Casey was curious why Gabe felt this way.

"I don't want to think that this murder has something to do with Heidi, from back when she was a Pritchard, but I'm afraid it might," Gabe admitted. "Which means ultimately it does have something to do with me." He gestured at Alfred and the boxes with the last of his pizza slice. "So it only makes sense that I'm the one who needs to get to the bottom of this capital F fuckery." He popped the pizza into his mouth and began to chew defiantly.

Gabe shifted his feet and stood up, then grabbed the empty plates and took them back over to the counter. "More pizza? Or should I break out the ice cream?"

"Gabe."

"What?"

"Why do you think there's a connection between your mother and this person's murder?"

Gabe pulled another piece of pizza out of the box and took a big bite of it.

Swallowing, he said, "The timing is fucking suspicious.

Monday, this Juliet person shows up. I send her away and head off to Westfort."

Casey made a disapproving sound in the back of his throat.

"Yeah, I know, the B and E. Bad Gabe. Then Elton brings that letter over in the afternoon, and suddenly I'm off to Seattle the next day to pick up stuff my mother didn't want me to have until she was dead." Gabe looked up, a mix of hurt and frustration clouding his expression. It made Casey's heart clench. "Why did she make sure I get to Heartstone in the first place and then get all of this"—he gestured at the boxes and the chair—"if she didn't want me to follow the trail to the bitter end? The timing is fucked. Juliet's appearance wasn't random, and I want to know how she found me and why she pulled the dad thing. I need to know. Heidi would be the first to point out that fucked-up timing is no coincidence."

Instead of returning to sit next to Casey again, Gabe stayed where he was in the kitchen, one hip propped against the counter, the piece of pizza dropped back into the box, forgotten.

"How did Juliet find me? I only put in a change of address a couple of weeks ago. Does that information immediately go public? Was someone sitting around waiting to find out where I really lived so they didn't have to use Elton as a conduit like our friend Lynn did?"

"Do you still have that envelope?" Casey asked.

"Yeah." Gabe swiveled his head to cover the entire kitchen with his gaze, as if the envelope would magically jump up and show itself. "It's here somewhere."

"Maybe you stuck it back into the fruit bowl?' Casey suggested. He was starting to learn that Gabe's filing system was less a cabinet and more whatever container was handy.

"Oh yeah, here it is." Gabe plucked the envelope out from underneath a bag of oranges. "And why am I looking at this?"

"To see when it was sent." Casey walked over to stand

shoulder to shoulder with Gabe, leaning in so he could see the envelope and offer support.

It was a regular letter-sized envelope, although a bit grubby and creased where it had been folded at some point. Gabe flipped it over to the front. There, in the middle of the front, just like Casey had learned in elementary school, was Gabe's name and Care Of Elton Cox above Elton's address. The handwriting was shaky, as if the person was ill, old, or both—much like Lynn Schmitt.

"Basic postmark from Seattle." Casey pointed to the top right-hand corner where the postage stamp had been affixed. "Nothing else looking suspicious."

"That doesn't explain if Juliet's tied to it. She showed up before he brought it over."

"So…" Casey said, thinking out loud. "They got their timing off. Or there are more unknowns in play."

"I do not like unknowns," Gabe complained.

Right on cue, Bowie let out a sharp bark and a growl, startling them.

"What's up, dog?" Casey asked.

Bowie shot to the front door to sniff along the bottom edge, his tail straight up and out, as if someone was on the other side. The hairs on the back of Casey's neck prickled.

"Maybe Alfred spooked him?"

The chair was several feet from Bowie opposite the door. Casey didn't think Alfred was behind Bowie's reaction, and he couldn't believe that Gabe did either.

"That's his 'there's something out there I don't like' stance. Although I wouldn't be surprised if he did distrust that chair, I think he heard something outside," Casey said quietly.

Gabe stepped around him and made for the door, then opened it an inch or so and peered outside. Based on the bit of outside that Casey could see above Gabe's head, dark had fallen hard. The sky was cloudy, not even a sliver of moon peeking out. The only light came from the few close-by porch lights that residents had flipped on. Bowie crowded Gabe's legs, scrabbling to get past him, but he held tight to the doorknob, for which Casey was grateful. He so much did not want to chase after Bowie in the dark.

"I don't see anyone out—"

"Shh!" Casey whispered as he crossed the six feet or so to Gabe and slammed the door shut again.

Casey would never be able to explain the sense of impending dread he felt in that second.

"Get down!" Lunging at Gabe, Casey dragged him to the floor while he stretched for the overhead light switch and flipped it off. They were plunged into near darkness, with only the ambient light given off by the stove and microwave displays for light.

Then there was a sharp *pop* sound, and the front window shattered and glass fell to the carpet.

"What the fuck?" Gabe hissed, outraged instead of terrified by the shooter. "Did some fucker just shoot out one of my windows? This is war. I'm fucking pissed off now."

He started to stand, but Casey kept a firm grip on his belt. "Wait."

The sound of rapid footsteps heading away from Gabe's home reached their ears.

"The fuck they're getting away." Gabe jerked out of Casey's grasp and surged to his feet. "The *fuck* somebody is coming here and fucking around with my house."

Before Casey could grab him again, Gabe had shoved his feet into a pair of Crocs—Casey wanted to point out that they might not be the best footwear for chasing after a gunman but kept his mouth shut—jerked the door open and was jogging past their parked cars out to the access road. Bowie, not to be left behind, was at his side.

Casey hastily jammed his work boots back on and raced after the two of them. In Gabe's own words, what could go wrong?

A fucking lot.

He caught up with Gabe a couple of hundred feet away from his house, out of breath and standing with his hands on his hips, staring toward the main road. Bowie was just a few feet away, still on alert but at least not sprinting into unknown danger.

"Did you see anyone?" Casey asked.

"No, dammit, I fucking did not. I'm not exactly Usain Bolt, especially not in these." He lifted one Croc-encased foot. "Look at you." He poked Casey in the chest. "You're not even breathing heavily."

Casey ignored him. Someone had taken a shot at Gabriel. Unacceptable.

"What the fuck was all that about? Why would anyone shoot at me? Or was it for both of us?" He scowled. "Fine, yeah. We both know it was me they were aiming for."

Across the road, Bill's living room light came on. Casey figured Gabe would rather not have to explain the shooting to his neighbor. Or he'd make up an outlandish story that no one would believe anyway.

"I can't begin to imagine what's behind this. But let's get back to your place. We left the door open."

"Crap." Gabe turned around and started back, Casey and Bowie hot on his heels.

"I don't think anyone got in," Gabe said, glancing around once they were back inside. "Does it look like it to you? We were only out there a few minutes. Shit, I didn't even hear a car driving away. Did you?"

Casey shook his head, hands on his hips. "Nope."

No car meant the guy either lived nearby or had parked close and the shooter had walked into the park. Sure, the shooter could have been a woman, but statistics said the likelihood of that being the case was pretty damn low. And Casey needed the stability of statistics right now.

If the point of the shooting had been to get them out of

Gabe's house, it had been a failure. They had been drawn outside but not far enough away that someone could have easily snuck into the mobile home.

Gabe's place looked the same to Casey, everything exactly as they'd left it. But he did a quick sweep of the rest of the rooms to satisfy himself that there was no one hiding in any of them.

"Okay, I think we're good. Exhibit A, leftover pizza still sitting on the counter. If someone did get in here, it wasn't hungry teenagers. And if it had been, they could have knocked. I would have shared the leftovers."

"Hey," Casey said, stepping into Gabe's space and settling his hands on Gabe's waist. "Do you want to stay at mine tonight? We'll have to do something about the window though."

Gabe may have been a grifter most of his life, but Casey was fast becoming a Gabriel Karne expert. He could tell that Gabe was shaken. And so was Casey.

"Remember, I have a nice, quiet sailboat moored behind a locked gate."

"Yeah. And look how well that gate kept out Rizzi and whoever."

He had a point.

"If the mysterious 'they' are after something here, it's not happening. The hell I'm hiding on *The Barbara*. I'm mad now. Pissed fucking off."

"And you're not gonna take it anymore?" Casey said, one eyebrow raised. The last thing he needed was Gabe on a rampage. Who really knew what kind of trouble he could get into.

"Something like that."

Casey only had to angle his head a tad to press his lips against Gabe's. He was rewarded with a little puff of a sigh, then Gabe loosely wrapped his arms around Casey's shoulders while they kissed.

Gabe, Casey had learned, very much enjoyed the act of kissing, and by proxy, Casey now did too. Having Gabe in his life was akin to opening an unexpected present every day.

Sometimes Gabe was wild and out of control, which, ironically, Casey had never thought he wanted in a partner, but he couldn't imagine Gabe any other way. Other times, like this one, he needed to be held and protected. Not worshipped, coveted. And Casey was happy to oblige.

"We'll stay here for tonight, then," Casey said. "Together." Stepping away from Gabe, he added, "But we need to secure the window and call TCSO's non-emergency number to notify them first. Do you have any plywood?"

"In what universe would I, Gabriel Karne, have plywood randomly sitting around? I don't even have a fucking saw." He spun around and pointed at Alfred. "That's the closest thing I've got, and with no saw, we are out of luck. And you don't know how sad that makes me right now." He threw in an extra glare at the monstrosity.

"How about the pizza box?" Casey suggested mildly.

"That's good enough for me. I'll hide it with the shade."

CASEY BLINKED, then squinted against the light that had dragged him awake. He was alone in Gabe's bed, the sheet and blankets tangled around his legs as if he'd gone several rounds with an imaginary opponent.

He lay there for a moment, listening for Gabe. The man wasn't particularly quiet, but he'd managed to get out of bed without disturbing him—except he'd left the bedroom door ajar and the light from the living room had woken Casey. Also the click-clack of Gabe tapping on a keyboard.

Casey rolled to the edge of the bed and sat up, his joints cracking and snapping as he stretched and set his feet on the carpet According to his watch, it wasn't even five a.m. yet. Slipping back into his jeans but deciding against a shirt, he padded out to the living room.

Gabe sat on the couch, his laptop balanced on his thighs and a cheap pair of blinged-out reading glasses perched on his nose. Whatever he was reading, it had his full attention, so much so that he didn't hear Casey's approach.

"What are you doing awake?" he asked.

"Jesus!" Gabe's head jerked around toward Casey. "Don't scare me like that again, you'll kill me." Gabe snatched the ridiculous glasses off his face. He insisted that he'd bought them as a joke, but Casey'd caught him wearing the garish rhinestone-festooned frames more than once.

"Well?" Casey said.

"Well, what?"

Oh, they were playing this game, then.

"Well, what are you doing up before daylight?"

"Couldn't sleep. I had to see if I could find anything. You know, research and so forth." Gabe set the glasses on the arm of the couch and started to get up. "You want coffee?"

"Yeah, but you stay where you are, I'll make it. Have you found anything interesting?"

"I don't know what I don't know, which makes this extra difficult." He slid the reading glasses back on and leaned close to the laptop screen again. "We're so used to everything being online these days, but not everything has been digitized, even if I wish it was."

Casey nodded and busied himself making an espresso. While he was at it, Keith emerged from hiding to wrap around his ankles. "Trying to assassinate me, are you?" Casey asked. Keith rewarded him with a gravelly meow, which Casey was taking as a solid *yes*.

"I miss physical phone books. Back in the day, a person could just flip through one and see how many people, say, named

Pritchard had Westfort addresses, give a person something to start with. But *noooo*. Now I have to slog through this crap. And most of these asshole companies want me to pay for a subscription—fucking outrageous!—for information that used to be free. They steal our information and sell it back to us, which is a scam I never considered. I'm rambling, but I need to know what I'm looking for first—and I do not." Gabe sat back again, arching his back and rolling his shoulders.

"Did you try the library archives? I think they're available online. Or the newspaper? I think the state archives also sometimes stores old phone books if that's what you're focusing on."

"Yeah, but what I want is before 1982, and I'm really trying to avoid adding a trip to Olympia in. It might be worth a try though. And I do have a fancy new library card in my possession. Well, a temporary one."

Picking up his cup, one with a Smokey the Bear graphic on it and the phrase *Please Help Smokey*, Casey crossed the room to sit down next to Gabe, unintentionally jostling the computer as he did so.

"Oops, sorry."

"No worries," Gabe murmured, focused on the screen. Casey took a sip of his coffee and skimmed the web page in front of Gabe.

"Have you searched like, uh, news headlines in Westfort from the late 1970s?" Casey asked him. "Or around the time of the yearbook? I mean, most likely Heidi-slash-Holly wouldn't have been in the news back then, at least I hope not, but what if something big happened, and that set off a chain of events? Maybe somehow the event was connected to her or to the name Pritchard. Could that have eventually led to her leaving town and changing her name?"

"Sure, why not? I was looking for Pritchards in a haystack. At this point, I'd use a damn Magic 8 Ball."

"Good luck. I'm going to put some more clothes on."

"Such a shame," Gabe said.

Casey chuckled. "You may appreciate the lack of clothing, but Greta will not."

"Fine," Gabe huffed. "Go ahead and get dressed if you insist."

EIGHTEEN

GABE – THURSDAY MORNING

"I'm heading out," Casey announced as he walked out of the bedroom. Out of the corner of his eye, Gabe saw him grab his empty cup and carry it into the kitchen. The water turned on, and Gabe knew he was rinsing the cup out and setting it in the dish rack. Casey was much tidier than Gabe, who just stacked dishes in the sink during the day and washed them all at night. Sometimes Gabe wondered if Casey was bothered by his messier habits, if this was going to be a sticking point if—*when*—they moved in together.

He looked up from the laptop and frowned. Casey had put a shirt on, dammit. His sexy, bare chest was always a pleasure.

"Alright," Gabe said, instead of complaining about the need for clothing when one had a real job. "I'm going to keep at this for a while longer, then I'll give Elton a call and see if he learned anything interesting yesterday. So far, the big news I'm finding is Ted Bundy's second arrest, but that was in Florida, and I doubt Heidi had anything to do with it anyway. She was more likely to have been a victim."

Coming back around the kitchen counter, Casey stopped in front of him, gently looming. Gabe dragged his gaze up Casey's body and decided for the hundredth time that his well-filled-out ranger uniform was as good as a sexy, naked chest. A happy sigh escaped him. There was almost nothing better than his man in uniform.

"If Heidi or her"—Casey seemed to be picking his words carefully—"relations were generally on the wrong side of the law, maybe that was an inciting factor? At the very least, I think we can assume she ran away from home. Since she may have been a minor, those records might not be readily available. I don't even know where you'd look. Maybe call the Westfort police?"

"Yeah, nope." Gabe set his laptop to the side and rose to his feet. "Anyway, have a great day at work, honey. Make good choices." The last bit he chanted, his voice pitched higher than normal.

Casey snorted, and Gabe leaned in and planted a kiss on his lips.

"I feel like I'm the one who should be reminding you to make the good choices."

"Yeah, yeah," Gabe said absently as he sat back down and returned his attention to the search.

Once Casey and Bowie had departed, the house was quiet, and Gabe wasn't sure he liked it that way. After a lifetime of moving around with Heidi and then living by himself for the most part, he was realizing how much he enjoyed companionship, how much he just plain liked Casey Lundin. What he felt was more than *like*, but he wasn't quite ready to say it out loud.

Three coffees and one trip to the bathroom later, Gabe abruptly stopped typing and stared at the screen. "What do we have here?"

At Casey's suggestion, he'd logged in to the public library site. After a steep learning curve, he had eventually figured out how to search the electronic archives. He also had developed an even healthier respect for librarians and archivists.

Keith, who'd curled up next to him to use Gabe as her

personal heater after her breakfast, did not have an answer for him. In fact, she didn't say anything at all.

WESTFORT, WA., AUGUST 2 (AP) – No Arrests In Local Gallery Art Heist.

The newspaper article wasn't even on the top of the page. He'd almost missed it because Gabe's eyes had started to water, and, frankly, his search for something interesting during the late 1970s had begun to feel futile. But then, there it was, the kind of news he'd been looking for, just below the fold on the front page.

The 201 Gallery, at 201 Water Street in downtown Westfort, was broken into sometime over the busy summer weekend, and several valuable paintings stolen.

"We don't know how the thieves got in," gallery employee Carla Pritchard attested. "We locked up after close on Sunday evening, and they were just gone when we came back Tuesday."

Noting the name of Pritchard, Gabe scanned the short article. The exhaustion he'd felt from getting up before 4 a.m. evaporated.

The paintings were the creation of world-famous Pacific Northwest-born artist Martin Crevan. Brilliantly talented, Crevan is best known for his moody landscapes that ask the observer to question man's purpose on earth and in the universe in general. Crevan is also known for his artistic female nudes. Notable for being part of the Lost Generation of Paris expatriates in the 1920s, Crevan was an associate of Pablo Picasso, Ernest Hemingway, and Modigliani, among others.

"Could this guy be more pretentious? Barf."

Crevan, eighty-five, could not be reached for comment.

"We've never had anything like this happen in our little town," Police Chief E. Jackson told the Gazette. "We're asking that anyone with information please step forward."

As if. In the real world, thieves did not step forward and admit to their crimes.

The 201 Gallery is widely known for hosting some of the more famous artists who live in our midst, and Martin Crevan is one of our own. "This is a tragedy," said one local artist. "Who can we trust? How did this happen?"

When asked if they had any suspects, Chief Jackson confirmed that they did not have anyone in custody or any clues. "As for a motive, we imagine it is nothing more than greed and money. The paintings will likely be sold on the black market and never again be seen by the public."

Gabe sat back. "Huh." Then he did a quick search and was not at all surprised to find there was no longer an art gallery or any shop in Westfort called the 201 Gallery. Also, as far as he could discover, there was no follow-up story mentioning any recovery of the artwork.

"Huh," Gabe repeated. But also, *so what*?

Maybe this Carla Pritchard was related to Heidi, but the theft had happened almost fifty years ago. Carla could be dead by now. She could have changed her name. Gabe briefly shut his eyes and rubbed his forehead. This search was giving him a headache.

What business was at 201 now? Gabe typed in the address and was rewarded with *Windward Kite Shop*. His phone chose that moment to vibrate against the coffee table, alerting him to an incoming call. His heart skipped what felt like several beats. Snatching it up, he saw that it was Casey.

"What?"

"Did you call the Sheriff's Office and let them know about the shooting? Don't think I didn't notice that you distracted me from doing so last night."

Gabe didn't tell Casey that he'd never intended to call Eagan. Involving law enforcement in his life was not on the top of his to-do list, wouldn't even make an appearance on page two. There would be questions he didn't have the answers to and no reason to think that TCSO would have better ideas. Best not to include them at all.

It could even be that the gunman had been Dirty Socks Randy. Maybe, like Juliet Carter, Randy had figured out who Gabe was and where he lived and had decided to pay him a revenge visit.

"No, I haven't. What difference is it going to make at this point? It's not as if the guy hung around."

"Make. The. Call."

Gabe smiled at the gravelly, demanding tone. It was nice to know that someone cared.

Still didn't want to call in the cops though.

"Casey, seriously, why bother?"

Casey seemed to hesitate before answering him. "If something else happens, if you continue to be harassed, they'll have a record of the instances."

"Me, Gabriel Karne, call the police, sheriff, whatever? I don't think so." At this point, he was arguing for the sake of it. And to keep Casey on the phone with him a little longer. The house felt too quiet without him there.

"Too bad for you." Casey sounded smug now. "I called them a few minutes ago when I figured out that you weren't planning on it. One of the deputies will be out to take pictures and talk to you later today. And no, I'm not sorry about it."

Well, at least that was cleared up. Casey had already called TCSO and had no regrets. Nice. That was a very Gabriel Karne move of him, act and ask forgiveness later.

"Fine."

"Fine?"

"Yeah, but hey, check this out. I found an article about an art gallery heist that happened in late July of 1978. And guess what? As an aside, heist is one of my favorite words."

"Of course it is. What am I supposed to guess?"

"One of the employees was named Carla Pritchard."

"Pritchard?"

"Yep," Gabe said, his tone smug.

"So what's the next step going to be?"

"As far as I can tell, there's no other mention of the theft. So next up is searching for Carla Pritchard. And, duh, I need to see if I can get a hold of Holly Pritchard's birth certificate. The issue, of course, is that I'm still not sure which year she was born in."

"Be careful, Gabriel. You seem to have ruffled a lot of feathers this week, and it's only Thursday morning. Personally, I like you best in one piece."

"I'll be careful."

"Why do I feel like you're saying that just to appease me?"

Gabe sighed and stared at the ceiling. "Okay, I will *try* to be careful, but obviously, I can't make any guarantees."

"That doesn't make me feel any better," Casey said quietly.

"It's the best I can do, Ranger Man."

Casey paused for so long that Gabe checked his cell phone's screen to make sure the call hadn't dropped. "At least send a text if you decide to head into Westfort today or talk to anyone in person."

"I can do that."

"You mean a lot to me, Gabriel. And I'd like you to stay alive and in one piece."

"Yeah—"

There was a knock at the door, followed by a voice saying, "It's Deputy Eagan."

"Look, I gotta go, Eagan's is here already."

"Take care and talk soon. And don't forget to give Elton a call."

Making a mental note to talk to Elton, Gabe closed the lid to his laptop and set it on the coffee table, then walked over to the front door to let Bree Eagan inside, narrowly missing Keith as she ran to the bedroom once again.

"Good morning," the deputy said, looking around.

"I suppose it is, seeing as I don't have a bullet in me. Only the window was damaged."

Gabe saw Eagan's eyes widen when she spotted Alfred lurking in his corner. "Are you collecting antiques now?"

"Hah, not likely. That is something I recently acquired from my mother. I want to chop it up into firewood, but I don't own an axe or a saw and don't have a fireplace. Would you like something to drink? I can make you a coffee."

"No, but thank you for the offer. Casey called and reported an incident last night, a shooting. Will you run through what happened with me?"

Gabe tucked his hands into the back pockets of his jeans to keep from waving them around like an air traffic controller.

"I think it was about ten p.m. Casey and I were talking and eating pizza, and Bowie started acting like he'd heard something outside. Next thing I knew, Casey was telling me to get down and the window exploded."

"Did you find the bullet?"

Gabe frowned. "To be honest, I didn't look for it. I was just glad none of us were hurt. We heard the shooter running off, and I was pissed as hell, so I ran after him but, obviously, whoever it was got away."

"Did you see a car?"

"No. And we didn't hear one either. If the shooter used one, they parked far enough away so we wouldn't hear an engine. Which means, at least in my mind, that they know the area."

Eagan nodded as she scribbled in her small spiral notepad. "I'd have to agree. Are you filing for damages?"

"No. Casey said we can fix it ourselves. I don't really want my renter's insurance to skyrocket."

"Walk with me outside?" Pivoting, she reached for the door handle.

With a grumble, Gabe slipped on his Crocs and purloined parka and followed the deputy out into the rain.

Together, they walked the perimeter of Gabe's home and his small yard. Since Eagan set the pace, it was slow, and Gabe had to force himself to stay with her. She was keeping an eye out for a clue as to where the shot had been taken from. Maybe she thought they'd find an empty shell? Gabe had no idea. He didn't know a pistol from a rifle except by shape.

"There don't seem to be extra footprints or any other evidence of an intruder other than the broken window. But with this weather, I would have been surprised to find much of anything."

"Nope," Gabe agreed. But then, he hadn't expected to find anything either. It had started to rain again during the night and hadn't let up. Even now, the rain was dumping down in unpleasant diagonal sheets.

"Do you think this has something to do with the young woman who visited you Monday?"

"You mean the one who is now deceased? How would I know? It's not as if I've made any recent enemies. That I know of."

"Seems like quite a coincidence."

There was that word again.

You know how I feel about coincidence, Chance.

He did. Way too much.

Gabe swiveled to look at Eagan. "You still don't know her real name?"

The deputy shook her head. "Her prints aren't in the system, and she hasn't been reported missing yet. It's early days though."

"Do you know anything about a family in the area with the last name of Pritchard?" Gabe asked.

"I know plenty families in the area with that last name. It's not that uncommon around here."

They'd returned to the front of the house. The rain abruptly began to come down harder, as if someone was pointing a hose directly at Heartstone.

"Jesus Christ," Eagan muttered, tugging her hood forward again to better protect her face. "I read somewhere that this is the wettest spring in recent history, and I believe it. If someone takes a shot at you again, or anything else out of the ordinary occurs, please call. I don't want to have to learn about this kind of thing from Lundin."

Gabe nodded. He chose not to point out that he'd pretty much been living "out of the ordinary" 24/7 since he moved to Heartstone. How was he supposed to identify something unusual when unusual had become his norm?

"Do you want to come back inside? I want to run something past you, and as I said before, I have coffee."

Eagan hesitated. Was it bribery to offer a cop coffee? Regardless, the temptation of a hot beverage must have been too strong for her to resist.

"A coffee would be lovely."

Gabe pulled his door open and, because his mother had taught him to, held it for Eagan to pass through.

"Make yourself comfortable."

"I'll stand, thanks." To prove her point, the deputy left her coat on but did unzip it.

"Yeah, I should work on getting a few more chairs. And a dining room table. Aside from Alfred, of course. No one in their right mind would want to use Alfred for sitting on."

Removing his jacket, Gabe hung it on the hooks Casey had installed, then toed off his Crocs and left them in a haphazard pile. While Eagan was not-so-subtly taking in his luxurious digs, Gabe busied himself at the espresso machine.

"I would marry this appliance if it was legal," he told her. "This machine makes the best coffee."

"Then why do I see you at Norskland almost every time I go in there?" Eagan asked, coming over to stand across from him at the counter.

"Ah, good question. For conversation. The only downfall of this thing is that it doesn't talk."

Eagan flashed a brief smile. "What did you want to run by me?"

"Here's the thing. I have reason to believe my mother's family name was Pritchard. Karne is something she came up with after she… disassociated herself from them. That's my working theory. Do you want steamed milk?"

"If you're offering."

"Done." He grabbed the milk out of the fridge and poured a small amount into the stainless pitcher he'd purchased just for this purpose.

"It's been a week, that's for sure. Juliet, for lack of a name, showed up first thing Monday morning with her claim that I was her sperm donor. That is not true. Also on Monday, I received a letter alerting me to belongings my mother had had in storage." He decided to skip past the Randy W. experience. He couldn't bring himself to believe it was connected to the rest of the craziness. "On Tuesday, Casey and I drove to Seattle to collect said belongings."

He nodded his chin in the direction of Alfred and the tattered boxes. "That's what we brought back."

Eagan looked over at the collection. "Anything interesting? Aside from the obvious."

"There's a Westfort High School yearbook from 1978. That's where I found out that Pritchard is the name my mother went by before Karne. Eli Rizzi was in there too. They were both juniors that year."

He poured espresso into a boring white mug, followed by steaming hot milk, and pushed it across the counter. "So, I'm just an innocent man trying to figure this all out." That earned him a splutter. "My mother left behind a mystery, one she clearly wanted me to solve, but not until after her death. Which makes me think that whatever led to her name change was not good. Perhaps not legal."

Eagan had her fingers wrapped around the mug as if she was hoarding its warmth. She took a sip and hummed appreciatively, nodding for him to continue.

"To that end, I've been poking around in the online archives this morning in search of some answers. Pritchard isn't an unusual name, but I was hoping I may see something about Heidi —or rather, Holly, which was her name in the yearbook. One thing that did jump out though was a newspaper story about a robbery."

"Oh, yeah?"

"Last day of July in 1978. The 201 Gallery was robbed, and several paintings were stolen. I don't know how many, the article didn't say. There was an employee whose name was Carla Pritchard."

"Okay."

"Anyway, I've searched for that name and found nothing. Obviously, Heidi or Holly was what, sixteen at the time? She wasn't working in a gallery, but maybe this Carla person was related. Maybe Carla was her mother, sister, or aunt. That's as far as I've gotten. Have you ever heard about this? Is this theft a regional urban legend?"

Eagan looked thoughtful, her brows drawing together. But she shook her head. "Nope. Mind, I wasn't even a gleam in my parents' eyes in 1978."

"Yeah, I wasn't for a couple of years yet, either. But the fact remains that Heidi Karne aka Holly Pritchard is not pictured in any Westfort Puffin yearbooks after 1978. From what Elton has told me, and I have no reason to think he hasn't told me everything, Heidi simply showed up one spring needing money. She proved herself to him, so he hired her."

Gabe paused and chugged down about half of his espresso. He was starting to feel the effects of his early morning.

"She didn't tell Elton much about herself, and he didn't ask. Fast forward a bit, and Heidi, uh, makes a poor decision, and whoops, I'm on the way. Elton says he knew what was up and that he'd figured out who my father was." He shook his head. "That's a whole other kettle of fish. Next thing he knew, she was gone from Heartstone, and he never saw or heard from her again. Then I showed up a couple of months ago. Yay, me."

"That's quite a lot to unpack." Eagan set her empty mug back down on the counter.

"You're telling me. So." He sighed the word. "You've never heard about this gallery robbery?"

Gabe would have been tempted to dismiss the robbery if he didn't have that decades-old memory of his mother removing artwork from a wall and sliding it into the trunk of their car.

"No, but I can ask around. There are a few old-timers who come into the station and shoot the breeze—I'm thinking of starting a coffee and donut fund for them. And don't forget that Althea's been there since the dawn of time too. Seriously, I don't know what I'm going to do when she finally retires. The institutional knowledge that woman has stored in her head is irreplaceable."

"Off to Westfort again, I guess. No rest for the wicked." The way things were going, Gabe wasn't sure he had time to wait for the old-timers to show up for free donuts. And why weren't they supporting Eagan for sheriff if she was making sure they got their sugar and caffeine fixes?

"Thank you for the coffee. We'll be in touch if we find anything out about the victim, and if someone takes another shot at you, call us immediately." Eagan set her empty cup down on the counter.

"Fine." Which, of course, meant *maybe*.

Eagan shot him a glare worthy of Ranger Man as they both walked to the door.

"Yes," Gabe huffed. "I will call the station if some asshole decides to take another shot at me."

Satisfied with his reply, Eagan pushed outside, but the infernal wind grabbed the door handle out of her grip and tried to slam it back on her. Being young and nimble, she avoided being squashed.

"Sorry about that!" she yelled over her shoulder.

Gabe grabbed hold of the door as the wind tried to sweep it closed again. "Just my luck, I'll get taken out by my own door."

Eagan started to open the cruiser door, which in turn had him squashing the memory of the last time he'd ridden in a sheriff's vehicle, with former Sheriff Eli Rizzi doing the honors.

Eli Rizzi, who'd gone to high school with Gabe's mother.

"Deputy Eagan," Gabe called out.

She paused, halfway in and out of the car, eyebrows raised.

"Any chance you might be able to ask Rizzi some questions for me? Since he was in high school with my mother and all."

What Gabe could only classify as a Complicated Expression slid across her face.

"Might be a bit difficult," she replied. "Rizzi was found dead in his cell this past weekend. I'm surprised you hadn't heard the news already."

With that, she finished climbing into the cruiser. Her lips were pressed into a thin line as she banged the car door shut and reversed out of the driveway, presumably to head back toward the Sheriff's Office.

For his part, Gabe stood on the tiny concrete pad that passed as his patio, with the rain and wind swirling around him, his mouth partially open.

The only thing you're going to catch is flies, Chance.

He slammed his lips closed and went back inside.

NINETEEN

CASEY – THURSDAY (UP THE VALLEY)

"I think I'm going to take a run up The Valley today, now that the storm has passed," Casey told Greta.

Eyeing him, his work partner set her coffee mug down on the desk.

"You want company?"

"No. I'll have Bowie with me. He doesn't pry into my personal life the way you do."

Greta snorted. "Any specific reason for the trip? Are you missing the potholes? I don't think the grader has been scheduled up the top of the road yet."

"Gabe told me he thought he saw Calvin Perkins's truck the other day, but he wasn't sure. What if Calvin, for reasons only known to him, hid out all winter and is alive? I think it's likely he'd head back to familiar haunts."

"Be careful, then. If he *is* alive, Calvin's dangerous."

"I've always thought Dwayne was the more unpredictable one. With him dead, maybe it will be easier to reason with his brother now that some time has passed. And besides, the driver could have been someone else. Gabe didn't get a good look. It's also possible that Calvin's dead and some opportunist stole his truck.

But I thought I'd take a long drive, see how winter treated the folks up that way."

"Just be careful, please."

Casey nodded, then pulled on his coat and knit Park Service winter beanie and grabbed Bowie's leash. Recognizing they were going somewhere, maybe a ride in the truck to happy-fun-doggy time, Bowie jumped up and headed for the office's door.

"I'm always careful. Come on, Bowie, let's go for a ride."

Casey decided he'd head up The Valley as far as he could go to low-key check for Calvin and then turn around, stopping at one or two of the friendlier homesteads on his way back. The folks up Crystal Creek were generally loners and stayed to themselves, but that didn't mean they didn't pay attention to traffic up and down the road.

"Christ," Casey muttered, steering around a spot where the road was close to being washed out.

Slowing to a complete stop, he grabbed his pen and water-proof notebook out of the glove compartment, then made a note of the exact location. As luck would have it, there was a handy mile marker. Sooner rather than later, the county would have to repair or at least shore up the road. There were more homesteads beyond this point, and they needed to be able to access their property.

Before those were Snowcap Estates and Gordon MacDonald's property, the last place Calvin was seen alive. Putting the truck in gear again, Casey pressed on the gas. The tires spun but caught quickly, thank god. The last thing he needed was to get stuck and be forced to call Greta for help.

"Yeah, no. I'd never hear the end of it. Isn't that right, Bowie?"

In the rearview mirror, Casey watched Bowie's ears prick up and his tail smack against the seat.

Half an hour later, he finally arrived at Snowcap Estates. The partially developed land depressed him. The so-called investment group had cut down the trees and installed electric hookups, but that was as far as they'd gotten before the shit hit the fan. Casey parked along the edge of the road and got out, thankful that the morning rain had lessened to a sort of enveloping mist instead of the downpour it had been when he'd left the ranger office. He held the door open for Bowie, who jumped to the ground.

"It's going to be a bath day for you after this."

Bowie eyed him briefly and then trotted off toward a pile of logging debris, following some scent that humans could not smell. Casey trailed after him, keeping an eye out for anything unusual that might suggest Perkins had been around—or just anything unusual in general.

He ducked under the ragged Do Not Trespass tape still looped across the site's access road. A forensics team had been contracted to search for Suzie Warner's remains, but conditions from December through February had been both cold and wet. For complicated reasons, some to do with the weather and others tied to the estimated age of the remains and not having an idea where they might be located on the acreage, the West Coast Forensics team was still not due in for another week.

At least that's what Casey had heard through the grapevine, the grapevine being Greta and her "sources."

As he walked further onto the property, a sense of unease began to overtake him. As someone who spent a lot of time alone in the woods and someone that lawbreakers didn't always welcome, he paid attention to the rise of the hairs on the back of his neck.

"Bowie." He snapped his fingers. "To me."

Already about fifty feet ahead of him, Bowie turned back and joined him. Maybe he was feeling the unease too.

"Good boy."

Regardless of who was out there, Casey wasn't leaving just yet.

"Calvin Perkins!" Casey shouted. "Are you out there?"

There was no immediate answer, which was not a surprise.

"Perkins, your mom is devastated and wants you home again." Even jerks like Calvin had mothers who cared about them. "I don't know if you've heard the news, but Eli Rizzi is in jail."

No response, just the drip-drip of rainwater falling from tree branches, Bowie sniffing around, and his own voice. Since the events of last fall, Casey had been wondering about the role Eli Rizzi had played in Dwayne's and Calvin's lives. Had their careers of petty crime been encouraged by their uncle? Calvin was the only one left who could say.

The hairs on his neck were telling him there was still someone—or something—out there. Casey stopped and turned in a full circle, scanning the area. With the leaves and other debris covering the ground and the copious amounts of mud and mud puddles popping up through them, it was hard to tell if someone had been there recently or if some sort of animal was watching him. There was no shortage of bears and cougars up this way.

Bowie let out a sharp bark.

"What is it, boy?"

Casey grabbed Bowie's collar and stood in place, his back to one of the few remaining fir trees, with Bowie between his legs. The space between his shoulder blades didn't feel so vulnerable in this position. He tried to convince himself that his imagination was making him jumpy, but it didn't work.

His cell phone vibrated, surprising him. It was rare for cell phones to have service up here unless there was a convergence of satellites and low cloud cover. Casey tugged the thing out of his inside pocket and saw it was Gabriel.

"Hello," Casey said softly.

"It's me."

It was ridiculous how the sound of Gabe's voice made him feel less jumpy. Who would've thought.

"It is."

Casey wondered why Gabe was calling. His tone didn't sound like "hey, was bored, whatcha doing."

"Guess what I just found out?" Gabe asked.

"What?" The various scenarios that Casey's imagination came up with ranged from Gabe's espresso machine had been recalled to he'd been called for jury duty.

"Rizzi is dead." Gabe put particular emphasis on the last d in dead.

Casey blinked. "What, seriously?"

"As a heart attack, as Elton would say. I don't know the details, but Eagan told me he was found dead in his cell over the weekend."

"Holy cow."

"And more. Where are you? You sound outdoorsy."

Bowie whined and tried to wiggle out of Casey's grip, but Casey wouldn't release him.

"I'm up at Snowcap. I thought I'd check up on your possible Calvin Perkins sighting."

"Oh." Gabe was silent, and Casey recognized that drop in tone. Gabe was worried. Now he knew how Casey felt way too often. Granted, Casey had come up here alone last fall and had been ambushed, so Gabe had a reason to feel concerned. "Have you found anything?"

"No, but I have that weird feeling you get when you're being watched. Could be a human, could be a wild animal."

"Would you do me a favor and get out of there? You don't need to be the hero who brings in Perkins—if he's even still alive. The truck just looked like his and I thought you should know about it. I didn't think you would head off on a one-man mission to find the man."

"Gabriel, if you thought the truck looked enough like Calvin's to bring it up in conversation, then I'm going to take it seriously. He and Dwayne hung out up here, he's familiar with the area, he's got the survival skills. It makes sense that he might here somewhere."

"The key word is somewhere. Just come back and we'll drive up there together, okay?"

Casey didn't want to hurt Gabe's feelings by pointing out that Gabe was probably more of a hindrance than a help.

"Okay, I'll head back." He'd ask Greta to come back with him. She was an excellent tracker and great shot.

There was a snick sound on the line, and Casey figured the satellite was moving out of range.

"That's Elton calling," Gabe said. "I need to talk to him."

"I'll text when I'm back at the office."

But Gabe had already clicked off. Casey tucked the phone back into his pocket and started toward the truck with Bowie at his heels. The sense of being watched faded the farther he got from the tree line. Was it a case of his imagination working overtime or had someone's attention been focused on him?

Another unpleasant shiver crawled up his spine, and Casey moved a bit faster toward the truck.

A CACOPHONY of barking reached his ears before he arrived at the log cabin. Although the word *cabin* implied something small and quaint, and the Clark-Allard home was huge. Three stories and constructed with logs from the property, it was set a mile or so back from the road. The driveway wound almost aimlessly through the remaining trees until it finally ended at the back of the house.

Casey wasn't a big fan of city folks moving out to the wilds of the Olympics. More often than not, they ended up smack in the middle of some tragic disaster, freezing to death, accidentally setting their own house on fire. The gap in expectations established by social media influencers, many who'd never actually lived off the grid, and the reality was wider than the Grand Canyon and about as dangerous.

The Clark-Allards were an exception to Casey's general experience. Now in his mid-fifties, Paul had moved up The Valley five or so years ago with his younger partner, Etienne. Casey wasn't sure what exactly Paul did to keep busy, but Etienne raised dogs. A lot of big, goofy Newfoundland dogs. Dogs who sounded scary from afar, but who were more likely to knock a person down out of enthusiasm and then snuffle them to death.

"Come on, Bowie, you can show these goofs what a real dog can do again."

Four Newfies, three black and white and one all black, wrangled for who got to greet Bowie and Casey first. Elbowing the door open, Casey started to slide off the seat to the muddy ground below. Excited for the fun and games, Bowie squeezed out from behind him and jumped into the fray. The sniff fest began. Casey wasn't worried about his much smaller dog; Bowie had always held his own just fine in the past.

"What brings you here today, Lundin?" Paul asked, stepping out from the shadows of the covered porch that wrapped around the entirety of their home.

Casey looked up at the older man. "Permission to come aboard?"

Paul rolled his eyes. "Yes. Do you need a coffee or tea? Etienne has a kettle warming."

"Whichever is easier," Casey replied as he made for the stairs.

CASEY WAS thankful he hadn't chosen to wear the socks Gabe had given him for Christmas. It was difficult to feel professional wearing pictures of your dog on your feet. Following Paul's lead, he'd left his boots in the mudroom so he wouldn't track dirt inside.

"Coffee?" Etienne asked, his soft French accent blurring the word.

"Yes, thank you."

The main floor of their home was an open space with a kitchen area at one end. This space included a nook dining area surrounded by windows and looked out onto the yard. Casey glanced outside where there was currently a five-dog rugby team roiling in the mud.

"Paul?"

"Am I breathing?" Paul teased.

"Tea is full of antioxidants and much easier on your stomach."

"Quit worrying about my stomach. I hate tea. I've always hated tea and knowing that about me, you still decided to move to America with me."

"Ah, the things we do for love." Etienne smiled.

Etienne vaguely reminded Casey of a kinder, gentler Jason Statham, quiet and careful but with an edge of danger. He might have been raising dogs now, but Casey suspected Etienne had a past that was best left undiscovered. In fact, he figured both Paul and Etienne were more than they appeared.

"Milk?" Etienne offered, waggling a small carton.

"Black is all right." Casey looked around, liking what he could see of their home. He was always impressed by how they managed to make it truly feel like a cabin in the woods, despite its size.

"Is black coffee what you prefer?" Etienne asked sharply.

Paul snorted. "You might as well tell him. He will keep asking until you confess. I don't know why you haven't figured that out by now."

"Life is too short to settle for second best," Etienne added.

That sounded like something Gabriel would say. He probably had, and Casey had shaken his head. "Café au lait sounds wonderful. And once again, you've forced me to utilize my entire catalog of French."

"Café au lait, it is."

Moments later, the three of them were seated around the large square oak table that took up the dining space. Outside, the dogs were woofing and whumping as Bowie took the lead and the Newfies chased after him.

"He's gonna be extra tired tonight," Casey commented before sipping at his drink.

Etienne said, "A tired dog is a well-behaved dog."

"Come on, out with it, what brought you up The Valley on this dismal day? Is it something about that nonsense from last fall up at Snowcap?" Paul asked. "We were visiting Etienne's family outside of Marseilles and missed all the action."

"How was your trip? One of these days, I'll make the effort to get out of the country."

"It was good," Etienne said. "My parents are not as young as they used to be—but then again, who is? I always enjoy our visits but equally enjoy being back here."

Not for the first time, Casey wondered what the couple's history was and what they did other than raise large dogs these days to keep themselves busy. Casey suspected both men were ex-LEOs of some sort. Paul being a federal agent or CIA tracked. Etienne could've been Interpol or something equally sneaky and secret.

"There was a possible sighting of Calvin Perkins earlier in the week. Since he used to spend a lot of time up here, I thought it wouldn't hurt to take another look around, see if there were any signs of him."

"You think he's still alive after the winter?" Etienne asked.

"I do, yeah. Calvin has the skills and knowledge to survive in these woods. Admittedly, he was more unhinged than usual the last time I saw him, but I think it was grief over losing Dwayne. Now I'm worried he's out for revenge. Not sure who on, but if he's alive, he wants someone to pay. It's the way the Perkins brothers always were. But I didn't find any evidence today that Calvin has been lurking up there."

"And you're wondering if we've seen him." Paul lifted his coffee to his lips and took a tentative sip.

Casey nodded. "Or his truck. It's one of those big Fords with Confederate flags flying."

"That's something I've never understood." Etienne wrinkled his nose. "This state had little to do with the American Civil War."

"I'm sure there are folks who have written entire dissertations on the subject," Casey said dryly. "But I'm going with ignorance. It's easier for me to tolerate."

"We haven't seen Perkins or his truck." Paul looked at his partner, and Etienne agreed with a nod of his head. "But the dogs have been hyperaware the past week or so. We both thought it was a cougar or bear that had them acting squirrelly, ended up keeping them in the barn for a few days. But I suppose their nerves could have been caused by a human."

Etienne tapped the table with his index finger, his eyes narrowing thoughtfully. "I have heard a few vehicles driving up the road. More traffic than usual for this time of year." He shrugged. "I didn't run out to the road and stop them to inquire what their business was."

Casey nodded and took another sip of his drink. It was delicious, and he felt like a bit of a traitor. Gabe's coffee was not as good as Etienne's. Maybe it was the French influence, but Casey was going to buy some different beans to test.

"There are only a couple of homesteads above you," Casey pointed out. And at least one of them was on his to-visit list.

Paul nodded. "True, but the Carlsons are in Mexico until mid-May. Denny Pritchard is the only one between us and the end of this road, and he doesn't get out much this time of year."

"Denny is the next stop." Casey had saved Denny Pritchard for last, wanting to pump whatever information he could get about him from Paul and Etienne first. Living as close as they did, they knew more about the old man than anyone else Casey could think of.

Pritchard wasn't that uncommon of a name, but Casey had been wondering if Denny was a relative of Heidi Karne's, an uncle or cousin maybe. He'd wanted to talk to Denny before mentioning his existence to Gabriel, just to confirm, and having the mystery of *maybe* Calvin's truck showing up had given him the perfect reason to come up The Valley today.

Denny Pritchard and Calvin Perkins at the top of his to-do list. Casey almost laughed.

THEY DIDN'T SPEAK for a moment, and Paul and Etienne shared some kind of complicated glance. Casey'd been framing his chat with Denny and didn't know what the two men were contemplating. He wouldn't have been surprised if they were silently discussing how Denny was not The Valley's most outgoing person and Casey's goal of talking to him may not be achievable. In an area populated by people who just wanted to be left alone, Denny was the most alone of all.

"He's been a bit jumpy recently. Give him plenty of notice, maybe honk your horn or something, so he knows someone is on the way," Etienne finally said.

Casey nodded. That was a good idea. No reason to risk being shot at.

"Denny's at least eighty-five now, isn't he?" Casey asked.

"Eighty-five and his hearing is going. We don't like him living up there alone, but he refuses to move. Says he'll die when and where he wants to," said Paul.

Casey had associated casually with Denny for a few years, but the truth was what he knew about the man was almost nothing, except that his family, a wife and several daughters, had died in a tragic accident years ago. And even that fact Casey had heard from the previous ranger. Denny did not invite curiosity.

"Do you know if Denny's originally from around here?" Casey asked. He assumed Denny was, but the old man just as easily could have been the Unabomber's unknown cousin who moved to Washington decades ago.

Paul and Etienne looked at each other again. "I have no idea," Paul said. "He seems to have taken a liking to Etienne. Who wouldn't though?"

Etienne smiled and added, "He doesn't say much about himself. We talk about the dogs, the weather. Why do you ask?"

It was Casey's turn to be vague. "The name Pritchard came up in something else. I'm just wondering what Denny's history is, if they may be tied together."

There was a likelihood that Elton knew something about Denny Pritchard. Casey made a mental note to ask him.

"He is one of those who keeps to himself. A loner old man." A Gaelic shrug punctuated Etienne's words.

Paul was nodding. "He's gruff and often rude. A true misan-thrope. Etienne and I joke that his retirement account must be stored under the floorboards." Paul frowned. "But folks here are private. Etienne and I moved here to escape the rat race. I've always thought he was a local though."

Etienne glanced over at Paul. "Remember when we first moved here?" He chuckled and looked back at Casey. "Denny asked Paul about our relationship."

"I told him it was a don't-ask-don't-tell situation," Paul explained. "Denny nodded and nothing has been said since. What's this about anyway?"

Casey briefly considered the pros and cons of discussing Gabriel's personal life with virtual strangers. These men were not longtime Valley residents; they wouldn't know anything about Heidi Karne aka Holly Pritchard. But Gabriel wasn't currently hiding from anyone as far as Casey knew. What was it that Gabe often said? Act first, ask permission later.

"My—" Casey hesitated. "My partner discovered earlier this week that his mother's name at birth was Holly Pritchard. As you said, Pritchard is not an unusual surname, but sometime soon after 1978, a teenaged Holly Pritchard chose to go by Heidi Karne instead, which is how Gabe always knew her. Gabe's trying to connect the dots between Holly in 1978 and modern Heidi. She recently passed away, and her legacy appears to be mystery and conspiracy. I'm just trying to help."

"You do know it's only Wednesday, right?" Paul said.

"Isn't it Thursday?" asked Etienne, then shrugged.

"It is Thursday," Casey confirmed.

All three of them began to laugh. Who knew what day it was. It was March in the Pacific Northwest.

"So," continued Etienne when they'd gotten themselves under control. "Are you thinking Denny could be related to Gabriel's mother?"

"If he's in his late eighties, he's old enough to have been Holly Pritchard's father or some other older relation, an uncle maybe."

"There's only one way to find out. You're going to have to ask him in person. Denny doesn't have a phone."

This fact did not surprise Casey in the least. Denny Pritchard seemed like the kind of person to shun modern life entirely. Although from previous drop-ins, he knew the man had a working generator, so maybe he was just allergic to communication with the outside world.

"If you'd like, one of us can ask him about this Holly person the next time we see him," Paul said. "Etienne has a soft spot for the old coot, takes meals up to him a couple times a week."

"I'm going to head over there now. Might as well since I'm up here." Casey tugged his wallet out of his back pocket, removed one of his business cards, and handed it to Paul.

"Here's my cell phone number and email address if you remember anything. Or if you see or hear anything suspicious."

"Thanks," Paul said, slipping the card into his shirt pocket. "We'll be in touch."

DENNY PRITCHARD'S place was even more remote than Paul and Etienne's. Dilapidated and forlorn, it was surrounded by a lifetime of broken and discarded machinery—truck chassis, an old yellow school bus, two semi-truck containers, and more—that also dotted the cleared area around it. The forest was creeping back as well, making a play for consuming the yard and all of its ornamentation with the help of its sidekick, the European blackberry. Casey didn't want to think how or why he'd brought those vehicles up here. A trickle of woodsmoke leaked from the stovepipe-style chimney at the roofline.

The gravel drive that led from the road to Denny's house had been regularly maintained, and Casey wondered if that was Etienne and Paul's work. As suggested, he'd honked his horn several times as he drew closer before parking next to the twin of Elton's pickup. He waited a few minutes for some kind of acknowledgment from Denny before getting out.

Gabriel would not be happy if Casey returned with extra holes in him.

The front door opened wide enough for Denny himself to shuffle out onto the porch. An ancient shotgun was loosely gripped in his gnarled hands and vaguely pointing Casey's direction.

Opening the door of his truck, Casey slid out and landed in the muddy churned-up earth at the end of driveway.

"Afternoon, Denny, it's Casey Lundin from the Forest Service," he yelled.

"I'm not so old I don't know who you are, Lundin. What

brings you by?" Denny grimaced, although it could have been that the man thought he was smiling. Casey figured he didn't give a shit and greeted any visitor with a menacing scowl.

"We're still looking for Calvin Perkins. Someone thought they saw his truck on the highway recently. I'm just wondering if you've seen or heard anything that might suggest he's up this way?"

Casey continued to stand by his truck—the way Denny was handling that rifle had him wary. At least, warier than he typically was when dropping in on Denny. There was something less controlled about him this time.

To his credit, Denny appeared to consider Casey's question for a few seconds before shaking his head and saying, "Nope, I haven't. Useless piece of shit, maybe he got himself killed. If the forest didn't take him outright, one of his buddies probably did."

A low rumble that Casey hadn't been paying attention to increased briefly in intensity. He realized that Denny's gas generator was running in the background and wondered why. But it wasn't Casey's business and Denny was what was politely called eccentric. The man probably had enough fuel to last until the weather changed for the better and past that point.

"Thanks, Denny. If you notice something, maybe let Paul or Etienne know. They can reach out to me." He knew full well that no one up The Valley would willingly call the Sheriff's Office, but they might contact Casey or Greta.

Denny gave him a chin nod and then went back inside his house without saying anything further.

"Alright then." Casey used the steering wheel to heft himself back into the truck. "I guess he's not answering any more questions today."

Bowie had no reply.

He stopped at a few more of the occupied homes on the way back down to the highway while Bowie slept like the dead in the back seat. His dog didn't even ask to get out of the truck. No one other than Paul and Etienne had noticed any traffic that could be remotely considered unusual, which only added to Casey's expanding theory about the Clark-Allards' past.

"Those Newfies could be special agents too, Bowie. Enforcers, maybe. What do you think about that?"

TWENTY

GABE – THURSDAY EVENING

Gabe didn't like that Casey had gone alone to Snowcap Estates. Why hadn't Greta gone with him? Weren't they work partners? The events of last fall, when Casey had been attacked and Gabe couldn't get to him fast enough, snuck into his mind. For a short period of time, he and Elton hadn't even known where Casey was, and that had sent his blood pressure skyrocketing.

He was pacing in his living room, but it wasn't at all satisfying seeing as he had to turn around again every three seconds. Giving that up, he stopped in front of Alfred and the stack of boxes and glared at them.

"Obviously, I've missed something important in you all, more important than the yearbook."

Lifting a random box, he carried it to the coffee table and opened it. This was the one that seemed to be the contents of a young woman's dresser drawer. Carefully, Gabe removed every-thing, setting the items on the table after examining each one. He even tried opening the lip gloss, but it was permanently sealed shut. Taking the empty box, he turned it upside down and shook it. A tiny, gold-colored hoop earring that must have been trapped in a crease dropped out with a soft *plink* sound.

He picked it up and peered at it. Had his mother worn this earring and then lost its twin? How? Had she been at a high school dance? Or hanging out with friends? Since he didn't know how to feel about the earring and what it said about a young Heidi or the fact that it had been in a box since the mid-seventies, he tossed it back and set that box aside.

Gabe repeated the process with three more of the boxes, finding nothing to note. Box number four was the one that held the spiral notebooks. He'd thought at first that they were full of teenaged Heidi's class notes and homework, but when he flipped the top one open this time and scanned the page, he realized it was a diary. They all were.

The earliest one began Saturday, January 1, 1977.

This is the diary of Holly Pritchard.

Heidi's handwriting was loopy but clear and fairly easy to read. To Gabe, it seemed similar to her handwriting as an adult. The entries were benign, Heidi declaring on page one that she was going to write every day. She managed that for about a month, then the entries slowed to two or three times a week. Heidi recorded daily life, what it was like being a sophomore in high school, the teachers, her school assignments, etcetera. It was almost a calendar rather than a diary.

There were no entries with heart-rending confessions of young love, crushes, or friend group issues, which did not shock Gabe. The Heidi he'd known had not been sentimental. She could turn on the charm when needed, and it rarely failed, but Heidi didn't waste time bellyaching. Heidi moved on.

She also didn't name names, which Gabe found incredibly irritating.

"Come on, Heidi. Not one 'Eli Rizzi is a pig'? I need some hints."

The second notebook was similar to the first: boring. Gabe wondered why Heidi had bothered. Maybe it had become habit for her? He certainly had no memories of his mother spending her evenings jotting down what had happened during her day. If she'd been a diarist as a teen, it was something she'd stopped. If that was the case, why? If she hadn't, was he going to get another letter leading to boxes sometime in the future? Gabe shuddered.

His eyes started to water. Gabe rubbed them and, with a sigh, picked up a third notebook. The beginning date on this one was September 1977. Heidi had stopped including the days of the week by that point, just a date and whatever she thought important enough to jot down.

LANDED THE JOB.

Gabe at first thought she was talking about working for Elton. But an entry two pages later disabused him of that idea.

Found a secret door!

There were no secret doors. Elton had sold his wares from a booth at summer fairs. Gabe's exhaustion vanished. Quickly, he flipped through the pages to see if anything else leapt out at him.

"Really, Mom, would it have hurt you to add a bit more detail?"

He found it striking that even at sixteen or seventeen years old, Heidi was already extremely careful about what kind of information she left behind. It was almost as if she'd been born that way.

Or *trained*.

As a child, Gabe had never questioned his mother's choice of careers. After all, food on the table was a good thing, and he didn't understand that Heidi was usually bending the law. As an adult, he hadn't questioned it either. They'd often worked together, a sort of family affair.

Once a grifter, always a grifter. *Kinda sorta*. Gabe was doing his best to leave that part of his life behind. Now it was becoming clear, or at least less opaque, that Heidi had spent her early years learning the art of the swindle. And she'd passed that knowledge on to Gabriel.

"Come on, I need more. Where was this job? What was up with the door?"

Flipping back to the first page, Gabe reread each entry. Maybe he'd missed a reference. He had not.

"Jesus Christ."

There were fewer notes in this book. Almost, for instance, like she'd gotten a part-time job and didn't have as much time on her hands. Gabe did find it amusing that many entries were a variation of *it rained today*.

Not that Gabe had read many teenaged girl's diaries, but he'd kind of expected *had a fight with my mom, she's dumb*. He tried to imagine what he would've written about, and the answer was that Gabe wasn't the type to write shit down. And Heidi was the one who had taught him not to.

The last remotely interesting record was sometime in June of 1978, not long before he was assuming that Holly became Heidi.

He came into the store again today!

He had been circled several times. Gabe squinted. It looked to him like the circle had first been a heart shape and then Heidi had done her best to obliterate it.

Gabe set the book down again and blew out a big breath of air. What the hell? Why did he have the feeling that *He* was David Delacombe? Was it possible that David Delacombe had been a part of whatever Heidi had gotten herself involved in? Gabe didn't think the idea was farfetched. From what he understood, David Delacombe had never been a paragon of virtue, not even close. Of course, if that was the case, that meant Heidi's from-beyond-the-grave letter hadn't exactly been truthful.

"Twenty when you met, Heidi? Really?"

Patting various pockets to search for his phone and not finding it, Gabe spun in a circle until he finally spotted the device just where he'd left it, next to the blessed caffeine machine. Snatching it up, he opened his contact list and stared at the screen for a moment, then pressed Call.

Shay Delacombe answered after three rings with a smooth, "Gabriel, how are things?"

"Ridiculous, as seems to generally be the case with me."

"Are you calling for legal help?" Shay asked with a chuckle. "I can offer a friends and family discount."

"Not really. Thanks though. I have a question about, er, our father, and I figure you or maybe Claribel are the only ones who might be able to answer it."

And while yes, Claribel undoubtedly had more information, Shay would be the source of least resistance. Gabe wasn't prepared to talk to the Delacombe matriarch this afternoon. Claribel was the eleven on a scale of one to ten.

Niall Hamarsson was also a no-go. Gabe and Shay's other brother had never known David, having discovered that David was *his* father when he'd moved back to Piedras Island several years ago. Shay, at least, had lived with the man until he left the island for college.

Additionally, to the surprise of literally no one, it turned out that David Delacombe had had at least one girlfriend in most major cities in Western Washington. The man had had issues being on his own. Gabe just hoped those issues hadn't led to more invitees to the next family reunion Claribel called.

"I'll do my best."

Gabe could hear more than one voice speaking in the background. Wherever Shay was, he wasn't at home or his office.

"Are you busy right now? I don't want to barge into your day."

"Please. I'm Claribel's acting handler today. Just waiting for her to fleece her best friends while she cheats at bingo."

Ah, yes. Gabe had been invited to bingo but hadn't taken Claribel up on it yet. He was curious though.

"Sounds like an adventure." Phone in hand, Gabe walked over to stand in front of the other living room window, the one he could still see through. As usual, there was nothing going on. A lone squirrel scrabbled across the access road and up a maple tree on the other side. "Do you know anything about what David was up to in 1977-ish?"

"I'm older than you, Gabriel, but not by enough to have any clue what David was doing. One sec."

Abruptly, the incoming sounds were muted, probably by Shay's finger over the phone's microphone. Gabe caught sight of the squirrel again. Now it was carrying something in its mouth and was definitely acting furtively.

"Stole your neighbor's snacks, huh?"

"I'm sorry, what was that?"

Great. Shay now knew that Gabe talked to squirrels.

"Nothing, just talking to squirrels, as one does."

"Okaaaay. I'm going to put you on speaker. Claribel is right here with me. She says to hurry it up, she's about to cover the board."

"Good afternoon, Gabriel. How are you doing? Shay says you have a question about my feckless nephew."

Gabe decided less explaining and just asking his question would likely get him a more straightforward answer. He had only met the woman twice and already knew not to give her too much leeway.

"Do you think it's possible that David first met Heidi"—he wasn't ready to reveal that she was likely born Holly Pritchard quite yet—"as early as 1977? She would have been sixteen or so."

While he waited for Claribel to answer, Gabe tucked the phone under his ear, stacked up the notebooks, and slipped into his Crocs. Then he took the books and his laptop out to his car and tucked them under the back seat. Paranoid much? Perhaps. But he still thought someone had been in his house on Monday, and if that was the case, the notebooks might be safer if he stored them at Casey's or Elton's.

Claribel snorted. "Sixteen years old? Of course, it's possible. He often preferred younger girls, the asshole. Probably because they fell for his line of bullshit. Older, more experienced women were more likely to see him for who and what he was, a damn predator. The more I learn about him, the more disgusted I am."

That made sense, although Gabe was disturbed to think that his sperm donor was a predator. Just as he was about to say something, a spatter of raindrops splashed against his face.

He hurried back inside, saying as he did so, "Do you think he could have been involved in an art theft?"

Shutting the door against the coming storm, Gabe was thinking about Heidi's scribbles. *I got the job* and *found the door.* Was it possible that she had worked at the 201 Gallery and was part of the theft? What about Carla Pritchard? Where did she fit in with all of this? Had this Carla person—a possible relative— gotten Heidi a job at the gallery or had Heidi worked somewhere else?

Then the most important question of all, what had happened to the artwork? Heidi and Gabe certainly hadn't lived a life of luxury. He'd done a quick search on Martin Crevan, and even his sketches were worth thousands these days. The Heidi he knew wouldn't have let that kind of income get away from her. And... what kind of business had a secret door anyway?

Apparently, the kind located in a one-hundred-year-old building in Westfort, Washington.

"David?" Claribel sounded thoughtful, and Gabe wished he could see her face. "Why not? He was involved with problematic moneybags people and set fire to his own property for the insurance. Seems to me that art theft is just a hop, skip, and a jump from that. Why do you ask?"

Gabe kicked off his shoes and plopped down on the couch. "It's a long story, and I don't know the end of it yet. Conceivably, there's stolen art involved, but that could just be me projecting."

It nagged at him that he'd only found the single story about the paintings taken from the 201 Gallery. Crevan was a big artist, big enough that the theft should have been a huge deal. What had really happened? They'd probably never learn the whole story. If Gabe hadn't witnessed his mother coolly removing paintings from an art gallery in Laguna Beach all those years ago, he might not have stopped scrolling. But he had, and now he couldn't stop thinking about it.

"Stolen art is certainly a possibility. The asshole was always on the prowl for his next big scheme. But if he was involved, I don't know if he ever reaped any benefits. Certainly not an influx of cash. He was quick to brag when that happened." Gabe thought he heard a gagging sound on Claribel's part.

Good grifters don't brag. They take the money and move on.

"If I learn anything worthwhile, I'll fill you in," Gabe promised.

"See that you do, young man. Keep me updated and let Shay know if the situation changes. I need to get back to my bingo card."

Young man. Gabe snorted. He had to admit that he enjoyed Claribel's roguish outlook on life.

"Enjoy fleecing your friends!"

There was dead air for a moment and then Shay was back. "Do you need one of us to come down to Heartstone and throw our weight around for any reason?" he asked.

Fuck no. The last thing Gabe needed was Shay and Claribel showing up and sticking their noses into whatever was going on. He was fond of Claribel, but from afar. Absence makes the heart grow fonder or something like that.

"Jesus Christ, no. I've got enough people minding my business. Not to sound ungrateful or anything."

Shay laughed. "I don't know, I might agree with Claribel on this one. You've been on your own for too long, it's time you let family give you a hand. Heartstone is just a hop and a skip these days."

Gabe's phone beeped, letting him know someone else was calling. Glancing at the screen, he saw it was Elton.

"I gotta go, there's someone pinging me."

"Sure there is. We'll talk later."

Did Shay practice sounding ominous in the mirror on a daily basis? Filing that thought away for later, Gabe quickly pressed Accept.

"Elton, what's up?"

"Calling to let you know I asked around at the boat shed yesterday."

"And? Did you learn anything new? Did any of the old codgers think they might have known a Holly Pritchard?"

"No," Elton said. "No one remembered the name. I could go back with a copy of the page from her yearbook with her picture and show it around."

That wasn't a bad idea at all, except Gabe hadn't told Elton that the mystery girl had been found dead, although Althea had likely said something to him.

Instead, Gabe asked, "Did you ever hear about an art robbery? Summer of seventy-eight, an art gallery in Westfort was robbed and several paintings went missing."

"No, but we didn't have the internet following us around back in those days, recording everything sunrise to sunset. And like I said a while back, Heartstone and Westfort don't feel as geographically separated now as they did back then. Do you think Heidi had something to do with the robbery?"

"Honestly, I haven't found much information on it, just the one article. There's no smoking gun proving she was involved, but it seems odd. However, the employee who was quoted in the paper was a Carla Pritchard, which only adds to my suspicions. Maybe a sister, an aunt, her mother? I'll need to head back to County Records now that I have another name."

"Pritchard again? The only Pritchard I know of is Denny, and it's been so long since I've seen him that I'd almost forgotten about him. He's older than me and lives up The Valley, ornery old mountain man."

Gabe mulled this information over for a moment, adding it to what little he knew and trying to come up with a plausible connection.

When the plausible fails, turn to the implausible, Chance.

"Did you hear that a body was found?" Gabe asked, changing the subject to something even more grim.

"Yep. Police scanner," Elton reminded him.

Ah yes, he would have learned about the body from his scanner, Althea didn't have to tell him.

Yes, because everyone but Gabe, and perhaps Casey, had a scanner and knew just about every emergency or infraction before Gabe did. Most likely, Casey *did* have one; Gabe had never had a reason to ask him about it.

"Right. Did you also hear that it's an as yet unidentified young woman?"

"Yep, that too. Why?"

"Well, what I do know is that the body belongs to that woman. The one who showed up Monday afternoon claiming to be my daughter."

There was a long pause before Elton responded. "This is not good, Gabe. Not good at all," he finally said.

"Yeah." Gabe had to agree. "I was at the Sheriff's Office answering questions for a little while yesterday because the only thing they found on her was some piece of paper with my name and address on it. Did Althea tell you any of this?"

"She doesn't talk much about work. If Deputy Eagan told her not to say anything, she'd have kept her mouth shut."

"That makes sense."

Neither spoke for a moment. Gabe's brain was working overtime trying to piece this last puzzle of Heidi's together. He and Elton needed to visit this Denny Pritchard person together and ask him a few questions. Denny Pritchard could be the key. What if he was Heidi's father?

Finally, Elton said, "How about you and Casey come over for

dinner? I picked up some chicken noodle soup. It's a big container."

"Sure thing. I'm happy not to cook. Casey said he'd be by, and I planned on inviting myself over to his anyway." Gabe looked at his phone and saw it was after six.

Crap, he'd lost track of time. Where was Casey? Shouldn't he have been back from his field trip by now? "We'll be by later, around seven? We can lay out this new information, maybe come up with an idea or five. I'm going to bring the notebooks with me. I found some possibly interesting comments in one of them."

Gabe quickly punched in Casey's cell number, but it went straight to voicemail. The likely answer was that he was in a dead zone. With a frustrated grumble, he tossed his phone down next to him.

Since he needed to do something that was not just sitting around waiting for Casey to show up, and pacing hadn't done the job, Gabe hopped up, shoved his feet into his boots, and pulled on a jacket.

Grabbing his keys off the hook—*thank you, Casey*—he headed out the door. Sometimes just aimlessly driving helped him think more clearly.

Maybe if he'd been paying attention to his surroundings, he wouldn't have been caught off guard. But he wasn't paying attention, he was thinking about The Current Fuckery.

About Casey, where was he? About a dead girl, who was she really? And an added nutty topping of What The Fuck had his mother been involved in all those years ago that made her flee her home and change her name?

He wasn't thinking about being ambushed.

Stepping outside, he turned to push the door shut and was ready to slide the key into the lock when a shuffling sound caught his attention. The scuff of a boot against gravel? Gabe twisted to see what the cause was.

A hooded figure, the lower part of their face covered, had slipped out from the darker shadows to Gabe's right.

They'd been waiting for him, hiding around the side of the house.

"What the hell?" he exclaimed. "What do you want?"

He hadn't seen a vehicle, so Dark Hood had arrived on foot or parked elsewhere, just like the shooter the other night had. "Are you the asshole who took a shot at me?"

An unyielding object slammed against the side of Gabe's head.

"The *fuck*." All Gabe could do was try and breathe through the pain. He was seeing stars, which wasn't good.

Dark Hood rushed him, and Gabe instinctively raised both arms to protect his head; he was already doubled over from the pain. Fuck. Someone from behind him walloped him a second time, and Gabe's world went black. His last thought before losing consciousness was that Casey had a point.

He was, in fact, breakable.

TWENTY-ONE

CASEY – THURSDAY EVENING

It had taken Casey longer to get to Gabriel's than he'd expected. First, the rain had started up again, and there were no windshield wipers that could keep up with the deluge. He didn't envy anyone venturing up Crystal Creek Road in this weather. Hopefully, the asshole driver who sped up the road at forty miles an hour didn't end up in a ditch or front bumper first in one of the canyonesque potholes. Then, once he was back on the highway, Casey had had to make a stop at the Park Office to trade vehicles and fill Greta in on what he'd learned about Calvin, which was not much.

While he'd enjoyed having coffee with Paul and Etienne, he never did get more than a *maybe* in answer to his questions, followed up with a vague promise to get in touch if they did suspect Perkins was in the area.

It was the curse of living off the grid and wanting to be left alone, Casey grumbled to himself as he drove into Smitty's and toward Gabe's. Although admittedly, living off the grid sounded like a curse for him but obviously not for the retired spies or other folks living up there. Their mutual agreement to not pay attention to other people's business was an issue when something did happen. Something like Calvin Perkins disappearing.

Gabe's place was inexplicably dark, but the Honda was parked in his spot out front, so he had to be home. Maybe he'd fallen asleep? After all, Gabe had been up since at least three or four a.m., searching for information about Holly Pritchard. Casey'd been up almost as many hours, and he was beat.

Still, something didn't feel right, and he wasn't sure what it was. For one thing, he couldn't imagine Gabe sitting around with all the lights off.

"Huh." Reaching down, he set the Wagoneer's parking brake and leaned forward, peering at Gabe's front door, which was illuminated by his headlights.

Casey narrowed his eyes, squinting at the house. Was the door slightly ajar?

It was. Gabe would never leave his door open, especially not this time of year. Just the other day, he'd scolded Casey for not making sure it latched because Keith was a bit of an escape artist and "no way was he chasing the damn cat around the RV park in this fucking cold."

Behind him, Bowie stirred and sat up to see what was going on. Casey could almost hear him asking why they weren't getting out of the car.

A gust of wind blew up. The door slammed with an audible bang and almost immediately swung outward again.

"Stay," Casey ordered Bowie, then elbowed his door open and got out.

"Gabe?" he yelled.

There was no answer. The tiny glimmer of hope Casey had that the open door meant Gabriel was inside and was about to pull it closed flickered out. A second gust of wind blew across the park grounds. Another weather system was moving in fast, and the next few hours promised to be wet and windy. Not an ideal time for Gabe to disappear.

Casey moved closer to the house, the unease in the pit of his stomach becoming a snake pit. An acid-producing snake pit. His foot landed on something that crunched against the gravel. Stepping back, he looked down and saw a glint in the darkening evening light.

"Shit." Bending down, Casey hooked one finger around the sparkly Hello Kitty keychain Gabe had picked up from Norskland General Store. Another of Mercy's failed purchases for her daughter when Brooklyn had been a tween, one that Gabe had found amusing to add to his collection of sparkly things.

The acid roiled. What was he going to find inside?

"Gabe, are you there?" he called out again, pocketing the keys and forcing himself to move toward the door.

Under normal circumstances, Casey did not allow his imagination to run wild. Imagination was just that—not wholly perceived reality. However, Casey's brain was churning out unwanted images. Gabe injured. Gabe dead. Charming Fucker, gone forever.

Life with Gabriel Karne, he'd learned, was never going to be normal. But this was even less normal than Casey was accustomed to.

Gabriel Karne was Casey's personal basket lightning. The phenomenon was something he'd only seen once in his life. Instead of striking the earth, one and done, a bolt of lightning bolt struck, then appeared to twist up and roll along the ground like a ball, sometimes for miles, wreaking havoc in its path. Casey wasn't sure he could revert to a havoc-less, Gabe-less life.

"Fuck."

Tugging the sleeve of his coat over one hand, Casey pulled on the handle and held the door open with his shoulder, then reached inside and flipped on the interior light.

Casey didn't know what he expected to see, but it wasn't this.

"Holy shit."

The front room was utter chaos, completely trashed. Ignoring the rubble, Casey hastily searched for signs of Gabriel. In the bedroom, he discovered Keith hiding under the bed but no Gabe.

"Good kitty for staying inside," Casey said to the pair of glowing eyes.

Leaving the cat there for the time being, Casey peeked into the closet and bathroom. Nothing. No Gabriel. No Charming Fucker.

At least he wasn't lying on the kitchen floor. Was the fact that Gabe wasn't to be found a good thing? Had Gabe decided to walk somewhere in this weather? Or had whoever was responsible for this mess taken him?

Gabe's standard level of mess was a stack of dishes in the sink and dirty laundry sitting in a pile on the bedroom carpet beside the bed. And, yes, the over-the-top selection of toys he'd purchased for Keith were often strewn about. What Casey was looking at now was far beyond that.

From the confines of the Wagoneer, Bowie started barking, demanding to be let out. "Sorry, doggo, no can do," Casey said, even though he knew Bowie couldn't hear him.

Before he tried to make some kind of sense of what might have happened to Gabriel, Casey made two calls. The first was to the Sheriff's Office to report a break-in, and the second was to Elton.

"I'm heading over," Elton said grimly. "I was just sitting around wondering when you two were planning on getting here."

"Were we supposed to come over? Eagan's sending someone by. Maybe we should let them do their job?" Casey suggested. Not that he wouldn't welcome moral support in the form of Elton Cox.

"Are *you* waiting around for them to get their act together?"

"Elton," Casey said with a sigh. No, he wasn't.

"Five minutes. I'll turn the stove off and get my boots on."

While he waited for Elton and law enforcement to show up, Casey walked the perimeter of the property but found no sign of Gabe. This was good, he told himself. He was tempted to investigate further, but it was dark, and he was more likely to destroy any evidence left behind than make a miraculous discovery.

Elton and one of the new-hire deputies arrived at virtually the same time. Casey was thankful the deputy had skipped the siren and lights. After all, there was no one in the house to scare away, and the neighbors would find out soon enough.

Rolling down his window, Elton leaned out and asked, "Have you tried calling him again?"

Keeping out of the deputy's way, Casey walked over to Elton's truck. "Only about twenty times. Wherever he is, he's not answering. Or he doesn't have control of his phone. I found his keys on the ground." Casey held them out as proof.

Elton's caterpillar-like eyebrows drew together. "I don't like this."

"You don't like it?" Casey asked. "I hate it."

"Mr. Lundin?"

Casey turned around as the young deputy approached him.

"Acting Chief Deputy Eagan is on her way. Um, do you think you can take a look and see if anything is missing before she arrives? Might help us get started on sorting out what happened here."

Casey glanced at Elton. "Wait here. I've already been inside once."

"Use that fancy phone of yours to take a video so I can see too."

Gabe was right, they'd created a monster. But taking a video was also a great idea.

"Will do."

Casey cringed again at the wreckage when he and the deputy re-entered the house. Pressing Record, he held his phone out to document the damage; when they found Gabe, he might find it useful. He refused to entertain the idea they might not find him.

The intruders had destroyed Gabe's secondhand Ikea couch, the cushion stuffing spread across the room. His small but growing collection of paperback mysteries and thrillers had been swept off the shelves and tossed to the carpet. Some of them had been ripped apart and stomped on, their pages violated. Had the intruders been looking for something or just trying to cause as much damage as they could?

"Gabe isn't going to be happy about this."

When they found him. When they found him *alive*. The alive part was very important.

The bedroom had endured the same sort of willful destruction. Drawers had been ripped out of the chest and the contents thrown across the floor. Casey couldn't tell if anything had been taken or not; it was all a jumble of socks and underwear and pillow innards.

Stopping the recording, Casey returned to the living room with the deputy, whose name he really should have tried to learn, but he couldn't be bothered at the moment. He let his gaze drift slowly around the room, taking in the minute details now that he wasn't looking for intruders.

"Shit."

He knew *exactly* what was missing.

The boxes they'd picked up on Tuesday were gone. Nowhere in sight. All six of them.

"Some moving-type boxes are missing," Casey told the deputy. "They were right here." He pointed at the empty spot next to Alfred.

"Gabe brought them here the other day. They were his mother's," Casey added, although he doubted the deputy cared much about who the boxes had originally belonged to. Gabe would probably be upset that the intruders hadn't taken Alfred too.

Through the window that wasn't obscured by a pizza box, Casey saw that another police cruiser had arrived, Deputy Eagan behind the wheel. The chief deputy got out and approached the front of the house, a flashlight clutched in one hand. Casey appreciated how she scanned the area, but he could have told her she wouldn't find anything.

He stepped through the propped-open door and met her outside.

"Karne going missing is very not good." She shot Casey a gimlet stare. "We have an ID on the victim from the beach."

"Oh? What is her name?"

"Mia Witherspoon. Does that name mean anything to you?"

"Did I hear you say Witherspoon?" Elton asked. He'd manifested himself from sitting in his truck to standing directly next to Casey.

Casey glanced at Elton and lifted his brows in a silent question. Were they going to tell Eagan about Gabe's side job?

Elton spoke up. "Gabe had a run-in with Randy Witherspoon on Monday. Is she a relation?"

Apparently, they *were* sharing Gabe's side hustle.

"And again yesterday. Gabe ran into him in Westfort," Casey added.

"But that doesn't explain why Mia Witherspoon showed up at Gabe's Monday morning," Elton added.

"Maybe we should head to the office and compare notes, see if we can come up with a narrative that makes sense. But before we do that, Deputy Wycoff and I will knock on doors around here, try to flush out a few witnesses, but I'm not holding my breath. Please, wait here."

The *don't do anything stupid* was inferred.

After getting a nod from each of them, Eagan and Wycoff headed toward the nearest neighbor.

"Why are we waiting here?" Elton asked out the side of his mouth.

"Because we are not Gabriel Karne?" Casey replied, equally quiet.

The truth was, Casey didn't want to wait either. Waiting felt wrong, but they needed a direction to search in.

"If it was one of us, Gabriel would not sit on his hands," Elton pointed out.

"Where do we start?"

"First, we go to the Sheriff's Office, like Deputy Eagan asked. We report Gabe missing. Then we think like Gabriel. He didn't leave under his own power but knowing him, he left us a clue if he could."

"What like, Hansel and Gretal?" Casey asked.

Elton's eyebrows twitched up and down. "Exactly like Hansel and Gretal."

TWENTY-TWO

GABE – LATE THURSDAY NIGHT

Gabe was cold. His head and back hurt. He was hungry, and he was pissed off. And his bladder needed relief.

He'd been unceremoniously packed into a vehicle of some kind. With his luck, it would turn out to be a cliché serial killer-style van, all black and no windows, the passenger seats removed for easier transport.

You are not the stereotypical serial killer's dream catch, Chance.

The vehicle was big enough that his abductors had been able to easily toss him inside. He'd rolled onto his side on a cold metal floor but didn't have much more space to move around.

A bag or a shirt—cloth of some type—had been pulled over his head so he couldn't see. Worse, Gabe was forced to breathe through his mouth because whatever the fabric was, it reeked of sweat and body odor.

Covering his head meant they didn't want him to know who they were and where they were going, right? Or that the kidnappers had watched way too much TV and thought covering his head was just something they needed to do.

That was not good. Or was it?

It bothered him that they weren't speaking. But again, could be the too-much-TV thing on the part of his kidnappers.

"If you tell me what you want, like by using your words instead of inflicting pain, I might be able to help you."

Nothing. Not even a grumpy *shut it*.

"I'm a nice guy, some even would say considerate. Maybe not everyone would say that, but lots of folks." Gabe paused. "Okay, so maybe only my close friends would say that, but they are very good judges of character."

He was greeted with silence. Which was disappointing.

His head throbbed where he'd been hit. Gabe was choosing to believe he'd been dazed and not knocked out because he hadn't been out that long. Coming back to himself while they were wrestling the disgusting rag over his head, he'd done his best to resist, but they'd bound his wrists and ankles.

He managed to roll one wrist and was rewarded with hard, pointy plastic.

Zip ties. Great. He wasn't escaping those.

"So, hey, did you guys watch a lot of Scooby-Doo as kids? *A Night of Fright is No Delight* was my favorite episode although *A Gaggle of Galloping Ghosts* was good too. I bet you wonder how I remember the titles. Can't explain it, there's a lot of useless information saved in my brain." While he talked, Gabe continued to try and free himself, but the way they'd thrown him in meant he was right up against some boxes with no spare room to be had. If he kept at it, he was going to end up being one large, Gabe-sized bruise. Casey would not be happy.

Gabe knew he should be frightened, but he wasn't. Maybe the odor of the bag was affecting his judgment. By his estimate, they'd been driving for at least thirty minutes, which meant they weren't on Heartstone any longer unless they were going in circles, but Gabe didn't recall bumpy roads, like this one appeared to be, on the island. He amused himself by imagining he was riding in the Mystery Machine while careening recklessly along the unpaved back roads of the Olympic Peninsula.

Twice the van slowed and the engine revved when the driver punched the gas, the tires struggling on what Gabe was going to assume was a muddy-ass road. The rain pounding down on the roof of the car sounded like they were in a car wash, making the already crazy experience even more surreal.

"I watched that show, like, a *lot*. I had a crush on Daphne, but didn't everyone? Admittedly, I thought Fred was hot too, and Shaggy had his own appeal. And Velma's glasses, wow. Okay, I had a crush on the whole gang." He thought he heard a whispered *Jesus Christ*, but he wasn't sure.

Good. Maybe he could annoy them into speaking, giving away something that would tell him who these fuckers were.

The van started to slow once more and then this time stopped entirely. A door opened with a screech, and Gabe heard someone jump out of the vehicle. Then the door slammed shut and the van started moving again, but at a snail's pace and for a much shorter period of time.

"Help me get him out," said the guy he'd labeled as Number One. Abruptly, Gabe realized the voice was that of Dirty Socks Randy.

Seriously, Dirty Socks had kidnapped him? Gabe was almost embarrassed.

"You know, I could walk myself out if you took the zip ties off me. There's no need for the rough handling."

"Don't you never shut up?" asked a second voice.

Dammit. He knew that was a voice he hadn't heard before.

"What can I say, it's a curse."

"Get him into the back now."

That last voice was female and another one he thought was familiar. He'd heard that one recently too. Sometime in the last few days, perhaps even in the past twenty-four hours, right around—

No. It couldn't be.

Gabe didn't want to believe that Althea Mortine was behind this. But Dirty Socks Randy certainly wasn't the mastermind.

Randy and his pal grabbed Gabe's feet, dragging him forward so that he dangled half in and half out of the van. Was there to be no dignity for him at all?

"Ow, mind my head," Gabe said when he was thumped against the unyielding side of the kidnap van.

"Cut those things off his ankles so he can walk on his own," said the woman.

Gabe tried to think who else the voice could belong to. He didn't want it to be Althea, but between the whack on the head, the hood, and the godawful stench, he was having a hard time thinking straight.

And he was fooling himself. That voice belonged to Elton's girlfriend.

With one kidnapper at each shoulder—and the Fucking Stinky Hood still on his head—he was led into what he presumed was some sort of structure. From the way everyone's footsteps echoed, he figured they were in a large but enclosed area, maybe a garage. There was no rain or wind that he could feel.

That's because you have a hood over your head, Chance.

Thanks a lot, Heidi.

"Does anyone want to step up and tell me what the fuck—and I cannot emphasize that particular word enough—this is fucking about?"

"Take that off him."

The foul rag was ripped off his head, and Gabe blinked. They were in a garage or office. Garage office? It was empty except for a single empty metal chair.

"This is all a little too Bond-like for my comfort. Can't we just go into someone's kitchen and talk this out over a cup of tea? I don't even like tea, but I'd drink it tonight. Make an effort to meet you halfway and all that."

A woman stepped out from behind him.

The woman.

Gabe squinted. Maybe he was feeling the effects of being hit on the head. He could literally feel his brain sputtering.

Standing in front of him was Althea Mortine. It was times like these that Gabe hated being right.

"Althea, what's going on? Surely, we could've had a civilized conversation?" About what, he had no idea.

"Cuff him to the chair."

The goons dragged him forward and started to push him down into the chair. He was right, voice number one had belonged to Randy Witherspoon, because of course it did. Here was Monday returning to kick him in the ass on Thursday. Or was it Friday already? Friday hadn't had a chance to really fuck him up yet.

"Is he yours?" Gabe asked Althea. "He needs to practice better hygiene."

Abruptly, he was dragged to standing again, with the person behind him saying, "We need to cut the ties off his wrists too."

Once that task was taken care of, Gabe was forced to sit again, and a handcuff was attached to his left wrist and then around the arm of the chair.

"Seriously, I'd like to know what is going on here."

"Where is it?" Althea demanded.

"Where is what? No one asked about anything. I have no idea why you brought me here or what you're looking for." He kinda thought he did have an idea but wasn't planning on letting on.

Gabe had always encountered Althea Mortine behind the desk at the sheriff's department, although in December he'd met her and Elton at the Geoduck for brunch once. Never had Gabe entertained the thought that the mild-mannered older woman was some kind of criminal mastermind. She'd been pleasant, made a decent cup of coffee. He thought they'd bonded when John Stevens took over the station and held Rizzi hostage. She worked for the Twana County Sheriff's Office, for fuck's sake.

"Your mother stole from the family. I want the Crevans back."

Ah. *The family*. But also, *I*, not *we*. Interesting. Not Colavito-style Family but her family. Blood. She wanted the artwork back for herself.

Really, Mom?

"I hate to be the one to break it to you, but my mother died last fall."

Althea's lips curved into the semblance of a smile. It wasn't a smile of comfort; it was an evil grimace that creeped him out.

"Elton told me you picked up some of her things that had been in storage."

Gabe's heart clenched. Elton was going to be devastated to learn that Althea was behind this latest fuckery. He wondered how long she'd been pumping him for information and when Althea had discovered that Heidi Karne was Gabe's mother. Maybe she'd known all along.

He figured she must have known about him almost from the moment he'd arrived on Heartstone. With her job at the front desk of the TCSO, Althea was positioned to find out a lot about the people of Heartstone. Her "friendship" with Elton was merely an added bonus.

"I did, and I went through it all. There was nothing interesting." Not unless you counted Alfred and the notebooks.

"You might not have realized that what you were looking at was important. But Randy and William brought the boxes, along with you."

Ah. Number Two was William. Good to know.

"I've been through those. There's not much there. Certainly not a hand-drawn map with X marking the spot."

Althea's left eye twitched, and Gabe smirked. An eye twitch meant he was achieving his goal of getting under her skin.

"I have so many questions. Why do I have to be cuffed to this chair? Why put a hood over my head? In general, why? Why can't we have a polite conversation? Why didn't you steal the boxes when I wasn't home? I'm just saying, this is what happens when you don't think things through."

He wasn't super excited to learn what they had planned for him when they didn't find the artwork. Randy and William reappeared, carrying boxes that Gabe recognized. Whether he wanted to or not, it looked like Gabe was about to find out just what their plan B was.

And what was wrong with William that he was Randy's *sidekick*?

"Set them there on the floor and pull everything out," Althea instructed, pointing to the spot where she wanted them to go.

"Auntie, it would help if I knew what we were looking for," Randy complained.

But he did as he was told, opening one box and dumping out the contents. The lip gloss fell out and rolled a few feet away.

Auntie? The word rolled around in his head like a wacky marble. *What the Fuck.* "Why the fuck did you task me to get your *granddaughter's* locket back?"

"I thought you already had the goods, didn't I?" Althea said. "It was a bit of a shock when we let ourselves into your house and there was nothing there. We needed another plan. When Elton mentioned that letter was about Heidi's crap, I figured we had another chance."

"Wait. You broke into my house while I was gone on Monday, didn't you? Before one of your clowns took a shot at us to get us out of the house."

He was trying to process the chain of events that had led to him being cuffed to a chair in a building in the middle of nowhere, an admittedly difficult endeavor what with all the banging his head had endured this week. And he was thirsty as hell.

He was never doing anything nice for a stranger again.

"Do you even have a granddaughter?" And here he'd thought Hero was such a great name.

"No." Her lip curled. "I managed to avoid bearing children." She shot a glance Dirty Sock's way.

"Which leaves me wondering, how do you fit into this amazing made-for-TV family drama? Do you have a starring role or are you a side character?"

Gabe watched her closely, wondering if she'd answer him. She had an ego, so he figured she wouldn't be able to resist telling him how everyone else had screwed up but how her primary plan was going to work perfectly. Plus, keeping her talking was better than having the gun waved in his face.

"Believe me, my plan was to get out of Nowhereville as soon as I could, greener pastures. Carla was the one who came up with the idea to steal some pricey artwork. She was pregnant by then, the father owned the gallery, which explains how she got the job. She thought they'd sell it, and the money would be her ticket out." Althea shook her head.

"It's hard to sell stolen art if you're twenty and have no connections. Fast forward a bit, Holly and the art disappear. A few years pass and I get a call. Can I come home and fix the mess? Carla kicked the bucket. Leaving behind grandkids. That one"—she pointed her chin at Dirty Socks—"and a girl. But the paintings are still MIA."

Lovely. Althea was the kind of woman who *hated* women. She probably hated Heidi for taking the money and running—because that was what she would've done.

"Twenty years had passed by then and there was still no sign of the paintings or Holly. All I could do was wait. When Elton told me that 'Heidi Karne's' son had shown up on Heartstone, I didn't think I'd have to wait much longer. Heidi was one of Holly's alternate names, and I just had to do a bit of digging on you to figure out it was Holly he was talking about. You may not have had a criminal history, but working at TCSO has its perks beyond what most can even imagine. Then it just became a matter of figuring out what could get it all rolling before Eagan found out anything about me."

"So, do you have a game plan? Take the paintings and disappear into the sunset? Maybe you could drop me off at home on your way."

If the abduction, cuffs, and gun weren't big enough hints, he was beginning to clue in that Althea was feasibly more cold-blooded than he'd initially estimated, and thus her answer might not bode well for his future.

On the other side of the storage space, Randy and his friend William were not so gently tearing through the contents of Heidi's boxes, which pissed him off more than he already was. While not attached to what had been hidden away for so many years, the tapes, the lip gloss, and so forth were still a part of his mother Gabe had never known.

"Hey!" he said sharply. "There's no reason to manhandle someone else's stuff."

"Nice shiner," Randy replied.

"It's people like you that make people like me look bad," Gabe said.

Althea reached down and slapped Gabe in the back of the head hard enough that he saw stars and tears came to his eyes.

"Jesus Christ. Be nice already. Haven't you heard that flies with honey quote? My head has been through enough the past few days."

"There's nothing here, Auntie." Randy tipped the last box upside down and shook it. "Just a lot of shit."

Gabe was offended for Heidi that this complete loser was judging her stuff like that. But he also felt sorry for Dirty Socks growing up with Althea as one of his role models. Such conflicting emotions. And dammit, it sounded like Dirty Socks was his cousin or something, so he probably should have been thinking better shit about him.

"I have experienced the inside of your house and think that maybe you have no fucking idea what you're talking about."

"Elton said there were notebooks, the spiral kind." Althea scowled at Gabe. "She was always writing stuff down, like she was some sort of Harriet the Spy. Where are they?"

Now there was a book Gabriel hadn't thought about in decades. Heidi had loved it and had bought Gabe a copy that he'd tucked away somewhere after reading once. When he got out of this hellhole, he was going to track down a copy and read it again.

"Where are the damn notebooks?" Althea demanded.

"No idea." Where they were was where he'd left them, under the passenger seat in the Honda, along with his laptop. Information Gabe did not plan on sharing with Althea or the losers she employed as henchmen.

"Carla and Holly were your sisters, then," Gabe mused.

"Carla," Althea said with a dismissive sneer, hatred gleaming in her eyes. "Carla is the one who fucked up the whole gig by telling Holly about it. Then she went and died—drove right off the road. I thought I'd freed myself of Westfort but no, I had to come back and mind her useless grandchildren for their useless father. I only agreed because I figured I could finally find out what happened to those drawings."

Althea glared at Gabe. "At least Holly had the decency to take care of her own damn messes."

"Except you still don't know what she did with the artwork," Gabriel pointed out with a smirk.

Let's keep it this way, Chance.

TWENTY-THREE

CASEY – FRIDAY EARLY

Hours passed and there was no sight of or word from Gabriel.

Casey tried to rest, convincing himself that driving around in the pitch dark with rain pissing down only meant emergency services would be pulling him out of a ditch, but staying inside hadn't stopped his brain from spinning. Elton's couch was a torture device in disguise, anyway, not meant for sleeping and certainly not for someone Casey's size.

Instead, he'd spent the last few hours wondering what had happened. Add in the young woman who'd turned up dead and—

Casey tried not to imagine the very worst but failed miserably.

As Gabe would say, what *the fuck*?

Yesterday evening, as requested by Acting Chief Deputy Eagan, he and Elton had visited the Sheriff's Office. They'd had nothing to add to the facts that Eagan and her team had already gathered.

"It's a bit early to report Karne as a missing person. He's an able-bodied, healthy adult," Eagan had told them. "But I am concerned. If he doesn't show up by midmorning, we'll rethink filing a report." She'd raised a hand, making a calming gesture. "I know you're both worried. And it is worrisome, but this is

Gabriel Karne we're talking about. We found no blood or signs of a struggle, and we all know Gabriel's good at taking care of himself."

They had found his phone though, half hidden underneath the remains of his couch. If Gabe didn't generally keep it on silent mode, Casey would have been able to find it when he'd called his number.

"How would you be able to tell if there'd been a struggle in that mess?"

That comment had earned Casey a stern look from the acting chief deputy.

"I'll have my deputies keeping an ear out tonight, and we'll talk again in the morning," Eagan had promised. "If either of you think of something or if he calls, feel free to call me. Don't worry about the time. It's shit weather out there tonight, so please don't do anything stupid."

She'd handed each of them a business card with her cell phone number and desk number.

"My updated number. You call that and you'll reach me directly."

Thwarted and hating feeling helpless and freaked out, Casey had loaded Bowie up in the Wagoneer and they'd followed Elton back to his place.

"I was already planning on you two being here. Gabe had found something."

"He didn't tell you what it was, did he?"

Elton shook his head. "Just that he was bringing the notebooks and wanted to show us something."

They'd eaten chicken soup paired with Sailor Boy Pilot crackers and rehashed the facts they had gathered as they understood them. Which was not many and not well. By the end of the meal, they had a list. It started with now dead Mia Witherspoon showing up on Gabe's doorstep Monday morning and the trip to Westfort that afternoon.

"Maybe somebody from his past saw him in town or some-place else he's been this week? We need to track it, just in case," Elton said. "Tuesday you drove to Seattle, which prompted Gabe to do some research at the library and Public Records on Wednesday. Westfort again."

"Where he ran into Randy Witherspoon, or Randy was following him." Casey had added. "He didn't find much, so he started digging around online this morning and found some article about an art robbery in the late seventies."

Casey then scribbled more on the list, muttering, "Gabe sure has been at the center of all the events that have happened on Heartstone since he showed up."

He could almost hear Gabe correct the word "events" to "fuckery."

Elton had chuckled. "We can't lay everything that's happened in the past few months at Gabe's feet, but I concur. His arrival seems to have coincided with a falling-dominoes effect when it comes to the criminal element that has been quietly operating in and around Twana County for years."

Now, lying on the spine-mutilating couch, Casey supposed that Elton had it right. With their uncle's help, the Perkins brothers had been running on the wrong side of the law while their mother looked the other way. John Stevens and Rizzi had been up to their criminal activities even longer. Who else was feeling the heat?

Beside him, Bowie released a deep, heartfelt, doggy sigh. After enduring a thorough hose-down, he'd scarfed down some kibble and crashed out on his "away" dog bed. Casey's restless stirring had woken him up.

"You're no help," Casey complained. "Isn't this when you run off and find Timmy in the well?" Bowie didn't acknowledge Casey's taunt. He didn't even bother lifting his head. All Casey got in response was another soft snore as the dog went back to sleep.

It didn't feel right to sit and wait for morning. Gabe was out there right now. *Somewhere*. That was the problem. Sure, Casey could hop in the Jeep and drive around, but where to?

According to his phone, it was 2:43 a.m. Sighing, he checked his weather app and saw that the storm was starting to wane. He decided to take another power nap and reconsider his options when he woke up.

A STRANGE SOUND forced Casey to open his eyes. He'd been dreaming, he wasn't sure about what. Mostly he'd been running around worried, looking for Gabriel and not finding him.

"Coffee?" Elton asked, shuffling into the living room.

"Yeah," Casey said with a groan. He sat up and immediately regretted falling asleep with his head in a funky position. "I could use the caffeine."

Automatically, Casey checked his phone. Again. It had been three hours since the last time he'd looked and he'd managed maybe two of whatever that had been, but it hadn't been sleep. No notifications. Nothing from Gabe since yesterday afternoon. Because duh, Gabe wouldn't be calling from his phone, which was now sitting on the coffee table. Elton needed to hurry with that coffee.

Pausing at the kitchen doorway, Elton asked, "Did you get any rest?"

"Not really. You?"

"No, but I'm old. I don't sleep like I used to."

Bowie bumped Casey's hand with his cold, wet nose, his way of informing Casey that rain or shine, it was time to go out and do his business. Rising to his feet, Casey tugged his boots and coat on.

"I'm taking Bowie out for his constitutional," he told Elton.

"Morning Joe will be ready when you two get back."

The rain had slowed down around midnight, but it hadn't

entirely stopped. The world was damp and cold, droplets of water that clung to naked tree branches catching the light from Elton's porch. Daybreak was on its way, slowly and occasionally seeming to retreat and dim a bit before the light would increase again. Casey inhaled a deep breath in through his nose and let it slowly out, reminding himself that remaining calm was imperative. He watched Bowie trot across the grass ahead, his nose just inches from the ground.

"Hurry it up. We're out here for you to take care of your business, not chase nocturnal squirrels and get soaked."

Bowie acknowledged Casey's comment with a brief glance over his shoulder, very close to an eye roll. Then, as if to say FINE in his best Gabriel Karne impersonation, the dog found the proper shrub for his purposes.

Even his dog had felt the Gabriel Karne Effect over the last few months.

"Here's your cuppa." Elton handed him a mug when Casey and Bowie returned inside, bringing a bit of the cold and damp early morning air with them. "Shut the door, it's cold."

Accepting the mug, Casey savored the warmth of it against his cold fingers for a moment before raising it to his lips and sipping at the molten liquid.

"What's the plan?"

Elton always had a plan of some kind. Casey often felt a bit like an interloper—Gabe and Elton were the ones to plan escapades together, and Casey was a poor substitute.

"I think we should go back over to Gabe's. We might see something, catch what the sheriff may have missed. Not to say that Bree and her team aren't adequate, but another set of eyes never hurts."

Casey glanced out the window; even since coming back inside with Bowie, it was lighter outside. Not bright but a hint that the sun was planning on rising regardless of the steady mist.

"Let's go." Action was better than sitting around waiting for news.

CASEY INSISTED on driving them both in the Wagoneer. The truth was, he didn't have the patience to wait while Elton climbed behind the wheel of his big truck.

"Let's get going," Casey said grimly, shoving the Jeep into gear and pressing on the gas pedal.

The drive was around fifteen minutes normally, but Casey pushed the speed a bit and they were there in ten. Elton didn't tell him to slow down.

Smitty's always looked a bit lonely to Casey in the colder months. Casey wasn't sure if it was the lack of seasonal RVers— because there weren't many to begin with these days—or the leafless maples and birch trees that dotted the area. Sure, there were some evergreens, but the bare branches of the deciduous trees seemed naked and a bit bereft. Gabe thought Bill needed to put up lights. Bill was not convinced.

"How do you want to do this?" he asked his passenger. "What's the next part of this plan of yours?"

"Plans are for suckers. Let's take a walk around his house. I know I watched that video you took last night, but I'd like to see the inside with my own eyes too."

Since they both had keys to Gabe's place, getting in wasn't an issue. By mutual agreement, they started at the concrete pad that acted as a porch and circled the house several times in ever-increasing loops, Elton wielding a flashlight to help their eyesight in the early morning light.

"I think someone may have stood here for a while." Casey pointed at a spot near the back corner of the house where grass appeared to have been crushed. "But there're no clear footprints and nothing worth doing a plaster cast for. Maybe they waited here until they could ambush him?"

Elton shook his head. "Hard to tell. Could be from a deer."

A deer, yes. He should have thought of that too.

They looked around inside the house but didn't notice anything that Casey and the responding deputies hadn't seen last night. The house was trashed, the boxes were still missing, and Gabriel was not there. Alfred glowered at them, entirely out of place in Gabe's minimalist—his word—living room.

"Oh, Gabe is not going to be happy about the coffee maker," Elton commented, noting the machine had been shoved onto the floor and maybe stomped on.

Casey stared down the remains of what had been Gabe's pride and joy. "Yeah, not happy at all."

Casey headed back outside. Gabe's house was small, the whole search had taken them maybe fifteen minutes tops, but he couldn't be there any longer. Not without Gabe.

Gabe was bigger than life—which Casey'd thought was one of the stupidest sayings he'd ever heard until he met him. Life was fucking huge, how could a human being be bigger than life itself?

And then Gabriel Karne materialized in living color, exploding Casey's preconceived notions, filling in every bit of space in his vicinity. Demanding Casey's attention. Courting him—fucking *wooing* him. Charming *Casey*, of all people.

The rock that had been squatting in the pit of his stomach since the night before morphed into a boulder, making it difficult to breathe.

He'd gone from being perfectly happy on his own to accepting Gabriel Karne into his life.

To loving the whole package.

"Dammit."

It was mildly irritating to fully realize you love someone when they're not around so you can't tell them. And now he didn't know if he'd get the chance.

"Stop it."

Casey snapped out of his thoughts. "Stop what?"

"Stop catastrophizing in that head of yours. It won't help us figure out what the hell is going on. Come on, let's get out of here before a neighbor decides to talk to us." Elton stomped out the door and back to the car.

"Nice bedside manner you have," Casey called to his back as he shut the door behind him. "Very comforting. I feel much better now."

Elton didn't even turn around. "You don't need kid gloves."

Casey automatically glanced inside Gabe's car as he eased between the Wagoneer and the Honda to reach his door. Had anyone checked it last night? He couldn't remember. Reaching down, he tugged the handle of the passenger door, and it opened easily.

"I'm just going to see if there's anything in his car," Casey said.

Unlike his home, Gabe kept his car tidy, no empty to-go cups or crumpled fast food bags littering the floors. Because Bowie rarely rode in it, there was no dog hair either.

A spiral-bound detailed Washington State map was tucked between the driver's seat and the center console, and a few random coins were in one of those holders that never fit anything useful. Why did car manufacturers bother?

Casey moved to the back but didn't see anything of note at first glance, then swiped a hand underneath the seat. He wasn't expecting to find much, and it wasn't as if Gabriel himself would fit in the small space, but his gut told him to be as thorough as possible right now. Thus he was shocked when his fingers bumped against something cold, something that was not the floor rug.

"What have you found?" Elton demanded.

"Jesus, Elton, scare the shit out of me, why don't you?" Casey straightened, cradling his find in his hands. "Gabe's laptop. Here, hold it while I check under the other seat."

Leaning across the back of the car, Casey shoved a hand

under the driver's side back seat and pulled out several decades-old spiral notebooks, protected by a plastic bag. Heidi's notebooks.

"Why are these in his car?" Casey wondered.

"Remember? You two were coming over for dinner last night. Maybe he was getting ready to leave. We'll ask when we find him."

Casey had to appreciate Elton's certainty. Gabe was coming back, and Elton wasn't considering other options.

THEY'D BEEN BACK at Elton's just long to fire up more coffee— Elton's words—and for Casey to get as comfortable as was possible on his sofa in preparation to dive into Heidi Karne's past. The spiral-bound books waited for them on Elton's puzzle table, along with the laptop.

For now, the laptop was going to remain powered off. Casey didn't know what the password was and risking being locked out of it seemed foolish. Plus, he still hoped that Gabe would show up soon and they wouldn't have to break into the thing.

Casey had just picked up one of the notebooks when there were several sharp knocks against the front door. Bowie leaped to his feet and began barking.

Rising to his feet, Casey glanced out the window. A glossy black SUV was parked behind Elton's truck. It was a big vehicle, with capacity for at least seven passengers.

"Expecting someone who owns a Lincoln Navigator?" Casey asked. "Bowie, quiet." Bowie stopped barking but not before he got one last snarl in.

"Nope. Pretty darn early for visitors though." Elton started to stand up.

"I'll get it." Casey cut past Elton and his chair to check out the window again. A man who wasn't Gabe but looked a great deal like him waited on the stoop.

What the hell was Shay Delacombe doing on Elton's front porch at this time of day?

"It's Shay Delacombe," he told Elton. "What do you wanna bet Claribel is in the car?" He couldn't really see through the tinted windows, but there appeared to be a diminutive figure waiting in the front seat.

"Might as well open the door, then. Claribel's released her flying monkeys."

"I heard that," Shay said with a sardonic grin as he stepped across the threshold. "I have to say, I've never been called a flying monkey before. At least, not to my face."

"Why are you here?" Casey demanded.

"Gabe called yesterday." Shay waved a hand that included the Navigator. "We both thought it sounded like he could use a hand. Claribel tried calling him several times last night, there was no answer, so here we are. Would have come last night, but the rain."

Casey appreciated that Shay was making it sound like Claribel was the one worried, that Shay was merely tagging along.

"Claribel is in the car?"

Shay nodded.

"If we tell you that we have everything under control, you won't just go away, will you?"

"Nope. We drove by his place on our way here, it looked like there was a break-in. You try getting the old woman to leave now."

"Let 'em in," said Elton. "Might as well."

"Actually, Claribel had me rent a house last night in preparation. It's on the backside of the island. Fair warning, Claribel is calling it a command center. It's large enough that we'll all be comfortable there." Shay rattled off an address that Casey recognized as being close to Greta and Abby's place.

Casey resisted rolling his eyes. He wasn't going to do it, he refused, but the urge was close to overwhelming. Shay and

Claribel Delacombe were incredibly presumptuous. Renting a house even. However, the fact was Elton's house, *The Barbara*, and Gabe's place at Smitty's were all too small to host any kind of extended family gatherings, even one centered on finding Gabe.

A thought that had been banging around in the back of Casey's mind made itself obvious. He was done with separate addresses. When this was over, he and Gabe would look for a place together if Gabe was agreeable. A place where occasionally, emphasis on the O-word, they might host family and friends like Gabriel would want to.

"Casey, your phone is going off," Elton said.

"Just a second." He turned back and grabbed his phone but didn't recognize the number.

Gabe was missing. He answered anyway.

"Hello, Casey Lundin."

"Casey," said a man's voice. "Paul Allard. I know it's early, but I thought you might want to know that there's been unusual activity up here since you left. A truck or large van barely made it up the road last night. We could hear their engine struggling. We think they may have stopped at Denny's place. The dogs have been going crazy all night, barking and wanting to get out. We're going to check on Denny, but Etienne insisted on letting you know first."

If Gabe hadn't been missing and Denny's last name hadn't been Pritchard, Casey might have disregarded the call. Calvin Perkins could wait. However, this was a red flag Casey wasn't ignoring, even if he wasn't sure how Denny Pritchard the hermit might fit into this current situation.

"Thanks, Paul. I'm on my way." To Elton and Shay, he said, "There's been activity at or near Denny Pritchard's place."

"What are we waiting for?" said Elton.

"Lead the way. We'll be right behind you."

Casey decided that arguing with Shay was not worth the lost

time, but he sure as hell wasn't stopping to dig the Navigator out of the mud if they got stuck.

TWENTY-FOUR

GABE – TGI FRIDAY

Gabe was beyond cold.

His ankles ached where the plastic zip ties they'd put back on dug into his skin, and his wrists hurt from the handcuffs. He was also well on his way to a caffeine headache. There wasn't any heat to be had in this place, which cemented his theory that they were in a garage or storage structure. He was firmly restrained, and no one had offered him any coffee.

The trio—duo, really, because Althea and Randy were obviously in charge—had continued to ask him the same questions for what felt like hours. A couple of times Gabe had convinced them to let him at least use the bathroom, which had been a total shitshow of them leaving his ankles zip-tied and handcuffing his nondominant hand to Randy. Fortunately, he'd broken his arm when he was fifteen and still had the muscle memory to unzip his fly and take care of business one-handed.

Sidekick William had just stood around trying to look tough, but he mostly seemed cold and scared.

Hours in, Gabe had been left to his own devices with just William as his keeper. William had sat in a corner, presumably watching Gabe to make sure he didn't do anything funny. For his part, Gabe had dozed and talked and tried to come up with an escape plan that wouldn't hurt too much. Who knew being strapped to a chair was so effective.

Althea and Randy had finally returned, and Gabe was curious to know what they'd been up to. Had they been napping? Was there an OSHA for criminals that required a lunch break? Was it morning and thus working hours for abductors?

"Can I get a glass of water?"

"Where are the paintings?" Althea demanded, ignoring the request.

"So that's a no?"

"Where. Are. The. Paintings. I know your mother took them. She must have still had them when she died or there would've been whispers. Where are they?"

Gabe repeated what he'd already told her last night, word for word, tossing in a few additional questions of his own to see if he could get a reaction out of her.

Until yesterday, he'd never considered how Althea resembled an aging Cruella Deville. Cruella before Disney had rehabilitated her—or tried to. She'd hidden her real self well, for what seemed to be years, but the mask was off now. She was a hateful conniving bitch.

"Did you know that repeating the same thing but expecting a different outcome is the definition of insanity?" Gabe was improvising, but he remembered the quote being something along those lines.

That comment pissed both Randy and Althea off. Excellent. Althea had a vein across her forehead that throbbed every time Gabe said something snarky, and Randy was a wonky bottle rocket ready to explode. They were both all talk at this point. They thought he knew where the artwork was and didn't want to jeopardize getting their hands on it. So, while they'd kidnapped him and were slowly freezing him to death, they weren't going to take it further—yet.

He could handle a few bumps and bruises, a knock in the head. But if this ass-backward gang of two-and-a-half physically hurt Elton or Casey or anyone else he cared for, Gabe was officially going to lose his shit. He chose to continue with what he did best. Keep talking.

"What I don't get, Althea, is how you managed to fool Elton. He seems to have a well-primed bullshit meter. Yet here you are, a terrible person who's used him to get some fantasy artwork back."

Althea eyebrows shot up, and her lips flattened into a thin line. "What are you talking about? I like Elton—I *love* him. All I want is that fucking art, and we'll have enough to live like kings for the rest of our days, somewhere it doesn't fucking rain all the time. Maybe Costa Rica."

In her psycho dreams.

"Are you so deluded that you believe you can spirit Elton away from here? Wow, further gone than I thought. And, I have to say, I already figured you were over the edge."

Althea's nostrils flared. She stepped close enough that he inhaled a whiff of the powdery perfume she must have bathed in. And he sneezed. Althea stepped away, a look of disgust crossing her face.

"Sorry, my hands are—" He wiggled them, clinking the cuffs against the metal arms of the chair.

"Let's keep talking about this. What are your next steps? What's going to happen when he learns that you're a terrible person? I don't know where these so-called paintings are, so whatever your endgame is, I can't help you. Elton is going to meet your real self, and it's going to be all over. He's not even going to look back. And to think he said you were going to make us fried chicken."

He had a figment of a thought that hardly counted as an idea about where the art might be, but he wasn't sharing with Cruella, and he couldn't check for himself until he got out of this situation.

"You were at the library, and the librarian didn't see any reason not to tell me that you were looking through old microfiche. What did you find? You found something, we know it," Randy said.

Randy was not top-notch accomplice material. Gabe knew from the malevolent glance Althea shot him that she was wishing he would disappear. Or—a hideous icy feeling akin to cold lightning crawled down his spine—she was *planning* for Dirty Socks Randy to disappear.

Gabe looked toward William, who was also probably approaching his expiration date as far as Althea was concerned. He saw shelves packed with boxes labeled *MRE* in permanent marker lining one wall and began counting them to hide his real thoughts. Without a distraction, he wasn't sure his best poker face could hide his utter disgust with this person.

No wonder you ran, Heidi.

He shivered, wondering if Carla had really died in an accident.

Gabe hadn't figured everything out yet, and maybe he never would, but he'd bet Althea's "idiot sister" Carla had been Althea's partner in the 201 Gallery heist. Something must have happened between the initial theft and the rest of the plan. Enter his mother.

Holly Pritchard got a job in town. Holly found a door because Holly was a big fan of *Harriet the Spy* and liked secrets. Then Holly became Heidi Karne. Neither Holly nor Heidi knew how to get rid of the paintings. She did, however—and Gabe was projecting here —know that Althea Mortine, née Pritchard, was a dangerous person, so after a few futile years of trying to fence them and thus risking exposure, she gave up and left the mystery to her son, figuring that he would be able to fend for himself.

I'm not so sure about that last part, Heidi.

"Who was the young woman who came by my house

Monday?" he asked. "The one claiming to be my daughter. Was she your great-niece or something?"

Gabe recalled the photographs he'd seen hanging in the hallway of Dirty Socks's destroyed home. Specifically, the one with a younger Randy and a toddler. That toddler could have been the young woman on his doorstep on Monday. Had she somehow been part of this plan or had she struck out on her own?

"Someone killed her and her body ended up in the bay. But you know that already, don't you? And I'd bet my right nut you knew it before the Sheriff's Office did."

He stared hard at Althea. Was he exhausted and fucking cold and in desperate need of coffee? Yes, but also oddly energized with this revelation. He had to get Althea talking more. She'd done such a good job hiding behind the TCSO front desk for years, privy to the underbelly of the entire county, but it was time to get that villain monologue going to help fill in some blanks.

"I'd bet my left nut that having Eli Rizzi exposed was bad for your business. Did it make you a little nervous? You know, Elton and Casey both told me that Bree Eagan and state investigators have been going through all the stored files. Will they find your influence there too? They will, won't they? I can't think of a person in a better position to help Rizzi hide what he was up to."

Althea waved the gun his direction. "Stop speaking now."

Gabe wasn't particularly worried she'd shoot him, at least not until she got the information she wanted. And Gabriel Karne excelled at talking a lot but not giving up any information.

"What are you going to do? Kill me before you figure out where the scribbles are? I don't think so."

"Auntie, what did you do?" Randy had gone a sickly shade of white. "You told me Mia was busy doing something for you."

"Should I be calling you Auntie too?" Gabe asked sweetly.

Darting Randy a glance that should have eviscerated him, Althea said, "Don't worry about your sister right now. And you" —she pointed the gun at Gabe again—"I told you to stop speaking. It's so obvious you're Holly's kid. Always thought she knew it all too, didn't she?"

"I'm worried, Auntie, very worried. Where's Mia?"

It was nice to see that Randy cared. Hopefully, Althea was the lone psychopath in the family.

"She panicked, didn't she? Came to the station when I've told you both never to approach me there," Althea hissed.

Randy stepped backward, his eyes wide and fucking finally, scared. "*Auntie.*"

"Don't you fucking *Auntie* me."

In the distance, Gabe heard dogs barking again. They'd been doing so on and off the entire time Gabe and his captors had been inside. They sounded big, ferocious. Seriously, why dogs? The only place locally that he knew of with a lot of dogs was Heartstone Veterinary Clinic, but he thought they were miles from Heartstone.

Eyes wide, Randy bolted. But before he got more than a few steps, Althea turned the gun she'd been pointing at Gabe toward him and squeezed the trigger. The first shot missed but not the second. It hit him high up in the arm, toward his shoulder, and the useless nephew went down like a proverbial sack of potatoes.

"Holy shit," whispered William.

He glanced wildly around, clearly assessing his chances of getting out.

"Stay right where you are, William. I have plenty of ammo left in this gun for you."

William stopped moving. He practically stopped breathing. If Althea hadn't been coolly holding her finger on the trigger, Gabe might have laughed. Chuckled anyway. William looked like he was the only player in a life-or-death game of Red Light, Green Light.

"Wow, and here I thought Rizzi was a POS," Gabe said casually. His mind raced, brimming with thoughts. He was right, Althea had to have been party to some of Rizzi's dealings. Hell, she probably was his personal assistant in all that mess even as she was working her own business too. Having Rizzi go down had to hurt.

Althea turned back to him, waving the gun Gabe's direction for the umpteenth time. "Have you tried growing old in this forsaken country? The rising cost of health care? Groceries? Housing? It costs, young man, believe me. I need this. Do you think working at the Twana County Sheriff's Office for as long as I have has done anything for me besides give me a few decent connections?"

"Probably sucks that Stevens grew a spine and confessed, really put you in a bind."

Randy was moaning and writhing on the cement floor, and an expression that informed Gabe she really wanted to shoot him again and shut him up for good this time crossed the old woman's face. Meanwhile, William had taken a step to the left. Gabe figured he was trying to get close to the side door without Althea realizing until it was too late to shoot him too.

Time to keep talking, Chance. This old bitch needs to go down.

"Not to judge or anything but if it were me, I'd have some mad money squirreled away, wouldn't have relied on a crooked cop or stolen artwork to finance my retirement. But as you pointed out, I'm not quite there yet. Have you considered investing in stocks or bonds? Does the term mad money bother you? Personally, I think it suits you."

"Shut the fuck up, or I'll pull the trigger."

"See, you won't. If you shoot me, I won't be able to tell you anything about the missing artwork. Not one single fucking word."

"So you *do* know something."

Gabe lifted one shoulder and let it drop again. "Maybe."

With her attention off William, Mr. Sidekick had edged a few feet closer to the exit. Gabe was trying very hard not to glance across the room at him. Damn it was difficult looking a killer in the eye.

Althea narrowed her eyes at him. The crow's feet from her years of living became even more pronounced. Gabe was tempted to point out that scowling had a negative effect on her countenance, but he was too busy watching William out the corner of his eye and trying to make sure Althea didn't notice.

Two more steps, William.

He must have given himself away or William made a scuffing sound. Regardless of what had alerted her, Althea swung around, and the gun went off a third time. Luckily for William, Althea's spin made the shot go high and the bullet hit the wall about six feet over his head. Lunging for the door handle, he wrenched the door open and disappeared into the early morning twilight.

Cold air rushed into the building, displacing the air that Gabe hadn't registered as warm. What he wouldn't have given for his Casey coat right now.

"You could have at least provided me with some of those pocket-sized hand warmers. If I freeze to death, you will—and I promise you this—never find what you're looking for. The secret will go with me to my grave. Nobody knows what I know." Deep inside, Gabe knew he shouldn't enjoy sounding mysterious in this fucked-up situation, but he did.

For his part, Randy moaned again and tried to roll to a sitting position, but one glance from his crazy relative and Randy lay back.

"Yeah, what he said."

The guy was in pain, and there was visible blood on the concrete flooring. He needed medical attention sooner rather than later, but Gabe didn't think Althea planned on calling in an ambulance. However, Gabe had noticed several boxes marked *First Aid* among the MRE storage.

"If you untie me, I could check his wound. He's still

conscious, so that's good, but you don't want him bleeding out, do you?"

Fuck, maybe she really was a psychopath and just didn't care.

"Stay right where you are," Althea ordered.

As if he could go anywhere zip-tied and handcuffed to a chair. When he did get free, he'd probably end up face down on the floor. He was seriously too old for this shit.

Without being obvious about it, Gabe was keeping his attention on the now open door. He thought he'd seen movement out there, something furtive in the shadowed morning. With his run of luck, it would turn out to be the world's last surviving werewolf or maybe Bigfoot.

Who was he kidding? With his luck, it would be Larry Colavito.

"If Holly didn't have the paintings in these boxes, where are they?" She returned her attention to Randy who looked suspiciously still. "You missed something." She waved the gun Gabe's direction, something Gabe really wished she'd just stop doing. "He has to have it. Holly made sure he did."

Althea crossed to where Randy lay, now curled up in as much of a ball as he could manage, and kicked him. He screamed and writhed again.

"Answer me when I'm talking to you."

"Nothing, there was nothing," Randy gasped.

Gabe didn't think it was his imagination that the tiny bit of sky he could see through the cracked-open door looked infinitesimally lighter. The trees outside were less dark, which meant it could be after six a.m., maybe even close to seven.

Gabe just hoped Elton and Casey had an idea of where he was although he didn't know how they would. He didn't even know where he was.

Gabe also hoped they'd bring coffee with them.

Out the still open door, Gabe thought he saw movement. Movement that wasn't tree branches dancing in the wind. Before he could focus on it, whatever it was faded away. He blinked. Was he hallucinating? Not out of the realm of possibility.

"So, I think I've got this sorted out, at least a rough draft. I've had hours to think about it, after all. Your sisters pulled off a heist fifty years ago and you knew about it, maybe you helped. At the very least, you were jealous they'd come up with the idea. Something went sideways, maybe there was disagreement? The art went poof. Into thin air. My mother was the smart sister, wasn't she? I've long suspected we came from a family of grifters, and I think I'm on the right track."

Too many grifters in the kitchen ruin the con, Chance.

Althea made an indeterminate grunt that Gabe interpreted as *go ahead and keep talking.* He was going to keep talking because he'd seen the movement again and was certain there was a person, maybe more than one, just outside. The gun was still pointed at him, and Gabe was ready for it not to be.

"Moving right along. Way back when you came back to Heartstone, you got into bed with Eli Rizzi for reasons only known to the two of you. Maybe he knew something or you had something on him, it doesn't matter now. Last fall, he fell from grace and now you risk exposure. All you have to help you get out of here is maybe some artwork that my mother may have left to me."

Gabe was enjoying this in spite of himself. Now he knew how those detectives felt at the end of the show, when they gathered the suspects and laid the crime out in front of them.

"Time's running out. You can't keep your deeds hidden from Eagan and the investigators she brought in. So you'd come up with this locket scheme so you could search my house, I guess, except that I didn't have any of Heidi's things at that time. Was Mia acting on her own? Or was that a contingency plan? I still can't figure out that part."

"Why'd you kill her, Auntie?"

"Fuck off with the Auntie bullshit, Randall. Even after the Crevans went AWOL, I thought I'd finally escaped this backwater by marrying Frederick Martine. But then Carla and her kid died, and I was stuck with Randy and Mia. Raising kids is expensive these days. I deserve the money from that artwork. Mia agreed to approach you, see what she could find out. When you sent her away, she came crying to me. At the station, believe it or not, like the utter moron she was."

Althea turned back toward Randy, her gun hand slightly lower than it had been, and three men burst in through the door. One took Althea to the ground and relieved her of the weapon, then spun her onto her front and used zip ties to secure her. The second headed for Randy, kneeling beside him, and set down a boxy first aid kit.

The third, Ranger Man, headed straight for Gabe. He'd never seen anything more magnificent in his life.

"I'd stand up and lay a kiss on you, Ranger Man, but I'm kind of tied up."

TWENTY-FIVE

CASEY – FRIDAY,
EARLY. UP THE VALLEY

Etienne and Paul had beaten them to Denny Pritchard's place, of course. But after much back and forth on the sat phone, they'd agreed to keep their eyes out and wait for Casey to arrive. While Casey drove like a man possessed, the couple scouted the property and discovered Gabe and friends in Denny's massive storage unit.

"The action is in Denny's storage structure back of the house. There's a lot of talking, but we can't hear everything clearly. The older woman has a gun and doesn't look afraid to use it. She shot one of the accomplices, looks like she got him in the arm. How far out are you?"

"Under ten minutes."

"In that case, we'll hold before we go check on Denny. If things go sideways ahead of your arrival, we're going in," Paul said. "To be honest, Etienne and I are kind of enjoying being flies on the wall. We've been listening to—Gabriel, is it?"

"Yes, Gabriel." Casey confirmed.

"We're listening to him verbally torture his kidnappers. He's quite impressive. Oh, hang on, the other one is making a run for it. We're going to intercept him."

The connection ended so all they heard over the speaker now was fuzz. Casey pressed the gas down, pushing the Wagoneer as hard as he dared. Behind them, the headlights of Shay's Lincoln bounced. At least the rain had finally stopped, for now anyway.

"I think we'll learn that Althea was a Pritchard before she married Fred Mortine," Elton said to Casey as they bumped over another exposed rock and forded a small river created by the storm. He sounded disappointed and Casey couldn't blame him.

Casey grunted his agreement; they'd started this conversation a few miles back, going over as many different scenarios as they could using the puzzle pieces they had. It all came back to who knew Gabe had Heidi's stuff, and process of elimination had led to Althea.

The only explanation was that Althea was a Pritchard and wanted whatever she thought Heidi had taken. Ahead he finally spotted the access road to Denny's property. Slowing to a crawl, he turned off the headlights in case there was someone keeping an eye out. Behind him, Shay did the same.

He pulled to a stop about fifty yards from Denny's house and turned off the engine. Shay parked as well.

"No lights on," said Elton.

"Nope. I need you to wait here or in the Navigator with Claribel."

Elton opened his mouth to argue, but Casey shut him down. "Nope. I'm not having it. This is as close to the action as you get."

The last thing, the VERY last thing he needed by the time they all arrived at Denny Pritchard's property, was Elton or Claribel getting caught in any possible crossfire. Or Shay, Casey supposed. Shay's strengths were presumably in the courtroom, not at the crime scene.

He led the way to the Navigator, where Shay had his window open and was looking at him expectantly.

"Elton is waiting here with you and Claribel. I'm going around back where Paul and Etienne are." He did not have time to explain his theory about the couple being ex-secret spy types.

With that, Casey pulled up his hood and jogged toward Denny Pritchard's storage building, and less than five minutes later, Gabe was making jokes about being tied up.

Maybe someday he'd look back and think that maybe this wasn't the most romantic scenario, place, or situation to tell Gabe he'd fallen in love with him. But Casey wasn't able to stop the words from spilling out.

"God, I love you, Gabriel Karne," he said, kneeling down to cut through the zip ties.

"Randy has the key to the cuffs in his pocket," Gabe informed him. "Unlock me, dammit, because I love you right back."

AS RANGER CASEY LUNDIN, he represented the acting law enforcement agency on the scene until the Sheriff's Office arrived. William and Althea had already been restrained by the Allard-Clarks, so he settled both of them near the door.

An ambulance arrived before TCSO, having taken the long, bumpy trip up Crystal Creek Road, and was about to drive away again with Randy Witherspoon in the back. He was going to live thanks to Paul's quick work with his first aid kit. Gabe refused to go.

"I just need a good rubdown," he insisted, pairing his statement with a suggestive grin and eyebrow waggle.

Casey stared at him, noting the red welts on his wrists. He probably had them on his ankles too. "At least let the EMT check you over."

"The only person I want checking me over is you. I'm fine. Just cold and stiff."

At that moment, Paul and Etienne reappeared, forestalling Casey's retort.

"We found Denny in his kitchen, zip-tied and spitting mad,"

Paul told them. "Etienne talked him out of coming out here with his shotgun."

"Denny claims no knowledge of stolen art or any such thing. Althea paid him to use the storage unit, and that was the extent of their relationship. He's an old man, the cash was handy, and Denny's not the type to ask questions. She's a cousin, maybe an in-law, he wasn't even sure about how they were related. Denny's a prepper, which explains the supplies," Paul said. "The storage unit is stuffed with everything he'd need to survive the end times. I'm pretty sure that's what he was using the extra cash for, more prep."

"We believe he's telling the truth. Not that Denny's blameless, but he didn't give a shit what his cousin Althea was up to. He just wanted the money she offered," Etienne added.

The deputies arrived a few minutes later, squeezing past the rest of the vehicles already there, the tires bearing witness to at least one battle with mud during the drive up. A stone-silent Althea Mortine was read her rights as official handcuffs replaced the zip ties, and a deputy helped her into the back of Eagan's cruiser.

But they weren't transporting her to her former place of employment. The Westfort police would be taking custody and were likely going to need to run the entire case against her. Considering her involvement with Rizzi, Casey wouldn't be surprised if state investigator Lane Boyd showed up again.

Casey didn't fail to notice that Elton, Claribel, and Shay had found their way to the sidelines of the action. At least they'd stayed away until all perpetrators were taken into custody.

"She has her fingers in too many pies at the station," Eagan told them grimly. "I think she panicked because we brought in an outside auditor to go through pretty much everything. I won't be surprised if, in addition to Rizzi's and Stevens's crimes, we find that Althea was influencing the outcomes of investigations too."

"What about Mia Witherspoon?" Gabe asked.

"Believe me, Althea will be questioned further. Just not by me. But we will need a statement from you, Gabriel, and sooner rather than later."

Deputy Eagan moved away from them, toward the cruiser where Althea was pointedly not looking in their direction. Minutes later, she drove away, Deputy Wycoff following in her wake.

"So? Where's this damn missing art?" asked Elton, his eyes on the sheriff's car disappearing around a bend in Denny's driveway.

Casey wondered how he felt about Althea playing him. As far as Casey could tell though, he was angry, not hurt.

Gabe spoke before Casey could broach the sensitive subject. "Can we have this confab elsewhere? Someplace warm? I need to take a shower and change clothes. And bathe in coffee, a fucking vat of it. That sounds glorious."

There was some discussion, but in reality, no one place was large enough for everyone. In the end, they agreed to convene at the house Shay and Claribel had rented—after Casey took Gabe back to his house for a few much-needed minutes of peace and quiet.

"Etienne, Paul"—Claribel batted her eyelids, and Gabe covered a snort with a cough—"do come along and join us. These family gatherings are always a good time."

Paul shot Casey a look, but Casey shrugged in response. They were adults and the Claribel Delacombe warning label was too long for a silent conversation.

"We would be happy to," responded Etienne, entirely too chipper at the prospect of time in Claribel's company. "Paul and I also must freshen up first. We will bring croissants. I prepared the dough two days ago."

Casey sent Elton along with Shay. "We'll be there as soon as we can."

Elton harrumphed but didn't argue.

Casey'd just maneuvered the Wagoneer out onto the ravaged dirt road when his cell phone pinged.

MICKIE: DO YOU WANT TO CASH IN THAT RAIN CHECK? LUNCH TODAY?

"YOUR PLACE IS STILL A MESS," he warned Gabe, yet again.

Casey didn't think Gabe was particularly attached to the mobile home. His gleaming espresso machine and Keith were probably the two most important things to him. And the espresso machine could be replaced. He'd have to ask Etienne what brand his machine was.

"Shower *with you*, sex *with you*, in that order. I need to wash the stench of Dirty Socks Randy and Sidekick William down the drain. My clothes are at my house, so my place it is," Gabe said.

Casey had offered to grab his clothes and head back to *The Barbara,* but Gabe had quickly nixed that.

"Shower together, I believe I said. Not happening on the damn boat."

"So, what you're saying is we're gonna need a bigger boat?" Casey teased.

Gabe turned his head slowly in Casey's direction. Casey could feel his eyes on the side of his face and let himself smile.

"Did you just make a joke, Ranger Man? A *Jaws* reference? I think there may be hope for you yet."

"Maybe I did. But seriously, I want you to be prepared for what you're about to see."

"I'm prepared. Who gives a fuck about stuff? Things can be replaced. You said you took Keith to Elton's last night."

"I did."

"Well then, nothing else fucking matters. I suppose I might be a bit pissed off if they damaged my espresso machine."

Casey stayed quiet, focusing on the road. He wasn't turning his head and looking at Gabe.

Gabe gasped. "They did, didn't they! Those assholes."

"I think you may need a new one."

He definitely did. The pieces on the kitchen floor didn't resemble anything like an espresso maker anymore.

"At least Keith is okay. She is okay, right?"

That was at least the third or fourth time he'd asked about his cat. "Keith is good, maybe a little jumpier than usual, but she wasn't hurt."

"Good."

At the house, Gabe refused to let Casey help him out of the car. Instead, he was forced to hover at Gabe's shoulder and watch him sort of shuffle to the steps, stiff from hours cuffed to a chair with his ankles zip-tied. He was, at least, faster than Elton.

"The door's locked." Casey dug in his pocket and held out the sparkly Hello Kitty key ring. "But hey, we found your set of keys."

Accepting them, Gabe managed a grin—Casey wondered how he did that—and plucked out the one to the door, then pressed it into the lock. "Here goes not a hell of a lot."

With Casey right behind him, Gabe stepped inside just past the door and paused for a minute. His head moved to one side and then the other, taking in the destruction. The damage seemed worse this morning, but maybe it was just Casey projecting his feelings. Gabe didn't seem all that upset. Maybe he really meant what he'd said about it just being stuff.

Maybe Gabe's upbringing had more of an impact on his way of looking at his environment than Casey had ever considered.

"Get in the shower. I'll be there in a minute," Casey said.

Gabe didn't argue with him, which Casey appreciated. He merely turned toward the hallway, stripping as he went, leaving a trail of dirty clothes behind him.

Fortunately, the bathroom was relatively untouched. The intruders had pulled the towels off the rack and dumped out the two drawers in the small vanity, but there hadn't been much in them to begin with.

"I'll grab clean towels."

Gabe's shower wasn't much bigger than his, which made moving in together that much more practical of a decision. Casey snorted. Greta would have scrunched her face at him and asked what the hell he was waiting for.

Get a move on. Hold that man tight. Get him that new espresso maker as a housewarming present.

After doing what he could with clean sheets and a blanket to remake Gabe's bed, Casey discovered a short stack of untouched towels at the back of the hall closet. Randy and his friend had been destructive, but not thorough. Even if Gabe had been hiding the Crevans here, they easily might have missed them.

The bathroom was hot and steamy when he returned. He set the towels on the counter next to the sink. Gabe was humming; who knew Casey would have appreciated the slightly off-key warblings of a partner in the shower.

"What's that you're humming?" Casey asked.

"Ah, what? How would I know? Songs just flow out of me."

"But only in the shower?" Casey stripped off his own clothes, leaving them in a tidy pile on top of the toilet lid.

"And when I'm alone in the car." He started up again, mumbling words this time in that way people do when they only remember the chorus. Casey caught something about secondhand emotions.

"Excuse me?" Casey pulled the shower curtain aside and stepped over the lip of the tub. The shower enclosure really was too small for both of them so taking them together hadn't happened often. This morning the effort was worth it. Even if it meant he had to witness each bruise and scratch that Gabe currently wore on his skin.

"*What's Love Got To Do With It.* Tina Turner. A classic, one of my all-time favorites. I blame my mother."

Casey's Grinch-like heart briefly stuttered, like it didn't fit properly inside his chest anymore. He sucked in a deep breath and allowed his gaze to run down the length of Gabe's battered body and back up to his equally battered face. There he found himself ensnared by a huge grin and a pair of grayish blue eyes sparkling with joy.

Only his Gabriel.

"I know this is probably terrible timing," Casey began, setting his hands on Gabe's hips and tugging so they were both half under the hot spray. "But I love you. I wanted to say it without you being tied up, and I'm not telling you this now because you got yourself kidnapped and nearly, very close to possibly, killed last night. It's been on my mind for a while, and I should have said something sooner. I love you, Gabriel Karne."

Gabe's smile grew impossibly brighter and bigger. He leaned into Casey, looping his arms loosely around Casey's neck.

"I love you back, Ranger Man. Casey Lundin. Protector of the forest and people—even those you don't like much. Are you sure I don't need to be kidnapped and threatened a few more times? This shower thing is nice."

"I'd rather you didn't."

Smirking, Gabe rose the half an inch he needed to reach Casey properly, then his warm, wet, lips landed against Casey's. Was this what was meant by "sealed with a kiss"? It sure felt like it to Casey.

Without Casey being conscious of having acted, his hands were cradling Gabe's head, pulling him in, erasing the last bit of space between them. Casey opened his mouth and let Gabe taste him, savoring Gabriel in return. Until Charming Fucker, he hadn't known it could be like this, a complete and utter surrender of his barriers. It was scary but perfect.

With five fingers wound through Gabe's wet hair, Casey ran his other hand down Gabe's body, reassuring himself that Gabe was okay. That he was really in his arms and not a figment of Casey's imagination. After holding it together all night, he had to remind himself to breathe.

"I can't tell you how scared I was for you. I just found you," he whispered.

"Admit it, you hated me at first," Gabe said between kisses.

Casey nodded. "But that changed pretty damn fast." He gave him one last kiss and pulled back slightly. "Um, we should scrub down and rinse off." Casey let go of Gabe and reached for the shower gel, pumping enough for two into his palm. "This shower is too small."

"You've never complained before."

"I'm not complaining. It's a fact. And you're injured, so I feel the need to check over the rest of you. And I bet you a dollar the hot water is about to go."

"Damn, point made. Cold shower, not good."

Casey soaped them both down and ignored his body's reaction. Their bodies' reactions. The sooner they were out of the shower and in Gabe's bed, the better.

"I'M RUNNING THIS SHOW," Casey informed Gabe when they lay back onto the mattress. He didn't generally take charge when it came to sex. Partly because of a lack of experience, but also, he had to admit, he very much enjoyed Gabe taking care of him. And Gabe always did. It shouldn't have been a surprise to Casey that Gabe in the bedroom was a juxtaposition to Gabe in real life.

That damn sexy smirk flashed across Gabe's face. Rising to his knees and straddling Gabe's hips, Casey laid a finger across Gabe's lips.

"No, hush, just let me take care of you."

"If you insist."

"I do insist."

Starting at his lips, Casey traced the lines of Gabe's body. Sideways across his cheek, down his neck, across his chest, circling both nipples.

"Dammit, Casey," Gabe panted.

It was Casey's turn to smirk.

"God, you're a monster. How did I not know this before now?" Gabe reached for Casey.

"Nope, hands to yourself. No touching."

Dropping his hands, Gabe's fingers scrabbled against the sheets searching for purchase.

"Not a monster, a fiend," he panted.

Shifting off his hips, Casey scooted down to take Gabe's erection between his lips. No warning, just a quick glance up to catch the needy gaze of his favorite pair of eyes, then sucking in.

"Oh, God," Gabe moaned. He thrashed his hands around but didn't thrust into Casey's mouth. "Oh, god, oh god," he chanted. "Don't stop."

They didn't have long before Elton—or worse, Claribel—might impatiently knock on Gabe's door, demanding to know why they weren't at the post-adventure confab. No way in hell was Casey stopping. Their opportunity window was small, and they were both going to come, dammit.

Hollowing his cheeks, Casey sucked Gabe down as far as he could, which was surprisingly far. He swallowed, working his throat muscles around Gabe's cock, loving the feel of him losing control. For his part, Gabe thrashed side to side, his hips moving back and forth.

"I can't," he rasped. "Fuck. Oh my god." Gabe's hands landed on his head, winding through his hair.

Casey wrapped his fingers around the base of Gabe's cock, holding it still while he sucked and dragged his tongue around the tip of Gabe's penis and then very gently dragged his teeth along his length.

He knew when Gabe had reached his limit. Casey had reached his too. One more wicked suck and Gabe exploded into his mouth, his fingers tugging on Casey's hair as he released.

Casey pulled off him, letting Gabe's cock slip from between his lips.

"Come here," Gabe slurred, waving a hand toward Casey's cock. "I want that."

Knee-crawling up Gabe's body Casey fed him his own weeping cock.

"I'm so close," he said as Gabe's mouth tightened around him. "So, fucking close."

Casey propped himself up on his elbows over Gabe's head and let himself fall into the bliss of Gabe's touch, of knowing Gabe was alive and, at least mostly, unharmed.

Even so, Casey's orgasm took him by surprise. One second, he was gently pumping his hips, breathing in the scent of Gabe and sex, trying not to choke him. The next heartbeat, he was coming so hard his vision blurred. His rock-hard balls pulsed and emptied, his come streaming out of him and into Gabe.

Gabe's eyes were closed, his cheeks working the last of Casey's orgasm. There was too much come, so some dribbled out the corner of his mouth and down his neck to the sheet. God, it was sexy. Casey pulsed one last time.

"Fuck, Gabe," Casey whispered against his forearm, shaking now from the effort of keeping himself from collapsing onto Gabe. With care, he pulled out of Gabe's mouth and fell to the side.

After wiping his face with the sheet, Gabe rolled onto his side, facing Casey. He was smiling. "We needed that," he said with a big breath. "I love you, Casey Lundin. So much. It's a bit scary, actually."

They were both covered with spunk and would need a second shower before leaving the house, but Casey smiled back at his partner.

"I don't know much but I think maybe love is generally scary," said Casey.

What the hell. Casey knew Gabe wouldn't bring it up—he knew Casey too well. "I was serious, we do need a bigger boat.

But maybe not a boat. What about a house together, big enough for us, Bowie, and Keith?"

"You're talking about a home. About living together, me and you," Gabe said, his grin huge.

"Yeah, I am."

"If we weren't in danger of being invaded by Claribel and crew, I'd take the time to show you just how incredible I think this idea of yours is. How vehemently I am saying 'yes.' Is tomorrow too soon?"

"Before we met, Gabriel, I hated doing anything fast."

Gabe raised an eyebrow and leaned in to plant a quick kiss on Casey's lips. "And how has that changed?"

It was Casey's turn to smile. "I'm still not a fan but I've learned that with you, I just need to grab on and hold tight."

TWENTY-SIX

GABE – FRIDAY AFTERNOON

The house that Shay had rented for the weekend was a beautifully restored two-story farmhouse that looked like it was originally built around 1900. The contractor had artfully expanded the ground floor to include a modern-style kitchen, two large bedrooms, a living room, a mudroom, and some other bonus room Gabe didn't know the name for. There was another bathroom and two more bedrooms upstairs, and a beautiful wraparound porch. He'd live there for the porch alone.

"This is nice," Gabe said, setting his half of Alfred down and taking in their surroundings. "Do you think we could afford something like this?"

It was close to Greta and Abby. And, he thought, also to Casey's brother.

Casey coughed. "On a ranger's salary?"

Gabe noted that Casey didn't scoff at the *we*, just the budget.

The house was gorgeous, and Gabe had no trouble imagining living in a place like this—with Casey. They could have friends and family over easily enough, and there were plenty of rooms to give themselves space when they each needed alone time.

"I have money." Actually, Gabe still had quite a bit of money sort of lying around. Why not buy a home where he and Casey would be happy living together? "We might as well put it to good use. Come on." He smirked across the top of Alfred. "I could be your sugar daddy."

Gabe knew he should be exhausted, having gotten no sleep the night before, but he was officially wired. After a shower, coffee, and that energizing session of *Casey checking to make sure Gabe was really okay*, he was ready for the rest of the day. And that included Claribel, Shay, Elton, and the rest of the crew who had been invited for brunch, or whatever this was.

"Bring that thing into the kitchen!" Claribel shouted.

Gabe rolled his eyes while Casey coughed and frowned, clearly trying to think of a response.

"You know there's nothing you can say except yes."

"Can we just get this into the kitchen and hash out living arrangement details later?"

"Only if it involves sexual favors from me."

"Jesus Christ," Casey whispered, his cheeks red.

They'd brought the chair along with them because if Alfred the Ugly was hiding a secret, Elton would be disappointed if he wasn't there when they discovered it. If Alfred wasn't hiding anything, the next stop was the building where the 201 Gallery had been housed.

Gabe hoped it didn't come to that. He wasn't looking forward to crawling around potentially spider-infested forgotten passageways between old buildings in Westfort.

They set Alfred down in the middle of the kitchen floor. "If I was a seventeen-year-old looking to hide purloined artwork, and this thing was all that was handy, where would I put it?"

"Do we want to know why this chair was handy?" asked Shay.

"We do not. That is called a detour. Maybe Heidi worked in an antique store? There still are a bunch of them along Water Street, even one next to Windward Kite Shop, maybe that's where the secret door led from."

"We've looked in the obvious places." Casey glared at Gabe. "*Don't* say it."

"Fine, I won't, but we clearly need to look in inconspicuous places."

Claribel stood from the table and moved over to stand by Gabe. "This thing is one of those gentleman's surprise chairs. They're worth quite a bit."

"Maybe she sold the artwork, and the money is in the chair?" That was Elton.

Gabe shook his head. "I don't think so. I'm pretty sure it's here, in the single ugliest piece of furniture I've seen. Alternatively, it's still where Carla Pritchard hid it, and Holly-slash-Heidi found it but left it there. I don't think Heidi would have made sure Alfred came to me if that were the case. This chair is not her style. The art being in here makes more sense."

"What are you waiting for?" Shay asked.

"Fine," sighed Gabe. "Let's do this."

Slowly, meticulously, Gabe and Casey began to search Alfred again. Gabe dragged his fingertips along the chair arms, legs, and back, seeking a hidden seam. A place that opened but wasn't obvious.

"This chair was made for secrets," he complained after not finding a fucking thing. "Maybe it is Heidi's style, after all."

"Let's turn it over," Casey suggested.

Carefully, they turned the chair upside down so that it was balanced by the edge of the seat and the ornate, throne-like back.

"Elton, would you come steady this?" Gabe asked.

With Elton making sure the chair wouldn't tip over, he and Casey went back to work. Gabe found the palpable tension in the room a bit amusing. Claribel hadn't stopped biting her fingernail since they started and Shay hovered on the perimeter like a referee. Even Paul had returned to the living area to watch the action while Etienne kept an eye on the croissants he'd popped in the oven.

The underneath part of the chair seemed to have nothing unusual, not that Gabe could find anyway.

"What if Heidi made her own secret compartment?" Elton asked. "What if it's not original to the chair? Have you tried checking where the leather is sewn into the bottom of the seat?"

Gabe dragged his fingers along the seat bottom. It was held in place by staples, but they moved under his touch along one side. Not much, but more than one would expect.

"I need pliers or something," Gabe said, patting himself down as if he'd find them in his back pocket.

Elton held out his pocketknife. "Use this."

Kneeling, Gabe forced the tip of the blade under one staple, then another and another until they were all out. The protective fabric still adhered to the wood. Gabe peeled it away and dropped it to the floor.

Everyone spoke at once. "What do you see?" "What's there?" "Is there anything?"

Gabe hushed them all. "Gimme a chance here."

Casey stood back while Gabe pinched the edge of the fabric and pulled it away.

"I need a flashlight."

Shay handed him a phone, the light already turned on. Accepting it, Gabe shone it into the cavity. Another piece of fabric was tucked inside. He pulled it out, revealing three cardboard tubes, each about eighteen inches long.

"Holy shit."

Prying the lid off one tube, Gabe turned it upside down and shook it. When nothing slid out, he stuck a finger inside and carefully eased out a single canvas. With shaking hands, he rolled the canvas out just enough to see what it was. Gabe hadn't heard of Martin Crevan and didn't know how to identify art in general, but this was a landscape like the article had described. It was beautiful, and the artist's signature was in the corner.

"No way." Gabe sat back on his heels and stared at Casey and Elton. "No fucking way."

"Now what do we do?" Casey asked.

It was Shay who answered. "You call your friendly family lawyer, or if he's in the area, handing him a dollar retainer will do."

Gabe pulled out his wallet; all he had was a fiver. He held it out to his half brother, "I suppose you don't have change."

Shay carefully tucked the bill into his wallet. "I'll be in the other room calling a friend of a friend." He whistled as he walked away.

"I'm not sure I want to know who Shay's friends are," muttered Gabe.

"Best not to ask," agreed Claribel with a doting smile.

Casey made a displeased grumble sound and pulled his phone out of his pocket to check the screen.

"It's Mickie again. I never got back to him."

"And who is this Mickie person?" Claribel asked. "Not a hookup, I hope. I've been planning Gabriel's wedding. I'd like to see all my boys happy and settled."

Before Casey literally forgot to breathe or Claribel started speculating out loud about throuples—*fine*, Gabe had no issue with throuples, but three just wasn't his magic number—Gabe said, "Not a hookup, Casey's brother, Mickie."

"Brother! Why didn't you say so? Invite him over. We'll have plenty of food for everyone. Shay called the pizza place and put in an order before you got here." She smiled at Etienne, who had brought in a platter of croissants. "And these will tide us all over till they arrive."

Gabe glanced at Casey. "I'm not sure Mickie is ready for prime time."

Casey stared back at him, then looked down at his screen again. Shaking his head, he typed something and pressed Send.

"I guess we'll find out."

TWENTY-SEVEN

CASEY – FRIDAY — LUNCH

Casey'd been anxiously listening for the knock at the front door, and when he walked down the hallway to answer it, he did his best to keep his emotions in check. Every time Casey saw his brother without plexiglass between them his heart clenched. He didn't know if it'd ever go away.

"Hey, brother," Mickie greeted him. His smile reached his eyes, which made Casey hopeful. Behind him stood Pedro, looking as nervous as Casey felt.

"Hey, Mickie, you look good. You too, Pedro." He was impressed that Pedro had accepted the invitation and then realized that neither of them had met Claribel.

"Thanks for inviting Pedro. I hope it's okay with everyone else that he came with."

"Of course it's okay," Casey assured him. It was. If Mickie was happy, Casey was happy.

Mickie looked good, really good. They were half siblings, and the resemblance between them was strong, but Casey'd always felt his older brother was the better looking Lundin. Mickie's auburn hair was darker, and he was also broader, probably from spending hours upon hours in the prison's gym. Today, Casey noticed the dark circles under his eyes had faded, and even though the days were still cold, wet, and too short, he had some color to his skin. Casey couldn't wait to take him on a few of his favorite hikes.

"Incoming hug," Mickie said. "I can't believe you're in your thirties and I still have to say this."

Shaking his head but also smiling, Casey leaned in so his brother could wrap him in a lung-crushing bear hug. Casey was taller than Mickie these days, but he still felt like the little brother when Mickie hugged him. It was a good feeling.

"I missed your hugs," Casey admitted.

What the hell, Casey thought, pulling Pedro in for a hug as well. He wanted Mickie to be happy, and it looked like Pedro was part of the equation needed for that result.

"Thanks for coming." Damn, could he sound any more awkward? Probably not. "Fair warning," he said quietly, "Gabe's family is... different."

Mickie grinned and slapped him on the back. "But a good different, right?"

"Quit lingering in the hall and bring your brother to meet me," Claribel called out imperiously.

"Don't say I didn't warn you. There's still time for you to escape." Casey gestured toward the front door.

Chuckling, Mickie and Pedro shook their heads, so Casey led them down the hall and back into the large farmhouse-style kitchen. "We're in for the long haul. The good, the bad, the just plain weird."

Mickie's happiness meant everything to him. He liked Pedro a lot—except when he and Gabe flirted, which was second nature for both men and harmless. Even Casey, who could be oblivious when it came to love and relationships and attraction, knew Gabe was his and his alone.

Which was actually pretty crazy in itself and caused a pleasant tingle in the center of his chest when he thought about Gabe being a permanent part of his life. Even if it meant hanging on for dear life when Gabe got a wild hair. Casey definitely planned on hanging on.

"Hey everyone, this is my brother Mickie and his—" Casey hesitated for just a second—"his partner, Pedro Morales."

From the smiles plastered on Mickie's and Pedro's faces, Casey knew that he'd said the right thing.

EPILOGUE — GABRIEL — MAY

"Gabriel?" Casey called his name, managing to pack exasperation, confusion, and affection into just three tiny syllables.

Gabe was in their new-to-them kitchen, putting the vintage dishes that he'd just unpacked and washed into the cabinets where they now belonged. Nothing matched, the plates weren't the same sizes, and a few were irreplaceable if they got broken. Gabe loved them all.

Three short weeks ago, they'd closed on their house. The very same house that Shay and Claribel had rented. Was it a bit big for two people? Maybe, but they'd already proven that they had plenty of room for guests. It was close to Greta and Abby, as well as Pedro and Mickie. There was a big yard for Bowie and lots of nooks and crannies for Keith. Gabe had declared Casey in charge of the outdoor stuff while he had dived into putting their stamp on the inside.

"What?" Gabe replied, knowing full well *what*. That's why he had picked up two packs of paper plates at the store yesterday.

Casey was returning from a last-minute trip to Norskland General Store because Barry had called to let them know a shipment with brand-new flavors of Jewel Creamery ice cream had arrived. Since Casey was the very best partner, he'd volunteered to pick up a pint or five for the housewarming party. Guests were expected in two hours.

Gabe listened to the sound of Casey's footsteps coming toward the kitchen. When he came through the door, he was carrying the bag with the ice cream in it.

"My hero, again," Gabe said dramatically.

"Barry said he'd see us soon. Are he and Mercy coming? Do I want to know who you haven't invited?" Casey asked as he crossed to the fridge and popped the ice cream into the freezer.

Gabe pretended to think about it. "The only people not invited are those who are behind bars. I can't say who's coming. Maybe no one."

"As if. Barry and Mercy are for sure. They said Brooklyn might stop by with her new boyfriend."

"Good, so at least two plus. I hope we have enough food. There's nothing worse than running out of snacks."

Casey stood there for a minute, then shook his head and leaned in to give Gabe a quick buss on the cheek. "So, the whole island is coming over?"

"I don't think Deputy Eagan will make it, not now that she's officially been tapped to be the sheriff."

The Piedras Island relations were coming too, but Gabe and Casey were both ignoring that fact. They weren't something a person could prepare for. They just happened, like a major storm system.

"A win all around," said Casey, leaning one hip against the counter, directly next to where Gabe had been working.

"Damn right."

Did they have time to head upstairs and test out the new mattress again? He figured not, but a guy could dream.

"When does this thing start again?" Casey asked, twisting to grab a glass out of a cabinet and fill it with water from the pitcher they stored in the fridge.

"Oh, Casey, babe, it's already started. Haven't you realized that it's always a party when I'm around? Twenty-four seven." Gabe shook his hips, mimicking a cheesy disco move, and sauntered close enough to trap Casey against the front of the refrigerator and plant a real kiss on his lips. Maybe they did have time to go upstairs after all.

The doorbell interrupted them, sending Bowie into a fit of barking.

"Bowie, quiet. Who's that?" Casey asked.

"I think the only way to find out is to answer the door." Releasing Casey, Gabe spun on his heel and headed to the front door. "Maybe we need one of those porch video things," he said over his shoulder.

Pulling the door open, Gabe was surprised to find the island's newly minted sheriff on the other side.

"Sheriff Eagan, are your ears burning? We were just talking about you. Official congratulations on the promotion by the way."

He noted that she'd parked her cruiser across the drive as if she was in a hurry, and there was a serious expression on her face.

Shit. His heart started to race. "What's up? Did something happen? Elton?"

Elton was as healthy as an older senior could be, but Gabe worried about him. He was as close as Gabe was going to get to a father figure.

"No, Elton is fine as far as I know," she assured him.

Gabe took a calming breath. "Thank fuck. Do you want to come inside? I can make a coffee or we have fancy water."

Because, yes, Casey and his new French friend Etienne had conspired and gifted Gabriel with a shiny new espresso machine. It was beautiful and if he wasn't planning on asking Casey to tie the knot, he'd marry it.

He heard Casey wander down the hall and stand behind him.

She shook her head. "No time today." The sheriff looked over Gabe's shoulder at Casey. "Calvin Perkins has been located."

"Located? The Valley?" Casey pushed past Gabe. "Who? How?"

"The Allard-Clarks. They were doing some rescue training with those dogs of theirs."

Casey frowned. "He's alive?"

"No."

"Was it exposure?"

Eagan shook her head. "Also no. He was shot."

"Where? I mean, where was he found?"

"Along a fire service road that runs behind Gordon MacDonald's place and Snowcap Estates. He was executed, Casey. Shot in the back of the head."

Gabe's attention flicked between Casey and Eagan. "Shot in the back of the head? Not accidentally killed by a hunter, then?"

"No. His hands were tied. Whoever did it rolled the body up in a canvas tarp and tossed or dragged him off to the side. If it hadn't been for the dogs, we might not have found the remains."

Casey asked, "Do we know how long?"

Eagan nodded. "We have a timeline of sorts. He was alive until after this year's maples lost their leaves. But how long after we don't know yet."

"I was up there back in March," Casey told her.

"Did you see something?"

"No. But I had the distinct feeling that someone was watching me. At the time, I thought it could have been Calvin." He shrugged his shoulders. "But it slipped my mind and I haven't been back since."

"He had your card in his wallet, Casey. When would you have given him that? You're sure he didn't reach out to you recently?"

"No." Casey shook his head. "Calvin and I were never on polite speaking terms. I have a difficult time coming up with any scenario where he would come to me for help. I would have though, you know. Helped him."

"Well," the sheriff said after a moment passed, "it seems that he was considering connecting with you and someone didn't want that to happen."

"Which means—"

"Which means," she said grimly, "we have a problem. And if where Perkins was found means anything, the problem has something to do with The Valley."

"Damn," said Casey

"Damn indeed," said Eagan.

"Fuck," Gabriel added. "This is definitely fuckery."

———

Book four, **The Drop** – coming late 2026.

Who killed Calvin Perkins? It's up to Casey and Gabriel to find out.

To keep updated on what Elle is up to and the progress of The Drop please consider joining my newsletter, the highway to Elle. In exchange please enjoy this FREE copy of Trusting the Elements Greg and Otto's story (set in Westfort!).

If you could leave a review for Skin Game, that would mean a great deal.

I hope you've been enjoying Hearthstone, and Gabriel, and Casey!

AFTERWORD